Dodging Raindrops

a novel

To Joe & Sarah,
Enjoy the story —
happy reading!
megan ciampo

Megan Ciampo

To Mom, Dad, and Nicole,
For believing in my story long before I picked up a pen.

Prologue

N atural light was a deciding factor in choosing this apartment, but as sunshine crept through my bedroom window on the morning of January 1, I knew I needed to invest in some blackout shades, or shades of any kind.

As much as I wanted to blame this hangover on something suspicious in my drinks, I knew that wasn't the case. Instead, I had to start accepting that I was getting too old to handle a night of nonstop partying.

A year ago, I was a senior in college who spent almost every night at happy hour or a frat party. Now, after only one night of partying, I feel like I have been hit by a bus.

Thankfully I knew enough, even after a night out, to leave some aspirin and a water bottle next to my bed. Grabbing my phone from under my pillow, I prayed there weren't any embarrassing photos or videos posted online and let out a huge sigh of relief when I realized I was in the clear.

Glancing in my bathroom mirror after reuniting with everything I ate and drank the night before, I was extremely grateful that nobody else was in my apartment. My roommate, a girl I found online, paid her rent on time every month but spent all of her time at her boyfriend's apartment in Brooklyn. Some days, our apartment got lonely but on this particular day, I was glad to be alone.

A sock covered only one foot, my hair was disheveled, and makeup was still smudged on my face.

Once my head stopped spinning, I stumbled from the bathroom floor to the desk in my living room.

Even though I moved away from home a few months ago, I felt like I still needed to partake in the Fitzpatrick family's New Year's Day tradition of creating a resolution list.

Every year for the past ten, my younger brother and I created a list of things we wanted to accomplish within the following twelve months. There was only one rule, the number of resolutions had to be the same as the age we were turning that year.

When we first started creating the lists, we purposely only included things that could be accomplished almost immediately, ensuring we wouldn't have to think about the lists much after the middle of January. But, as the years passed, we recognized the significance of resolutions and started putting some effort into our lists.

The past few years had been a complete whirlwind. I graduated from high school, started college, graduated from college, made and lost friends, mentally made it through two of my father's deployments, moved to a new city on my own, and started my first real job.

Year after year, resolution lists helped keep things in line, especially as I tried to figure out what life had to offer.

Grabbing a blank notebook and a pen from the desk drawer, I wrote the date on top of the first page, thinking of twenty-three things I wanted the upcoming year to include.

This was my first full year living on my own and every part of me wanted every part of it to be perfect.

An hour later, my list was complete – twenty-three things to be accomplished before New Year's Eve, in no particular order.

<u>Maeve's Resolution List</u>
Spend more time with genuine people
Reconnect with an old friend
Fall in love
Do something that scares you
Donate blood
Send handwritten letters
Volunteer
Travel without posting on social media
Meet new people
Ask work for a raise/more responsibility
Invest some paychecks
Find a new hobby
Stay in touch with yourself
Clear out the clutter at home
Find a new job you love
Talk about feelings
Learn to cook
Be a New York City tourist for a day
See more live music

Go somewhere you've never been
Do something kind for others
Go an entire day without checking emails
Enjoy the little things

I purposely chose resolutions that would likely take all twelve months to complete, but they were all things I thought I wanted, and needed, to accomplish.

With the list created, I signed my name at the bottom of the page and placed my notebook back in the desk drawer.

Chapter One

Palm trees, a pool boy with washboard abs, incredible weather, and the most obnoxious noise in the world?

My unrealistic dream of home was cut short by my screeching alarm clock. The blaring continued for about thirty-five seconds before I threw the clock across the room.

Returning to work on January 2 should have been illegal.

I just spent the past nine days out of the office but sitting in a cubicle for eight hours was still the last thing I wanted to do.

Reluctantly, after prolonged social media scrolling, I stumbled out of bed, showered, picked out a semi-decent outfit, grabbed a granola bar, and headed out of my apartment.

I also tripped over a pair of shoes on my way to the bathroom, ran out of conditioner halfway through my shower, couldn't find the shirt I wanted to wear, and dropped the last granola bar in the box onto my kitchen floor. I had been awake for less than an hour and I could already tell it was going to feel like the most Monday of any Thursday ever.

The elevator was empty for the entirety of my seven-story descent, a real blessing. I wasn't in the headspace to make small talk with my neighbors, but that silence disappeared as the elevator met the ground floor.

I locked eyes with Ralph, my apartment building's doorman, as soon as I stepped into the lobby.

Ralph was the first person I met in New York City. From our very first conversation, I knew he was someone I wanted to have on my side as I tried to figure out life in an unfamiliar city. He reminded me of a grandfather. Almost immediately after we met, I knew he was caring, protective, and could be counted on in times of need.

Shortly after moving in, I learned Ralph had been a police officer in the NYPD for thirty-five years, serving and protecting the same streets he was born and raised on. He only started working as a doorman after retiring and "driving his wife crazy" in their "cramped apartment." He insisted the doorman job was a way for him to continue helping the community, but in a much safer capacity.

Ralph and I spent nearly a half-hour last night chatting about the holidays. I told him about my trip to my grandmother's house outside of Chicago, and he told me about the trip he took with Miss Ruth, his wife of fifty-four years, to Seattle to meet their first grandbaby.

I loved hearing stories of their family, but on this particular morning, I was glad I heard them the night before while in a better mood. Plus, that meant this morning, a simple "Hi Ralph, have a good day" on my way out the door would suffice.

I tried to start my work weeks by walking to the office, convinced some fresh air would make everything more bearable. But today was a cold and rainy Thursday, so the train beat out my usual walk.

Subway platforms quickly became some of my least favorite places in the city.

Ahead of my move to New York, my parents drilled the importance of staying aware of my surroundings. They never spent an extended amount of time in New York City, but they insisted it was extremely common for people to be pushed onto the train tracks by other passengers, usually complete strangers. After taking the subway at least once a day for the past seven months, I had yet to see that happen. I questioned the validity of their insinuations.

Doubts aside, I saw news stories almost daily of people getting slashed while on the subway, usually just minding their own business. So, with the fear of getting slashed or pushed onto the tracks, I was on high alert every time I stepped onto a subway platform.

The New York City subway system was the first thing Ralph explained while teaching me what (he thought) I needed to know about living in the city. He told me things got hot underground, even in the winter months, and explained that the doors would close on anyone who stood in their way. He showed me the correct way to swipe a MetroCard and insisted skipping fares was usually the quickest way to get questioned by the police.

The most important lesson about the subway he taught me was about empty subway cars, a lesson that came with a strong warning to never enter one.

"You might think you hit the jackpot if you see an empty car," he said, "but I promise that with one step on board, you'll find out exactly why it's empty, the hard way."

Early on in my subway riding tenure, I came across an empty car and although his warning crossed my mind, I assumed Ralph exaggerated. Stepping on board, the smell so was unbearable, I had no choice but to get off at the next stop, only six blocks from where I got on and twenty-eight blocks away from where I needed to be. That was the first, and only, time I didn't take one of Ralph's warnings seriously.

Thankfully, on my first day back to work, the wait on the platform wasn't longer than a minute and my nineteen-block ride to the office was nowhere near full.

Arriving at 96th Street, I made my way up the station stairs and back to the crowded New York City streets, trying to avoid muddy puddles on my two-block walk.

1207 Park Avenue was a giant building with a washed-brick exterior, on the corner of East 94th Street, that housed over three dozen companies.

Seven months ago, I started my first "real" job at Sampson West, one of the largest and most-successful print and digital publishing firms in the country. I accepted an assistant position after college graduation, without hesitation, and thought it was going to be my dream job. On paper, it seemed like the perfect place to get my foot in the door for a successful career in New York's cutthroat journalism industry. But that was far from reality.

I spent the past four years working toward a degree in journalism and I never questioned that I wanted to be in a big city, especially one with as many dreams and possibilities as New York, but I wasn't sure Sampson West was the answer. In the weeks leading to my start date, I imagined my days would be full of meetings, conference calls, press tours, and editing. It didn't take long to realize my days would actually be spent fetching coffee orders, staring into space, organizing files, answering phones, and watching the clock.

I was told I'd have to go through three months of training before I could get a title change and a raise. It had been seven months, I still had the same title and I hadn't seen an increase in the number that hit my bank account every two weeks. It felt like I was running in circles, giving my all to a boss and company where I wasn't appreciated. It seemed like my only responsibility was to do the seemingly unnecessary work nobody else wanted to do.

Noise echoed throughout the office as soon as I stepped off the elevator. People were scattered around, catching up after an extended winter break, but each conversation was full of small talk that I had no desire to participate in. I kept my headphones in until I reached my cubicle, giving a silent smile to everyone I passed, but not stopping to join any conversations.

Being back at work wasn't easy. The morning continued the same way as every other morning at the office. I caught up on emails, answered the phones when they rang, cut all of the necessary media clippings, and spent a lot of time staring into space.

I *knew* I shouldn't act like an 'entitled millennial' and should have been grateful to even have a job, but I put in countless time and effort for very little return. I knew something needed to change.

I sent my boss, Declan, an email asking if we could meet before the end of the day, knowing if I slept on it, I'd wimp out.

After hitting send on the email and refreshing my inbox, I was startled by the sound of an incoming video chat from my cell phone. I stood from my cubicle after reading my little brother's name written across the screen.

When his face appeared on the screen, I knew something was wrong. He didn't look like his usual: a too-cool-for-school teenager. His eyes reminded me of the time he accidentally threw a baseball through our garage window or the time he tattled on himself for forging our mom's signature on a report card in fourth grade.

There was no question those days, or today, that he was on the verge of tears.

"What's wrong?" I asked.

"It's not fair," he said after a few deep breaths and noticeable frustration.

"What, Wyatt? What happened?"

"Did you see the news today? There was another attack today and now I have to go back to school tomorrow and people are going to stare at me with pity because I'm the kid with the dad in Iraq," he said, getting choked up. "You got to leave Gulfpoint. I bet you have friends who don't even know what Dad's job is."

I didn't know what to say. I hadn't seen the news, or the latest attack, but he was right. It wasn't fair. But I also couldn't change it.

10

Our dad, George Fitzpatrick, was a Staff Sergeant in the United States Army and although deployments became our normal, they never got easier. The older we got, the harder they got. I was never able to escape my own mind during deployments, but I did avoid a majority of our small-town's whispers.

"Wyatt, we don't know if he's in Iraq or on a mission," I said, trying to ease the tension or make him laugh.

"You know what I meant!" he exclaimed.

He was right, again.

I understood his frustration.

He had to step up and become the 'man of the house' a lot earlier than any young boy should have to. And, through all of that, it was easy to forget Wyatt was still just a kid trying to navigate high school with a not-always-present father.

Our dad did his best to stay involved in our daily lives, but thanks to the seemingly never-ending War on Terror, it was nearly impossible to talk to him as often as we would have liked.

"I know, I know, I'm sorry. I really am. But I'll come home soon, okay? And dad will too." I reminded him.

"You guys both need to hurry up," he said. "Okay, I gotta go, Maeve."

"Bye Wyatt, love you," I responded.

And, just like that, my little brother's face disappeared from my phone's screen.

Back at my desk, I resumed staring into space before receiving a reply from Declan. He said he had ten minutes to spare right now, leaving me no time to prepare exactly what I wanted to say, and my nerves skyrocketed in the twenty-step walk from my cubicle to his office.

I wasn't afraid of Declan, but I was intimidated by his success. He was a no-nonsense kind of guy and it was no secret that he came from nothing. He always told jokes that weren't funny, wore clothes that were a little too big, made unnecessary petty comments, and acted like every employee owed him something. Although he was one of the most well-respected men in the industry, I found his entire presence frustrating.

The Sampson West office was open and bright, with no real sense of hierarchy, but Declan's office told a different story. The dark wood walls, ceiling, and floor were accompanied by an aura of class, dominance, and power.

"Have a seat, Miss Fitzpatrick," he said, "What can I do for you?"

That was another thing that bothered me about Declan Danvers. He always insisted on calling me 'Miss Fitzpatrick,' but it wasn't out of respect. On the contrary, he didn't respect me enough or care enough to remember my first name. During my first few months at Sampson West, he called me May, Marie, Eve, and Margie more times than he ever called me Maeve.

Sitting in front of his desk, I took a deep breath.

"Can we talk about my future and my pay scale?" I asked.

It was met by an eye roll.

"Well, I'm not a psychic and you know the budget is tight," he replied.

He was lying. The budget at Sampson West didn't exist. Executives spent unnecessary money on a regular basis. Lunches were catered, clients were treated to five-star experiences, print copies were selling better than ever, and every non-management employee was underpaid.

"Okay, never mind," I responded. "Thanks for your time."

The psychic comment confirmed this wasn't a conversation worth having right now. Declan wasn't going to be open-minded about the situation until I had done research on why I deserved a raise. For now, he made his decision and it wasn't going to work in my favor. I needed to go back to the drawing board before revisiting this conversation.

"Miss Fitzpatrick?" he asked on my way out the door.

"Yes?"

"Can you make sure there's coffee ready for the three o'clock staff meeting?"

I didn't answer, walking out of his office, seeing red.

I busted my ass for this man time and time again, going above and beyond for almost everything, but I shouldn't have been surprised that he didn't have the common courtesy to at least *pretend* he would think about my request.

I wanted to walk right into Human Resources with a letter of resignation, and I would have if it were two months ago, but I was trying to keep my impulsive decision-making tendencies under control.

Instead, after filling the coffeemaker, I sat at my computer and typed an email to both Declan and Maribel, the head of Human Resources. It was an email composed and deleted a dozen times, each written nastier than the one prior. I eventually settled on the subject line

Taking some time off:

Just wanted to let you know I'll be using two PTO days (tomorrow and Monday) and heading back home to Florida for an

extended weekend. I'll be back in the office at 9:00 a.m. on Tuesday.

Maeve.

Normally, I would have filed an official paid-time-off request, at least two weeks in advance, but I was fed up and needed to get away for a few days, as soon as possible.

Chapter Two

L anding at Florida's Gulf Coast International Airport the following morning, I dialed the ten-digit phone number I memorized in sixth grade.

Like always, Austin Packard, my best friend, the blue-eyed boy I met on the first day of kindergarten, answered on the second ring. That was our thing. The week before high school graduation, we agreed to answer each other's phone calls before the third ring, no matter what. Shortly after getting to college, we realized we had horrible timing, so a majority of our second-ring pick-ups were rushed "I need to call you back later" conversations.

But, on this particular day, Austin's infectious laugh filled my ears before I even had the chance to say hello. It was a laugh I missed with each passing day while in New York.

"Fitz, is it time? Did you land? I'm almost there!" he exclaimed, calling me a nickname only he was allowed to use.

Austin was the only one who knew I flew in for the weekend, making him my ride from Gulf Coast International to Gulfpoint.

His Audi coupe was parked in front of the terminal and, within seconds, I was engulfed in the tightest hug – one that made me realize just how much I missed home. I just saw my mom and brother a couple of weeks ago in Chicago but reuniting with Austin confirmed I made the right decision in spending an unexpected, but much-needed, long weekend back home.

It was a twenty-minute drive from the airport to Gulfpoint, a twelve-square-mile town where everyone waved to each other, house doors were left unlocked, and neighbors were always looking for ways to help. Most importantly, it was the town I would forever call home.

Austin and I chatted for a few minutes, but there wasn't much we needed to catch up on. We were best friends who spoke every day, no matter what, so a majority of the ride was spent in an enjoyable silence as I tried to take in my surroundings, immediately noticing how much changed but equally relieved by how much had stayed the same.

A few years ago, Gulfpoint started an overhaul with the intention of making everything in town look more uniform. The project stalled for a while as committees debated designs and budgets, but it seemed like everything came together since I last left town. Building exteriors were updated, sidewalks were expanded to accommodate outdoor seating, landscapers were tending to flowerbeds, and faces I'd never seen were scattered among familiar ones.

"Which of these did you help build?" I asked Austin.

He had moved back to Gulfpoint after college graduation and spent the past few months working for a local construction company.

"Almost all of them," he laughed.

Changes aside, the memories created on these streets remained the same. I grew up in this town. The school district I left on the last day of senior year was the same I entered on the first day of kindergarten. I learned how to play sports on these fields. I made my first friends within these borders. I learned how to drive, how to drink, how to cry, and how to love in this practically unknown spot on the map.

"How does it feel to be back?" Austin asked, his voice interrupting my trance.

"I'm not sure yet."

But, once I saw it, nothing else mattered.

6293 Del Ray Lane.

It was the first address I learned, the place I took my first steps, and the only house I ever called home.

The black trim of the windows and doorframe popped against the home's white siding. The landscaping was practically perfect in every way. The flowerbeds were my mom's pride and joy. The swing set, last used decades ago, remained in the backyard. The oak double-doors that separated the home from the outside world were oversized yet inviting.

"Maeve?! What are you doing here?" My mom exclaimed, with a genuine smile plastered across her face, opening the doors almost immediately after I knocked.

I thought Austin's airport sidewalk hug was tight, but even that was nothing compared to how quickly and how hard my mom wrapped her arms around me.

"Got space for me to crash for a couple of days, mama?" I asked.

"Oh my god, yes!" She said, surprise and excitement still evident in her voice. "Come in!"

With that, Austin and I followed her through the foyer and into the kitchen. My parents put a lot of love and labor into making this house a home, with most of their effort going into the creation of the kitchen. It was my mother's dream. From marble countertops and an abundance of storage space to a giant farmhouse sink and stainless-steel appliances, it had everything she wanted. It was the place you were almost guaranteed to find my mother during the years Wyatt and I were slowly but surely becoming respectful and halfway-responsible adults. It constantly smelled like fresh-baked cookies and cleaning supplies. The oversized room was the central hub of my childhood home, witnessing every major milestone and every mundane daily activity.

As Austin and I sat at the countertop, I asked my mom how things have been back home. With just under seven-thousand people calling this coastal town home, everyone knew everyone else's business. Austin kept me updated on our former classmates and Wyatt shared details about things happening in the high school, but I knew my mom would have the real scoop.

From neighbors to acquaintances, she filled me in on how everyone was doing, telling me about this week's book club drama, the latest mom-and-pop shops to close their doors, and which high school students had gotten into trouble for underage drinking at the latest school dance.

Before I could start asking questions, my mom's cell phone rang. She said it was work and she needed to answer. Susanna Fitzpatrick was the hardest working woman I knew. She was a stay-at-home mom turned lawyer who, over the past few years, spent countless hours at the office working on cases. She'd been practicing law but always thought she needed to put in more work than the others in the firm. She insisted she was "a few steps behind" after taking some time off to raise Wyatt and me.

With all of her focus back on work, I was impressed by how well she kept up with everything going on in everyone's social life, but that was one of those things that came along with life in a small town. Gulfpoint, Florida was the *epitome* of a small town.

Knowing it would be a while before my mom was off the phone, Austin followed me upstairs to my childhood bedroom, a room that had seen it all, from toddler temper tantrums to late-night sneak-outs meant for meeting up with high school hookups.

"Fitz, look!" Austin exclaimed after walking over to the far side of my room. "Can you believe we were this small?"

He was standing at my closet, pointing to the doorframe scattered with tick marks.

New marks were added each January to show how much Austin, Wyatt, and I had grown over the previous year.

"Didn't take long for you to pass me," I laughed.

My tick marks remained at the five-foot-six spot for years while Austin's and Wyatt's continued to rise.

"It's okay, you'll grow one day," he laughed, patting my head.

I rolled my eyes but his nonsense was one of the many reasons we had been the best of friends for nearly twenty years, becoming more like family than friends.

Growing up, Austin spent a ton of time with our family. He went on vacations with us and ate dinner at our house most nights. Once my parents started signing his permission slips and report cards, they turned the basement guest room into his bedroom.

Austin was an only child, his dad recently retired as a point guard in the NBA. His mom was really great at spending his dad's money, but not so great at raising a child. So, Austin was raised by an au pair, a chauffeur, and a chef, a far cry from the way Wyatt and I were brought up.

With a single glance, Austin and I knew when the other one needed a hug, a laugh, a shoulder to cry on, an ear to listen, or all of the above.

So, when I saw him staring out my bedroom window, I knew something was going on.

"What are you thinking about?" I asked.

"Your mom seems like she's doing alright," he replied.

I knew playing the role of both parents wasn't easy, but while my dad was deployed, she didn't have much of a choice. Although it was never easy to talk about, he was right, and I smiled. She seemed like she was in a good place or was just really good at faking it.

She was the strongest person I knew. She was the glue of our family, a parent when she needed to be and a friend when I needed one. There was no question that Wyatt, Austin, and I put her through a lot. Yet somehow, between carpools, missed curfews, teenage attitude, and harmless rebellion, we rarely heard her complain. She never complained about putting us first. She never complained about having to be the good cop and bad cop for so many years. She never questioned her ability to make it through whatever situations we were thrown into on any given day. She was superhuman in every sense of the word.

"You know I still try to check in on her as much as I can, right?" he asked.

"I know," I answered.

I knew he still stopped in at least twice a week. I knew he brought flowers to my mom at least once a month. I knew he tried to attend as many of Wyatt's football, basketball, and baseball games as possible. I knew he talked to my dad almost every Saturday morning.

He never told me when he was doing any of it, but I knew. And I slept better at night knowing my best friend was back at home, caring enough to keep an eye on my people.

A few minutes later, Austin's phone rang. He rolled his eyes as soon as he looked at the screen and I could only hear his side of the conversation.

"No. Yes. No. No. Stop. Okay. No, stay there. I'll be there soon. I'm leaving now."

Hanging up, he grabbed his jacket off my bed and insisted he needed to leave.

"Everything okay?" I asked.

"Yeah, I just have to help my mom with something," he said, hastily. "See you tomorrow?"

"Yeah, call me later."

With that, he was gone.

I knew his parents had been fighting a lot. I knew his mom had been spending a lot of time at a bar in Sand Harbor, a town a few miles from Gulfpoint. I knew it was probably safe to assume the call meant Austin had to pick her up, but I didn't want to ask too many questions. I knew Austin well enough to know we would talk about it when he wanted to.

With Austin gone, my mom on a conference call, and Wyatt at basketball practice, I opened my closet, and made piles of clothes that needed to be brought to New York, clothes that needed to be donated, and clothes that needed to be thrown away.

Closet organization turned into an 'organize my entire room' domino effect.

Most of the time was spent moving things from one box to another, somehow convincing myself that I was making progress.

I dug through boxes under my bed, tossed shoes that hadn't been worn in years, threw away papers and receipts that had been kept for no reason, and got distracted by the contents of various drawers. Opening the top drawer of my nightstand, I found the fake ID I retired a few years ago, a bunch of loose change, the hospital band from the time I drank too much, enough hair ties to last a year, and photos of old friends whose names were lost and of friends I still kept in touch with.

Running out of energy and bored of organizing, I thought about how much happened in this room. I completed homework assignments at this desk, cried over high school romances on that beanbag, laid in bed binge-watching too many TV shows, and left the floor messy more times than I could have counted.

Reminiscing turned into scrolling through social media and before I knew it, I heard a knock on my door.

"What're you doing here, Maeve?!" Wyatt asked.

"What're you already doing home? I asked back, wrapping my arms around him.

It looked like he grew at least an inch or two in the few weeks since I saw him last.

"Uhm, can't practice on a wet field," he replied, laughing.

I was so caught up in my afternoon, I didn't realize it was torrentially downpouring.

"Seriously though, why are you here?" he asked again.

"Just needed some time back home," I said. "I'm here for the weekend."

"Oh good, so we can catch up later?" he laughed. "I need to get food right now."

I laughed.

My mom mentioned a few times over the past few weeks that she couldn't keep the refrigerator stocked, occasionally referring to Wyatt as a garbage disposal.

"What?" he asked, walking out of my room. "I'm a growing boy."

Making my way downstairs, I sat at the counter, listening to my mom and Wyatt talk about something that had happened in the cafeteria today. I came into the room halfway through the story but, from what I gathered, a senior and sophomore girl were unknowingly dating the same senior guy and, apparently, their Internet pettiness turned into a full-blown fist fight in the middle of the school day.

I didn't want to ask for too many details, unable to get invested in more small-town drama. It drained me so I tuned them out, a skill I learned years ago.

I snapped out of my daze when mom mentioned a new barbeque place that opened on Main Street.

"I haven't been there yet but the ladies at Bridge are raving about it!" she said. "It's called Bailey's BBQ."

The women in my mom's Bridge group were exceptional card players but, more importantly, they were well-respected critics around town. Any recommendation from them was to be taken seriously.

"Should we try it tonight?" I asked.

"You fly, I buy?"

I wasn't going to turn that down, especially because I knew Wyatt's driver's license was so new that he wouldn't turn down an opportunity to drive.

That night, our meal from Bailey's BBQ ended up being another successful recommendation from the Gulfpoint moms.

I thought we ordered more food than three people would ever be able to eat but, before long, the pulled pork, brisket, spare ribs, baked beans, macaroni and cheese, and biscuits were gone.

My mom was right. I had only been away from home for a short time and had completely underestimated how much Wyatt could eat.

After dinner, Wyatt asked if I could help him with his trigonometry homework, a feat easier said than done. I dug through my old high school notebooks, trying to find the same lessons from my tenure but, apparently, they changed how to do trigonometry sometime during the past few years.

Once we realized I was of no help in the homework department, Wyatt suggested we call our dad. I sent him an email last night to let him know I was headed back to Gulfpoint for a long weekend but I still hadn't gotten a response. Wyatt dialed his number and the call went unanswered. Then, it clicked. It was nearly 8:00 p.m. in Florida which meant it was just around 3:00 a.m. in Baghdad.

Defeated, tonight was added to the long list of times our father was noticeably absent. I knew I would have driven myself crazy if I only focused on everything he missed because of deployments, but I hated that he missed birthdays, holidays, and random weekdays. Those sacrifices became part of our 'normal' long before I understood what war was.

Chapter Three

I promised Austin we could spend the following day together but I didn't realize it would be starting so shortly after the sun rose.

"Ready for a full day of fun?" he asked, walking into my house. "We're doing all things Gulfpoint."

"Slow down, tiger," I laughed, noticing the two cups of iced coffee in his hands. "Things in town aren't even open yet!"

Austin Packard and I shared a lot of unspoken rules but 'bring iced coffee' had always been near the top of the list.

Leading him into our family room, with every intention of enjoying every sip of coffee, I settled on our oversized couch, my favorite spot in the house.

"Look at what my mom found," I said, handing him a stack of photos.

There were pictures of Austin and me in line at Disney World during elementary school, in a third-grade play, at eighth grade graduation, at summer pool parties, on beach trips, at junior prom where we looked our best, and the following morning where we looked far from it.

I had a tendency to cherish places instead of people, absentmindedly leaving most of my hometown friends in high school. That was never the case with Austin. We were instant best friends, by each other's side from the days of playing pretend to the nights of playing drinking games. We trudged together, sometimes begrudgingly, through every situation, good and bad. Things between us remained the same while the world around us changed significantly.

"What do you have planned for today?" I asked as Austin reached the final photo in the stack.

It was our first full day together in months and, knowing him, I was sure he planned on doing as much as possible.

"I'm thinking a hike, the beach, the movies, SaraBelle's, and Penny's," he replied.

I was tired just thinking about it but, I didn't dare say no to any of it.

Walking out of my house and to the end of my street, we were at the entrance to Gulfpoint Town Park, ready to hike.

Most legitimate outdoorsy people would have scoffed at this hike. It only took about fifteen minutes to reach the end of the trail and the amount of required effort never exceeded 'minimum.' But, from Main Street to the beach, the view from the top was the best around.

During middle school and high school, Austin and I would gather our friends, come to Gulfpoint Town Park, and get into as much trouble as we could find. It didn't take long for Gulfpoint Town Park to become the hangout spot for almost everyone in our grade, or at least everyone we cared about. Afternoons were spent at the basketball court and skate ramp; I had my first kiss behind the equipment shed; Austin got into a few fist fights on the back field, knowing he couldn't get suspended from school or sports teams if the fight happened off school grounds.

But Austin and I didn't start taking advantage of the hiking trail until our junior year of high school, on the day Austin made his first purchase from Malakai, Gulfpoint's go-to weed guy. Austin picked me up after school, packed a bowl, and told me he knew a spot we could smoke without getting into trouble. We never became consistent smokers, but we both agreed that marijuana took the edge off every so often. It also didn't take long to realize bowls were better suited for garage parties and, after that first day, Austin only rolled blunts before hikes, leaving the bowl hidden beneath his bed.

The hike on my first full day back in Gulfpoint was weed-free, mainly because Malakai upgraded to hard drugs and had been recently busted for selling cocaine to an undercover cop.

But, although I was completely sober, I was as mesmerized on the trek up the cliff as I would have been after a few hits. I'd been spending so much time in New York lately, surrounded by concrete, I started to forget how unsurpassed Florida nature is. I always told people I missed the palm trees, but I seemed to overlook the rest of the Florida foliage, forgetting about mangroves, spotted horsemint, and wild sage. Surprisingly, and possibly for the first time in my life, I wasn't even bothered by the geckos or beetles we saw on the hike.

There was very little meaningful conversation on our hike up the hill. We'd be spending the entire day together and Austin could tell I was appreciating everything we were passing.

Sitting on a bench at the top of the hill, I looked down at Gulfpoint and realized things here were a world away from the life I had become accustomed to in New York.

New York City had multiples of everything. Gulfpoint was a town of one.

There was one school district, one grocery store, one movie theater, one gas station, one laundromat, and one run-down car dealership. But we only needed one.

And I only needed one best friend, a best friend who was getting more impatient the longer we sat.

"Fitz, it's getting hot. Can we go to the beach now?" he asked four times in what felt like less than a minute.

Laughing at his restlessness, I stood, and we started making our way toward the bottom of the hill. The walk down took almost twice as long as the walk up. Tourists were scattered throughout the trail, I got distracted by three puppies, and Austin got distracted by the girls walking the dogs before continuing to complain about the heat.

Arriving back at my house, I was surprised to see my mom's car in the driveway.

I had no idea why she would be home in the middle of a workday.

We startled her as we opened the front door.

"Mom, what're you doing here?" I asked.

"Your brother forgot his basketball shorts," she said, rolling her eyes.

I chuckled to myself at the double standard, remembering one day during sophomore year when I left my soccer shorts at home. I called my mom in a panic and begged her to drop them off at the school before kickoff. She told me it was my responsibility to remember my uniform and that it was up to me to find a solution to the problem. I ended up borrowing a pair, about three sizes too big, from the Athletic Director. I played all ninety minutes pulling up my pants. It was the only game in my entire four-year high school soccer career that I didn't score a goal. It was also the only time I forgot any part of my uniform.

But now that Wyatt was the only one left at home with my mom, he was her favorite and it was no surprise that she was dropping his forgotten shorts at the school on her lunch break.

"So, you don't mind if I steal Maeve for the rest of the day?" Austin asked.

"Go for it," she said.

Susanna Fitzpatrick never said no to Austin Packard.

After our hike and quick stop at my house, Austin and I headed to his house to go to the beach. There were dozens of public access beach entrances throughout Gulfpoint, but the best beach was, undoubtedly, the one that was only accessible through Coral Manors, Austin's neighborhood.

A few minutes later, sitting on the cold sand, Austin and I chatted as waves crashed against the shoreline.

To neither of our surprise, nobody was home at Austin's. The chauffeur got a new job after Austin got his driver's license, the au pair found a new placement when Austin turned eighteen, and the chef took on the role of house manager, only popping in every so often if Austin's parents were traveling the world.

Although I assumed Austin picked up his mom last night, I still hadn't asked about it. As much as I wanted to know, I understood that was a conversation that needed to be on his time.

"Where are your parents now?" I asked instead.

"They flew out this morning," he said. "To Costa Rica, I think."

One time in high school, he told us his parents were in the Caribbean for a week, but I was skeptical when they returned home without a tan, so I asked how the trip was. Turned out, they had been in Seattle and the sun hadn't come out once. Since that trip, I was convinced Austin just picked a random country or city whenever someone asked where they were.

"Remember that time I tried to teach you how to surf?" he asked, changing the subject.

"How could I forget?"

It was the summer after our freshman year of high school. Austin was the best surfer on the varsity team, and I had the biggest crush on Gavin, one of his senior teammates. Austin invited me to a Saturday morning session, and I made sure I was there. The surfing part of the session had been incredibly unsuccessful. Surfable waves were practically nonexistent, which Austin still insisted was somehow my fault. But, with no waves to surf, there was plenty of time for Gavin and me to get to know each other. That was the start of an eventual eight-month relationship.

The beach at Coral Manors wasn't just responsible for my most serious high school relationship. It was also where my friends and I trained for high school sports seasons, where we hung out on days we decided it was too hot for school, and where we worked on our tans all summer.

I was about to make a comment about how much time we spent in this sand growing up when we were interrupted by a voice I would recognize anywhere.

"Austin, is that you?" her voice screeched.

There was absolutely no reason for Missy McHale to be on the beach alone in the middle of January. With the exception of Austin and me, the beach was completely empty, but she also lived in Coral Manors and it was clear that, like always, she was just being nosy.

Missy and I never got along. She had a huge crush on Austin for as long as I could remember and when they dated for about thirty seconds during high school, she wasn't the biggest fan of he and I spending so much time together.

My relationship with Austin was always strictly platonic but Missy, and most people in our school, didn't believe us then and likely didn't believe us now.

"Hey Missy, what's up?" he asked as I rolled my eyes.

"Want to hang out tonight?" she asked, completely ignoring my presence.

"Can't, sorry," he said, looking toward me. "I'm spending the day with Maeve."

"Oh, my goodness," she shrieked. "Maeve Fitzpatrick, is that you?!"

"Hi Missy, it's good to see you," I said, lying.

"Wow, you look so different. But in a good way!" she said.

Missy McHale, still as fake and petty as ever. She knew what I looked like, we followed each other on social media, but she thrived on dramatics.

"What are you doing with your life?" she asked.

"I'm living and working in New York City," I replied, not wanting to give her too many details.

"Oh, just here for the weekend, then?" she asked with a smirk as she looked toward Austin.

"Yep," I shook my head.

"Well, it was good to see you," she said. "See you soon, Austin."

"See ya," he said, clearly not paying much attention.

"What was that about?" I asked once she got out of earshot.

"She hasn't changed," he laughed. "Don't worry, that's a situation I'm not getting myself back into."

Austin and Missy's relationship was short-lived, even by high school standards, but it was full of drama. Aside from her issues with me, she got mad every time he looked in another girl's direction, every time he chose a family night over a night with her, and every time he had practice or a game when she wanted to hang out.

"I think I'm going to check out the waves," he said, picking up his surfboard. "Want to come?"

"I'm good, thanks," I laughed, laying down as he walked toward the ocean.

I woke up a few minutes later, or so I thought.

According to Austin, I had been asleep for the last hour and a half, but he didn't want to wake me because I "looked so relaxed."

That was the result of reuniting with the Florida sun after months away, I insisted, even in January.

"Ready to get going?" he asked.

"Where to next?" I replied.

"Midday movie, duh!" he said.

For as long as I could remember, Gulfpoint Cinema played the newest releases for five dollars on Friday afternoons. Throughout high school, we spent most Fridays in the winter leaving school to watch movies.

I didn't recognize any of the titles on the marquee this particular day so, like during high school, Austin picked the movie. It was, of course, an action movie that I didn't pay too much attention to.

"SaraBelle's?" he asked two hours later as the credits appeared on the oversized screen.

"Let's do it!" I said, getting excited.

SaraBelle's Ice Cream Shoppe witnessed every major friendship, and life, milestone for Austin and me. We celebrated birthdays there, opened our college acceptance letters there, and drove straight there after every Friday night football game.

I got lost in my mind on our drive, distracted by unexpected nostalgia. Gulfpoint was my hometown and the only place I knew for my first eighteen years of life. Yet, driving down the streets felt different this time, like I was an outsider instead of a native.

After getting to SaraBelle's and ordering black raspberry, my favorite, for me, Austin led me to our usual table on the outdoor patio.

Sitting across from Austin, I knew he was holding something back, so I bit the bullet and asked the question that had been on my mind since overhearing last night's phone call.

"How are your parents doing?"

"They're good," he said.

"And now the truth?" I asked.

"Fine," he sighed, pausing. "It's terrible."

"Talk."

"She's drinking nonstop, he's sleeping with a girl barely older than us, and I'm apparently the only adult in the family."

His eyes filled with tears and my heart broke.

My parents were no-nonsense, the complete opposite of Austin's. They cared about us and put our well-being ahead of theirs, where his parents tried to buy his love. If he wanted something material, he got it. And, as much as he wanted them to act like responsible parents, we both knew that wasn't going to happen.

I reached across the table and grabbed his hand, giving it a squeeze before sticking my spoon into his ice cream cup, desperate to make him crack at least a small smile.

He swatted my spoon so fast and all of the ice cream landed on the table, sending both of us into fits of laugher.

"Well, on that note," he said. "Let's get going."

The next few hours were spent back at my house. Austin and Wyatt played video games and I took another nap while my mom cooked dinner. I considered checking my work emails, but it had been such a great day and I didn't want anything to ruin my mood.

"Penny's tonight?" Austin asked after we finished dinner.

Gulfpoint was one of those towns where, growing up, excitement came from walking around the mall (at least until they set that curfew back in 2008), driving aimlessly in someone's car, or drinking in a basement. But that changed when we were in high school and Austin's parents bought Penny's Pub.

Penny's was where most of my friends spent Friday and Saturday nights, first illegally then legally.

With only one Saturday night in Gulfpoint for the foreseeable future, there was no chance I'd miss the opportunity to spend some time at Penny's.

Even with the changes that happened in Gulfpoint over the past few years, Penny's Pub remained the same.

The warehouse-like space was small with scattered pillars and high-top tables. The bar, a pool table in one corner, and a makeshift stage in another were the only stagnant parts of the place. The tile floors were still sticky and the faucet in the girls' bathroom still leaked. But it was home, so like the rest of Gulfpoint, it was perfectly imperfect.

Although most of our high school friends moved away from Gulfpoint, avoiding former classmates was a hope that was shattered as soon as we walked through Penny's door.

Seated at the center table were a group of girls we went to school with from kindergarten until senior year. They, like most people we ran into post-high school, were surprised to see Austin and I were still friends, almost as surprised as we were to hear one of them was engaged, one was pregnant, one was dating her high school arch-nemesis, one was married, and two were in college for another year. They were part of the super smart clique during high school and we were never close friends so, thankfully, our small talk was quick and painless.

The rest of the night continued the same way. As expected, there was a lot of small talk, a lot of catching up, and very few meaningful conversations.

Things that happened at Penny's Pub were, I'm assuming, the same things that happened at high school reunions. Everyone spent hours trying to look their best while bragging about their accomplishments when, in reality, everyone was lost in a seemingly never-ending tunnel of confusion and self-doubt.

But that was the thing about small towns – whether you were trying to break the bubble or live a life of simple routines within the county lines, it was always a competition and always a priority to portray yourself in the best light.

Chapter Four

G etting ready for bed on my last night in Gulfpoint, eight knocks rattled against my bedroom door. Normally, I would have yelled at Wyatt to go away, but this particular sequence signified so much more than an annoying little brother. This knock pattern was reserved for hard nights and special occasions, starting when Wyatt was eight. I told him that if he pounded on my bedroom door eight times in a row, we could stay up and hang out all night.

For the most part, all-nighters were reserved for nights before our dad returned home from base or nights we realized we hadn't heard from him in a while.

And on this particular night, when Wyatt peeked his head into my room, the look in his eyes brought me back ten years. For a split second, he was eight again, not eighteen and taller than me.

"Can we pull an all-nighter?" he whispered, trying not to wake our mom.

How could I say no to that?

Growing up, all-nighters were often spent playing Wyatt's favorite video games and eating too much candy, because as soon as I understood why our dad was rarely home, I made it a priority to use these sleep-free sessions to distract my younger brother from the uncertainty that our daily life had become. I wanted him to keep his innocence. I wanted him to see the world through bright eyes, not shattered glass.

The night before my flight back to New York was more or less the same. His schedule was about to become crazier than ever as the end of high school would undoubtedly fly by but I wanted him to enjoy everything the next year of his life was set to include.

Between rounds of video games, I asked how things were going at school and he explained the drama surrounding social media posts and semi-friends unfollowing semi-friends. I was so grateful that social media was only becoming a thing while I was in high school. Instead of worrying about who was following whom, our gossip and drama came from who hooked up with whom the previous weekend, whether our varsity football team won last Friday night's game, and which of our classmates were the latest to turn a casual hookup into an eighteen-year commitment.

According to Wyatt, nobody in the high school had been pregnant within the last two years but, apparently, things were still dramatic at the garage parties Wyatt attended almost every weekend.

Wyatt was a superstar athlete and a great student, but during his freshman year, I let him in on my not-so-secret "look how easy it is to sneak out of the house" revelation from high school. Although it may not have been the most responsible thing to share, I knew firsthand how tough Wyatt's childhood was. He deserved a night out every so often. I was happy to hear he was still taking advantage of the not-so-hidden back hallway.

Sitting in my room, reconsidering my flight back to New York, I realized how much Wyatt grew in the past year. He wasn't just a little kid anymore. We were peers now, officially at the point where he could be considered a friend, instead of just a little brother.

The longer we sat there with tears, fake fighting, and uncontrollable laughter, the more my body filled with a twinge of regret. I regretted the moments I called him annoying or immature. I regretted yelling at him for eavesdropping on my conversations. I regretted ignoring his pleas to play when we were kids.

My bedroom door cracked open again three hours later, startling Wyatt and me out of a deep sleep, proof that, all-nighters were harder to pull now than they had been a decade ago.

"I'm pulling out of the driveway in an hour, with or without you," our mom threatened.

She wasn't bluffing.

During my sophomore year of high school, she left the house without me a dozen times. She never made the point she intended to though, because thanks in big part to Austin Packard and his car, I never learned my lesson. Instead, every time my mom and Wyatt would leave without me, Austin would stop at my house on his way to school.

Unfortunately, I knew Austin wasn't an option for an early-morning airport drive so, somewhat reluctantly, I got out of bed, took a quick shower, pulled together a sweatshirt and pair of leggings, and made my way down to the kitchen.

Twenty minutes later, with a piece of toast in hand, I got into my mom's car and we were headed to the airport.

Gulf Coast International was one of Florida's quieter airports, but it seemed unusually busy today. Businessmen and tourists alike were checking bags, printing boarding passes, and scanning the Departures board for their flight status.

As we approached the security lines, the hallways got more crowded and I noticed a woman with three small children headed in the same direction as a majority of the crowd.

With a single glance, I knew exactly why they were at the airport.

The woman looked no older than thirty and like she just stepped off a billboard. The three little ones accompanying her could have come straight out of a children's clothing campaign. The oldest, the only boy, looked to be around nine years old and was tossing a foam baseball in the air. The middle child, a five-or-six-year-old girl, wore a pink shirt bedazzled with the phrase "My daddy is my hero." I had a similar one when I was her age. The youngest, another girl who couldn't have been older than two-years-old, wore a red, white, and blue tutu.

By the time they reached the security exit and held up their "Welcome Home Daddy" signs, everyone stopped looking at the cell phones that previously captured their attention, all eyes shifting between the hallway and the waiting family.

As each person passed by, the middle child's blonde curls bounced with excitement. The boy's focus was on his youngest sister, repeating "Daddy's almost here" over and over again. A few seconds later, his combat boots were the first thing I saw, followed by a smile I would never forget, a smile bursting with genuine happiness.

As the three children sprinted to their father, I put my arm around Wyatt, met by his glistening eyes.

My heart broke for these kids but I also resented them. They were the lucky ones. For the most part, they wouldn't remember their father's absence or how much family time he missed. If they were older, like Wyatt and I were during the first deployment (and every deployment since), they wouldn't be able to ignore his absence.

"He might know Dad," Wyatt said.

He was right, but as much as I wanted to ask, there were a lot of soldiers at local bases and a lot more in the entire United States Army. Either way, my heart probably wouldn't be able to handle his response.

"We should go thank him, right?"

For only eighteen years old, Wyatt was wise beyond his years.

Our parents always reminded us the importance of thanking the troops for their service so we headed toward the newly reunited family.

The soldier was the first to greet us. I felt bad for interrupting his homecoming but, out of an abundance of respect, we started things off with "welcome home" and "thank you for your service."

He thanked us then looked toward his children and that attention-grabbing smile reappeared. He was clearly ecstatic to be home with them again. Turning to his wife, I told her to remember this moment because some families wouldn't get to experience joyful homecomings. The look of sincerity in her eyes told me that she knew exactly what I meant.

Wiping uninvited tears from my eyes, I turned toward the three kids and asked how excited they were to have their dad home.

The older girl started jumping around before telling me about the welcome home tea party she planned to have with her dad and her stuffed animals. Her older brother interrupted, showed me the baseball in his hand, and insisted he was going to play catch with his dad in the backyard until the sun went down every night.

With that, the smile on the soldier's face was now mirrored on mine.

Not wanting to take any more time away from the excited children or their newly reunited parents, Wyatt and I apologized for interrupting, thanked the soldier once again, and made our way back to our mother.

Knowing my mom had to get to work and Wyatt had to get to school, I knew it was time to say goodbye and my tears returned. No matter how many times I said it, it never got easier.

We kept our goodbyes short and sweet.

Wyatt pulled me in for a hug almost immediately and reminded me that he was only a phone call or plane ride away. My mom reminded me that she would always be there to push me through any struggles that presented themselves. She was wearing one of my dad's old sweatshirts, one she asked him to get rid of a million times, one that still smelled like him, one I was so glad he kept.

"I'm so proud of you, honey," my mom said before I walked away. "I love you."

That was all I needed.

I couldn't look back on my way to the security line, afraid a single glance would send me into a downward spiral, the same way it did so many times in the past.

My eyes were clouded with tears through the entirety of the security process. I don't think I took my laptop out of my backpack. I wasn't even sure I took my shoes off. I was in a complete daze from the time I left my mom and Wyatt until I found an open seat at Gate C2.

As I sat and waited for some indication to board my New York-bound flight, I pulled a pen and notebook out of my backpack, jotting down some thoughts and lists.

I wrote down things I wanted to remember about this trip, things I wanted to do when I got back to New York, things I needed to pick up at the corner store, and things I needed to do at work.

Then, running out of list ideas but not out of time to wait, I started to write a letter.

Wyatt and I started writing letters to our dad during his first deployment, and although the Internet and emails became part of our daily lives as the years passed and deployments continued, we never stopped exchanging handwritten letters.

With my notebook flipped to a blank page, I started to write.

Dear Dad,

I know it's been a while since I've written an actual letter and I know it's not a valid excuse, but life has been pretty crazy lately. I'm sitting at Gulf Coast International waiting for my flight back to New York and I wish it were ten years ago when we were here as a family headed on vacation. Now as at least somewhat of an actual adult, I realize more than ever how much those trips meant. Family time has always been my favorite but even more so now that I've started a life of my own in New York City – a life I'm proud of, even if I've questioned a few times if it's been the right move. Okay, maybe more than a few times.

But, as much as I enjoyed this weekend in Gulfpoint, it proved a million times over that I made the right decision by leaving. Sure, I miss seeing mom, Wyatt, and Austin every day but, in the words

of my incredibly smart father, "that's why they make FaceTime," right?

Turns out you were right about a lot of things.

Remember that time you told me I was too ambitious, too curious, and too restless to settle for a life of normalcy in Gulfpoint?

I do. And, you were right about that, too.

Gulfpoint was the perfect place to grow up. I give so much credit, probably more than you realize, to you and mom for giving Wyatt, Austin, and me an incredible childhood. But I needed to move on. I needed to move to a place outside my comfort zone. I needed to start making decisions for myself, especially ones that are difficult to make.

So, Dad, I guess the point of this letter is to say thank you. Thank you for giving me a place that was so hard to leave. Thank you for making sacrifices so that we didn't have to. Thank you for teaching us firsthand what hard work and courage look like.

Thank you for everything.

They've started to call groups to board so I have to go but I can't wait to see you – hopefully soon!

I love you more than you know.

Love,

Mae.

I signed the note with the nickname only my dad used, along with "I love you more than you know." Those seven words were our thing and how we ended every single letter written. The phrase was key in successfully getting our family through deployment after deployment.

Chapter Five

Turbulence as we descended into New York startled me out of a sleep I didn't remember entering.

New York City was the melting pot of the world. There were millions of people on the oversized island at any given moment – each with a story of their own – yet everything looked so perfectly put together from the clouds. Looking out the window, I was mesmerized by the skyscrapers that looked minuscule from this high.

After deplaning and texting my mom, Wyatt, and Austin to let them know I arrived safely, I made my way to the airport's designated ride-share pickup location. Walking through the crowd, I couldn't help but think of the people surrounding me. Where were they from? Were they just passing through, waiting for a connecting flight? Did they have loved ones awaiting their arrival in New York? Was it their first, or hundredth, time visiting the big city?

Curiosity aside, I found comfort in not knowing the answers to those questions. Everyone was going about their day, stuck in their own world, but their imprint would remain in New York City forever, even if just in the smallest way.

Sitting in an Uber, stuck in traffic about halfway back to my apartment, my phone dinged.

A text from Greyson, a guy I recently started hanging out with, appeared on the screen.

Welcome back. Dinner tonight?

We met through a mutual friend nearly two months ago and had been casually hooking up for a few weeks. But we were at the point where I saw no harm in spending time together during hours that weren't in the middle of the night.

I replied almost immediately.

Thanks! Sounds good, where are you thinking?

His response came quickly.

Rod Iron Grill at 7pm?

Perfect. Meet you there!

I responded, avoiding any possibility of him picking me up from my apartment.

I was intrigued by him and wanted to know how, or if, our two stories could fit together, but I didn't want things to move too quickly.

Traffic cleared after we passed an accident and we were back at my apartment building quicker than I expected.

"Miss Fitzpatrick, how was your trip?" Ralph exclaimed as soon as our eyes met.

Like my boss, Ralph always called me Miss Fitzpatrick, something I insisted was one thousand percent unnecessary and something he insisted was part of the way he was raised. But, unlike when Declan did it, I smiled every time Ralph called me Miss Fitzpatrick. His delivery was genuine and never included the same condescending tone that usually accompanied Declan's.

"It was so great to be back home," I told him. "Small town living is just so different than life in the city."

"You know, back in the day, growing up in the city probably wasn't much different than your little town," he said, chuckling.

"How do you mean?" I asked, confused.

"You grew up going to the same places for the same things with the same people, right?"

I nodded and he continued.

"My life in the neighborhood was the same," he insisted. "This city is just a bunch of small towns mixed together."

I never thought of it like that.

He laughed, opening the door for a delivery and signing for the building's packages. I took that as my cue, gathered my two bags, and headed up to my apartment.

Ralph's words stuck with me longer than expected. I assumed you'd never see the same person twice in Manhattan. But, on the elevator ride up to my apartment, I thought of my life on the crowded island. With the exception of days where I decided to venture to different neighborhoods, I spent most of my time at the same places. I had my usual bodega, my usual Starbucks, and my usual takeout restaurants.

Just like when he taught me the importance of owning a sturdy umbrella, comfortable shoes, and a good pair of headphones, I started to think Ralph was right about Gulfpoint and Manhattan being more similar than different.

The New Yorker described the Rod Iron Grill as "the go-to spot for recent college graduates and out-of-town businessmen," citing its half-priced specials, happy hours, Taco Tuesdays, and trivia nights.

Despite passing it countless times, I never made my way into the Rod Iron Grill. I found comfort in the reviews posted on *The New Yorker*'s website and thrived in places known for happy hours and trivia nights, even if I never participated in the latter.

I also found an unexpected comfort in knowing Greyson knew what I looked like already, clothed and not.

So, with my hair blown out and makeup already put on, I pulled a pair of leggings, white tank top, and jean jacket out of closet, deciding less was more tonight.

Looking at my phone, I was surprised to see it was already 6:40 p.m. The Rod Iron Grill was fifteen minutes from my apartment and Ralph would be back from his dinner break at 6:45 p.m. meaning I had to leave my apartment immediately if I wanted to make it out of the building without answering questions about where I was headed.

Rushing to the elevator and through the lobby, successfully avoiding Ralph and his curiosity, I was met by a burst of sharp air as I walked through my building's oversized double-doors, a big difference from the weather I had just left back in Gulfpoint.

Like most trips out of my building, I had two options – walk or take the subway.

It was cold, but not too cold, and I didn't want my date outfit to be ruined by smelling like the subway. If it were date three or four, I would have swiped my MetroCard and stood in a cramped subway car, but it was only real date number one, so I walked from my building to the restaurant.

Tonight, the streets were flooded with tourists and businessmen, coming alive when the sun went down, but I wasn't focused on slow-walkers or dodging briefcases.

Instead, I was freaking out, realizing I couldn't remember the last time I'd gone on a date.

I had boyfriends in the past, but in Gulfpoint, I never had to tell anyone about myself. Everyone knew my business, whether I wanted them to or not. During college, I somewhat responsibly had my fair share of fun, but rarely before midnight. Instead of going on dates, I chose the casual scene over longtime relationships, knowing most college guys were looking for one thing and that wasn't a serious relationship.

I began to second-guess everything. How was I supposed to act? Was I supposed to order a beer or a mixed drink? How much was I supposed to share about my life now and my life back in Gulfpoint? How would I know if things were going well?

My nerves disappeared when I saw Greyson standing outside the restaurant. He smiled and pulled me in for a hug. He was about four or five inches taller than me, his arms wrapping around me with an immediate comfort. He smelled like boy, rugged but clean, strong but not overpowering. His dark jeans and burgundy button-down brought out the richness of his eyes.

Walking into the restaurant, we were greeted by the hostess, a young girl standing behind an oversized podium. She looked at Greyson with wide eyes before leading us through wooden barstools and thick pillars, stopping at a two-person high-top table. The dining room was lined with tables close enough to each another to make you aware of other diners, but far enough away that you didn't feel like you were part of everyone else's conversations.

"Does this work?" The hostess asked, looking directly at Greyson.

"Perfect, thanks," he replied with a smirk.

She giggled all the way back to the server's station, obviously smitten by my date.

He seemed unfazed.

"Used to that?" I asked, smiling.

"What? The hostess?" he asked. "She was like maybe eighteen!"

"That girl would have given every penny in her piggy bank to switch places with me!"

"What are you drinking tonight?" Greyson asked, changing the subject but still laughing.

"Surprise me," I told him. "Anything but tequila."

Like most people, I saved tequila for nights there was something or someone I needed to forget, leaving the intoxicating liquid inappropriate for my first mostly sober night with Greyson.

While he was waiting at the bar, I realized just how little I knew about him. I knew he moved to New York a few years ago from a small town in Massachusetts; I knew he worked in Murray Hill, but wasn't quite sure what he did; I knew he preferred dive bars over a five-course set menu; and I knew he was really fun to hook up with. But I didn't know his backstory yet. I didn't know how he liked his burger cooked, what kind of student he was, what shows he watched, if he had pets growing up, or if he had a good relationship with his family.

A few minutes later, Greyson returned to the table with two bottles of Bud Light. He saw me order vodka drinks during our nights spent at clubs, but I thought I knew what he was doing. He wanted to see if I was low maintenance enough to throw back a beer and hang with the guys. As the bottles clinked against the metal table, I made a mental note to call Austin in the morning. Although it was never my first choice, he taught me to like beer when we were in high school.

"I ordered a bunch of appetizers from the bartender," he said. "I figured we could split them, is that okay?"

I nodded and we made small talk before Greyson asked what I learned while living on my own, a question that took me by surprise.

People often asked how I liked my life in New York, but nobody ever asked me what I've learned in the busy city. And the more I thought about it, the more I realized I learned a lot, some things easily and some the hard way.

"The dark gets scary. Spiders won't kill you. You always need an emergency plan. Things don't clean themselves, *especially* showers. You can't blame someone else if things go wrong when you live alone. Clothes get wrinkled if you leave them in the dryer for too long. The refrigerator doesn't refill itself. It's important to always keep your medicine cabinet stocked. Making your own coffee will help you save a lot of money."

He chuckled as I rattled off my list.

"It took me at least a year to learn half of that! How long have you been here?" he questioned.

"Since June," I replied.

Conversation between Greyson and I flowed easily. He laughed again, and I realized there was no reason for me to be so nervous.

"What was before New York?" he asked.

"College," I said.

"What was that like? Was it the 'best time ever?'" he asked, rolling his eyes.

College was where I became independent in almost every sense of the word. It was the backdrop to my best and worst days. It was my place to grow, my place to figure out who I was, my place to make mistakes, and the place I discovered my inner strength. But I couldn't get that deep with Greyson yet. It was only our first date and I didn't want to scare him away.

"Not quite," I laughed. "It had its fair share of ups and downs, but I never questioned that life would get better than overcrowded frat houses, not-cancelled 8:00 a.m. classes, rarely opened but overpriced textbooks, and group projects, right?"

Time disappeared as our conversation continued and, before we knew it, three hours passed, and it was time for us to call it a night.

Greyson insisted on walking me back to my apartment. I tried to tell him I could get a cab or take the subway, but he was adamant that it was too dangerous for a girl in her twenties to be wandering around New York City alone at night.

I knew he was right, that was the first thing my parents insisted before my move, so I didn't put up too much of a fight.

Conversation continued easily on our walk toward my apartment building as Greyson explained a project he was working on at the office, causing him to spend more time at work than he liked. He had said, over sliders and quesadillas, that he worked in analytics, tracking progress for some of the most recognizable companies in the country's biggest industries.

Standing outside of my building, he pulled me in for a hug, and our lips met. It was a sweet, soft kiss, different than the ones we shared in the past. Our nights spent together were usually rushed, but tonight's kiss was gentle. It was a nice change, one I could get used to, and one I didn't want to end.

If I were still in college, I would have asked him to come upstairs but after this dinner, I wanted to take things slow. I wanted to see if this could last longer than a usual hook-up.

So, instead, I gave Greyson one more kiss at the doorway and headed up to my apartment.

Chapter Six

I thought my trip back to Gulfpoint was a mental and physical reset, but standing in front of 1207 Park Avenue on Tuesday morning, I was back where I was last week: dreading having to go into the office. I spent the past few days surrounded by some of my favorite people, old and new, so I wasn't ready to go back to the place that added so much stress to my life over the past few months.

Before graduating from college, I spent week after week scrolling through what felt like one million job-search websites. Each page left me questioning if I chose the right field to pursue. I loved my college classes, acing them with ease, but it felt like I applied to hundreds of jobs and hadn't heard back from any. It felt nearly impossible to find a job that had anything to do with journalism near Gulfpoint.

Running out of options and not wanting to start my post-grad life working in retail in my hometown, I started looking for job openings in faraway cities. Denver, Boston, Dallas, Miami, Los Angeles, New Orleans, Atlanta, Phoenix, Baltimore, Chicago, and

Nashville had desirable characteristics, but the further I searched, the quicker the cons outnumbered the pros.

I must have looked at one hundred openings in nearly a dozen cities before typing 'New York, New York' into the search box.

In my mind, New York City was an untouchable mecca. I watched countless television shows and movies based in the oversized city, but I never saw it as a place I could live until I started researching it. I fell in love immediately and knew I needed to do whatever was necessary to move to New York City after college graduation. I applied for anything and everything that had even the slightest resemblance to journalism.

Unlike the jobs I applied to in Florida, I started hearing back from New York-based companies. For the first few weeks I only heard 'no,' but I kept applying. A few weeks later, after about twenty "we're moving forward with other candidates" emails, I got discouraged and took a break from applying.

Graduation was approaching and although it wasn't my original plan, I figured it wouldn't kill me to spend a little time back in Gulfpoint.

But that plan changed on the morning of graduation when I received an email with the subject line "22 Job Recommendations for You" from one of the many websites I signed up for.

The recommendations were in scattered locations around the country; only one of the twenty-two was based in New York City. It was for an administrative assistant position at Sampson West. Reading through the description, I assumed they were looking for someone with more experience but saw no harm in applying anyway, still set on starting my post-grad life in New York City.

Two days later, I received a positive email response and scheduled a phone interview. A week after that, I was on a flight to New York for a third round, in-person, interview. I walked out of the interview with an accepted offer.

My dream of living and working in New York City became my reality. But that was seven months ago and the dream-like ambiance that once surrounded a career at Sampson West disappeared.

Walking into the office on my first day back in town, I headed straight for my desk, opening my inbox for the first time since midday Thursday.

On an average day, I'd receive anywhere from seventy-five to one-hundred emails so, as the page loaded, I knew I was going to be overloaded with requests, assuming I'd have to spend at least a few hours filtering through my inbox.

560 emails.

Eyes widened, I hoped a majority didn't need a reply, but either way, I knew I had a long day ahead of me. There was only one way to tackle so many unread emails – start at Thursday afternoon and respond in the order they arrived.

About three emails in, my computer dinged with a reminder notification.

Monthly Planning Meeting – 15 minutes. Conference Room.

Shit.

It was the first Tuesday of the month, so the morning was reserved for a three-hour planning meeting, far from an ideal way to spend my first day back at work. It also meant my email purge would have to wait until this afternoon.

I thought I was going to be early to the meeting, for once, but four guys were already sitting around the table as I walked into the room. I wasn't sure of their names, but I knew they worked in finance. I also knew they did everything together. As the door creaked, they turned in my direction, smirking, before continuing their conversation. They were complaining about their girlfriends 'making them' volunteer at a soup kitchen this past weekend. I was tempted to make a comment about compassion and helping people, but I don't handle confrontation well and the conversation came to a halt when others started filing into the room.

The planning meeting went the same as every other. Declan sat at the head of the table, spewing nonsense about upcoming projects and recent releases. He spent far too long discussing things everyone was doing wrong, followed by very little time discussing everything we were doing right.

After listening to himself talk for long enough, he started calling on people around the room. Each department head had to explain everything they did since the last meeting, everything they planned on doing before the next meeting, everyone they met with, and every meeting scheduled – the bigger the name, the better.

The longer they spoke, the harder it was to pay attention, especially as everyone tried to one-up the person who spoke ahead of them. One of the first things I learned was how much people in New York City, or at least in New York's publishing industry, loved to brag about their careers, who they knew, and how often they visited the city's hotspots.

As an administrative assistant, I wasn't expected to talk during planning meetings, making paying attention that much harder. I tried to take notes during most meetings so it would at least seem like I was interested in what was being discussed, but today, even that was impossible. I was too distracted. I was replaying details of my date, wondering what was in the 557 still-unread emails sitting in my inbox, and thinking about where to get lunch once this meeting ended. With my mind everywhere but the conference room, I was flustered when I saw everyone looking in my direction.

"Miss Fitzpatrick, do you have any ideas to add?" Declan asked, getting annoyed, leading me to believe it wasn't the first time he had asked.

Last I heard, the group was discussing things we could do for some good PR, something I recommended a few times in the past.

A few of our authors had gotten themselves into trouble with the press lately, making off-the-cuff comments to reporters and sending drunk tweets, and the firm was starting to take a hit. Some underground independent websites started insinuating that we were losing control of our clients and, although that was likely true, we needed to make sure that narrative didn't make its way to mainstream media or our competitors.

I hadn't heard Declan's infamous "onto the next," yet so I assumed we were on the same topic.

"Why not a day of volunteering?" I asked, hesitating, in case I was a few topics behind.

"Actually, that's not bad, Eve," Declan said. "How would it work?"

"Well," I started, ignoring that he got my name wrong again. "We could have our clients and staff at a food bank or animal shelter for a day. We'd just need to invite the press or some sponsors and we could turn it into an entire social media campaign."

"I like it," he said. "Make it happen."

Declan liked my idea? That was a first.

Maybe he thought about our last conversation over the weekend. Maybe he was taking my concerns into consideration. Probably not, but a girl could dream.

Looking around the room, everyone moved on to the next topic, but I caught a few looks of disdain from the frat-bros-turned-finance.

Be careful who you complain in front of, boys, I thought.

The rest of the meeting, and the rest of the workday, dragged on for far too long. I got through nearly half of my unread emails, simultaneously deciding which from today could be ignored for now and which were time sensitive.

At six-thirty that evening, I packed up my belongings, turned my computer off, and made my way down to Manhattan's busy streets.

Skipping the subway, I dialed Austin's number on my walk toward my apartment building, hoping a phone call with my best friend would do some good. Thankfully, he answered almost immediately.

"Fitz!" he exclaimed. "How was day one back at work?"

"Do you think it's too soon for a trip back to Gulfpoint?" I asked.

"You're so dramatic," he laughed. "It couldn't have been that bad!"

"Declan called me Eve in front of the entire staff," I said.

"Stop! What'd you do?"

"Gave an idea that he ended up loving that he'll definitely take credit for."

"That's my girl!" he replied. "This is what you signed up for, remember?"

He was right. We had this conversation countless times during the spring semester of our senior year of college. We were prepared to do the work no one else wanted to, trading frat parties and keg stands for cubicles and rush-hour commutes at a time when the job market wasn't ideal and the cost of living was skyrocketing.

"I know, I know," I said, annoyed that he had been right so often lately.

"Listen Maeve, I gotta go. Your brother's calling," he said. "I'll text you later, okay?"

"Yeah. Talk later," I replied before hanging up.

Four hours later, my phone buzzed and a text from Austin appeared on the screen.

> **Wake up early tomorrow. Do your hair and makeup and pick out a good outfit.**

Another text came in almost immediately.

> **Buy an iced coffee on your way to work but sit and enjoy it. Call me when you're finished.**

Even from miles away, Austin knew exactly what to say when I needed a mood boost.

I sent back a couple of hearts and climbed into bed.

At Austin's request, I woke up extra early the following morning, grabbed my favorite sweater out of my closet, matched it to a pair of jeans and riding boots, did my hair and makeup, and headed out of my apartment toward Logan's Luncheonette, a quaint and secluded coffee shop not far from my building.

I assumed Logan's would be full of businesspeople looking to grab a cup of liquid-lifeline, but the shop was unusually quiet. Confused, I looked at my phone. It wasn't even 8:00 a.m. Most people I saw here on a normal day were most likely just waking up, getting ready for another day, or still commuting into the city.

It was unseasonably warm for January and deciding it was awkward to be the only person sitting in the shop, I walked out the back door to a partially hidden patio.

I was in the middle of a city that housed 8.5 million people, a city known for 'never sleeping,' yet silence seemingly engulfed the streets surrounding Logan's Luncheonette on this particular morning. Right before leaving Florida for the first time, everyone warned me that I would be overwhelmed by the constant flow of New York City, but it wasn't until sipping on my iced caramel macchiato this particular morning that I realized just how much I took the stillness clouding Gulfpoint for granted.

Silence didn't exist for long in New York City. Taxis were screeching, horns were beeping, and sirens were blaring by the time I finished my coffee.

I was supposed to call Austin after leaving Logan's, but I needed a few more minutes of quiet. I sent him a quick text instead.

Coffee/alone time was exactly what I needed, thanks! Call you after work!

Skipping the subway again, I walked toward 1207 Park Ave with my headphones plugged into my phone but no music playing, focusing on the sounds of the city instead of the latest playlist curated by a social media influencer.

Undistracted by music, I looked up at the passing skyscrapers and appreciated the tenacity seemingly programmed into every

New Yorker. Offices were already occupied, well before the start of a normal nine-to-five workday. People were already sitting at desks – some protecting the city, some creating content, and some providing essential services – impacting people all over the world, in one way or another.

Chapter Seven

Between pre-scheduled releases, meetings, and deadlines, it took a few weeks to coordinate the Sampson West 'Day of Volunteering.' By the first Monday of February, schedules had been cleared, press had been contacted, and almost the entire company was set to spend the end of the workweek volunteering at a dog shelter on the Lower East Side.

We arrived at the shelter shortly after 10:00 a.m. on Friday. We were greeted by an overweight man named Calvin, who introduced himself as the shelter's founder and "the dogs' biggest advocate." He explained that he started the shelter four years ago after he and his boyfriend found a dozen stray puppies behind The Museum of Natural History, not wanting the dogs to become victims of the environment. We met Stefan, the now-ex boyfriend, next. He insisted he and Calvin were great business partners even if they hadn't been good life partners. Stefan explained that he was responsible for animal transport, volunteer coordination, and media relations.

Before separating us into groups, Stefan asked if anyone had volunteered at an animal shelter, or anywhere else, in the past. I was shocked by how few hands raised. Never volunteering before was a concept I couldn't grasp.

Growing up, my parents placed considerable value on helping others. They believed our actions, big or small, had the power to change lives. Wyatt, Austin, and I spent a dozen afternoons and weekends every year at food pantries, animal shelters, children's hospitals, and fundraisers to benefit local charities.

Based on experience, I had a general idea of what to expect during our day at the shelter but, within an hour, I realized I had an almost-unfair advantage over most of my colleagues.

The morning was spent cleaning pens, listening to stories about the dogs in the cages, and getting to know some of the volunteers.

At one point, Savannah, a trust-fund baby from Connecticut who worked in marketing, asked how to get a dog out of its cage then questioned if the leash and collar were hurting the pup. Taking care of dogs was second nature to me – our family fostered dozens of shelter and military dogs during my childhood years so it took a minute for me to grasp that someone could be so inexperienced while dealing with the four-legged friends.

By lunchtime, almost everyone, including Declan, had the hang of the whole 'helping others' thing. I knew most people would figure it out eventually, but I would have bet every dollar in my savings account that Declan only knew how to care about himself.

Everyone from the press left after lunch and I assumed Declan would be right behind them but, much to my surprise, he stayed and helped take care of the dogs for the rest of the afternoon, leading me to believe he was starting to realize playing with puppies was the ultimate form of stress relief.

The afternoon was a lot less work and a lot more play than the morning. Calvin and Stefan brought out two cases of cold beer and must have thanked us fifty times for spending the day at the shelter, grateful to have received the help.

Our entire staff and the shelter's volunteers sat around for the last hour telling stories, playing with puppies, and getting to know each other. I even caught of glimpse of the four frat-bros-turned-finance-guys playing fetch with a few of the dogs. Looking around the room, noticing there wasn't one face without a smile, I had a feeling it wouldn't be my – or Sampson West's – last time at the shelter.

Gathering my stuff, ready to head back to my apartment, I ran into Declan at the door.

"How do you think the day went?" I asked.

"Maeve!" he exclaimed. "It was great! Did you see the numbers?"

Shaking my head, he explained that between the social media campaign and the press that earlier in the day, Sampson West was dominating the Internet in the best ways possible. He also told me that two of our biggest sponsors were so impressed by the day and wanted to join our efforts. One company decided to donate fifty pounds of dog food to the shelter for every fifty shares on social media, and the other pledged to pay the adoption fees for every dog adopted from the shelter in February.

"So yeah," Declan said with the biggest smile on his face. "Overall, a really great day for us, our sponsors, and most importantly, the shelter! Thank you for the idea!"

Another compliment from Declan? It was a miracle!

When I got back to my apartment, I called Wyatt and Austin, excited to tell them about my day and about Declan's compliments.

But, when Wyatt answered the three-way video chat, I could tell he was in a mood. It wasn't an angry or sad mood; it was the rare 'Wyatt didn't get his way' mood.

"What's wrong, Wyatt?" I asked.

Austin rolled his eyes.

"Mom's the worst," Wyatt said. "I'm so over this. I want to go away to school right now."

"Be careful what you wish for, bud," I replied. "Going away to school means paying most of your own bills and making your own doctor appointments."

Austin, thankfully, nodded in agreement.

"Your sister's right, dude," he said. "What'd your mom say no to?"

"She won't let me go to the old Riverwalk tonight," Wyatt said, annoyed.

"Wait a second," I interrupted. "You're mad because mom won't let you, her underage son, go to a party at the old abandoned Riverwalk Hotel?"

He nodded.

"I wonder why," I responded, sarcasm dripping in my tone.

"You guys used to go there all the time!"

"Yeah," Austin said. "Until someone literally died."

It was the night of our high school graduation and a bunch of us decided the drug-and-alcohol-free all-night party put on by the PTO was going to be lame, so we hosted our own party at the abandoned Riverwalk Hotel. We had been drinking for hours when Simon Atwood, a quiet kid who always just tried to fit in, fell through an unstable staircase and cracked his head open. He was dead before the ambulance could get through the chain link fence surrounding the building.

That was five years ago and I still couldn't drive or walk past the Riverwalk.

Clearly annoyed that Austin and I were siding with my mom, Wyatt hung up.

"Can you do something with him tonight?" I asked Austin.

"Already on it," he said. "I'll call you later!"

I understood Wyatt's frustration, but I'd been to plenty of Gulfpoint High School parties at the Riverwalk Hotel and knew they weren't worth the risk.

Not getting the chance to tell Wyatt and Austin my good news, I texted Greyson.

> **Shelter went great AND Declan was nice to me! Was so tempted to bring home a puppy!**

He responded less than a minute later.

> **Yes! That deserves a drink – have one for me, stuck at the office late tonight. Don't pick out a puppy without me!**

I hoped he was just making conversation, not actually serious about sharing a dog, but either way, I definitely needed that drink.

Opening the refrigerator, the Ground Rules letter I received from my father right after moving to New York caught my attention.

Growing up, Ground Rules letters made an appearance before every deployment. My mom would leave the list of expectations attached to the refrigerator door from the day my dad left until the day he returned home so I was doing the same with this letter.

The letters changed with every deployment, modified based on which grade we were in or which sport season was happening, but they always included ten rules to follow, usually in a numbered list.

This one was no different.

Grabbing a drink and settling on the couch, I re-read the letter.

> Dear Mae,
>
> The day has finally come. You're officially on your own, nearly 1,000 miles from home. Fair warning before I even get into the rules – this isn't going to be easy for any of us.
>
> You're going to have nights where you want to cry yourself to sleep, and some where you actually do, and days where you want to give up, but we both know you're not a quitter.
>
> More than anything, I need you to remember that you're not alone. You will never be alone. I promise we will be there every step of the way as you experience anything and everything your heart desires. We will be there to encourage you, comfort you, push you, and support you. But, while you figure out what's included in "what your heart desires," I need to lay some ground rules. If we've done as good of a job raising you as I'd like to believe, these rules will be second nature in no time, most of them probably already are!
>
> 1.) You're not in New York City to find Prince Charming, you're there to find yourself. If you find your future husband, it's on you to be a good judge of character. For my sake, and yours,

remember that you deserve the world and, most importantly, never lower your standards for some guy.

2.) Call home every so often. Your mom, Wyatt, Austin, and I are excited you made this move, but we're going to miss you more than we might be willing to admit. We don't need minute-by-minute updates, or even day-by-day, but please try to keep us in the loop about what's going on!

3.) Spread kindness. You're in a big city where you're going to meet different kinds of people with different backgrounds, different dreams, different perspectives, and different attitudes. You're going to run into rude people but please remember, kindness is key. Karma is real, Mae. It's not hard to do things for the less fortunate, even if it's just smiling at a stranger who looks like they're having a rough day. This move is about finding yourself, but one day, you'll realize those strangers were essential players in your journey.

4.) You might be out of school, but that doesn't mean the learning stops. If anything, it's only beginning. Try opening yourself up to new experiences as often as possible. You're only given one shot at life and I don't want you to have any regrets.

5.) There will be days where you don't see your own greatness but it's there, I promise. Please surround yourself with genuine people, Mae. Their reassurance and support will make a world of difference.

6.) Remember, flowers don't exist without some rain. Speaking of flowers, buy some when times are tough. They can brighten even the darkest of days.

7.) No matter where you end up, never forget where you came from. Del Ray Lane might be one thousand miles away but less than three hours on an airplane will bring you right back to a town that will always welcome you with open arms.

8.) Write everything down. There will be days where life feels like a complete blur and sometimes, it will be. Write down big events and small observations. Write down what you had for dinner, what you wore, and what you love about each day. Write down your arguments and your laughing fits. Write grocery lists and thank you notes. Just keep writing.

9.) Quick-fire round: Never say 'maybe' if you want to say 'no,' your happiness always needs to come first. Trust the timing of your life. Be a team player. Don't settle for second best. Remember, you get what you work for, not what you wish for.

10.) Most importantly – have fun.

I know you're overwhelmed right now by the move and the boxes that are probably still all over your apartment, but I hope you know we're so proud of you and we're cheering you on from afar. I love you more than you know.

Love,

Dad.

Reaching the end of the letter, I wiped the tears from my eyes, taking a minute to appreciate how lucky I was to have my dad in my corner.

Although his work schedule was incredibly unpredictable, and it seemed like we only had a few minutes to talk every week, I was beyond grateful that video chats were an option. They made it easier to pretend he was nearby instead of an ocean away. Plus, talking at least once a week wasn't anywhere near as rough as it could get. There were times when video chats during deployments happened daily and times where they were separated by weeks.

A few minutes later, as if scripted, a noise dinged from my laptop. The screen read Incoming FaceTime from Dad before being replaced by my father's face.

"Hi, Dad!" I exclaimed.

"Oh shoot, I meant to call your brother!" he laughed.

I loved his laugh. In a lot of ways, it matched his personality. It was strong and could quiet a room, making everything around him stop.

To outsiders, my dad was strong, courageous, and brave. But to us, he was so much more. He was my most-trusted confidant, my most-supportive cheerleader, my harshest critic, and my first phone call if I aced a test or crashed my car. He was the coach on the little league field, the guy who stopped to help broken down cars on Elm Street, the Sergeant leading our troops into battle, and the friendly neighbor waving on the streets of downtown Gulfpoint.

"What are you doing, sweetie?" he asked.

"Just hanging out," I laughed.

"So, procrastinating on whatever you're supposed to be doing?" he asked.

As a professional student for the past sixteen years, procrastination was my specialty. During junior year of college, it was a talent that increased tenfold, becoming a running joke between my father and me. For all four months of fall semester, I'd call him every time I was procrastinating, and eventually, he told me I couldn't call more than four times in one day.

I started to respond with some wise comment but was cut off by a radio noise on the other end of the line. I didn't know what the transmission meant, but I did know our call was ending.

"Honey, I have to go," he said. "I love you, talk soon."
I barely said "I love you too" before the screen went dark.

Chapter Eight

As February continued, Greyson and I started seeing each other regularly during daylight hours. Instead of only late-night booty calls and "you up?" messages – although those were still happening– we went out to dinner a few times, watched movies together at least twice a week, and spent most days texting back and forth.

Earlier in the week, we ventured around SoHo, browsing through stores we couldn't afford to shop in, trying on clothes we couldn't afford to buy, and pretending to be tourists. We laughed the entire time. Everything about us felt effortless and natural, completely different than my previous pseudo-relationships.

For the past few years, I was okay with being someone's "sometimes" but, the more time I spent with Greyson, the more I realized I wanted to be his "all the time." I wanted to find out what made him smile and what made him tick. I wanted to learn his guilty pleasures and his biggest pet peeves. I wanted to know about his family, his aspirations, his childhood, and his fears. Most importantly, I didn't want to spend my time entertaining anyone else.

But, desires aside, there wasn't an official title on our situation, so we decided not to do anything crazy for Valentine's Day. Instead of paying for an overpriced set-menu dinner-for-two at a crowded Manhattan restaurant, we treated it like a normal Friday night. He came over to my place with pizza, beer, and chocolate cake – a combination that led me to believe he already knew food was the way to my heart.

As we sat on the couch, watching some sappy chick flick neither of us was paying attention to, his fingers rubbing circles along my leg as mine rubbed his bicep, our lips met. I wrapped my arms around his neck and pressed my body against his chest, his tongue wandering freely in my mouth, our bodies fitting together like perfectly matched puzzle pieces, only to be interrupted by my phone ringing.

Looking at the screen, I saw Austin's name and, going against our 'answer before the third ring' rule, I ignored the call, feeling Greyson tense up under me.

"Do I have competition?" he asked.

"Not even a little," I insisted. "He's my best friend."

"Don't most girls usually end up falling in love with their best guy friend?" he asked, skeptically.

"Maybe," I laughed. "But I'm not most girls."

Greyson had a valid point, but Austin and I weren't like most boy-girl best friends. He was always more like a brother than a best friend.

There was only one conversation, in tenth grade about potentially becoming more than friends, but we realized neither of us was willing to risk a broken friendship as the result of a broken romantic relationship. We hadn't spoken of it since. Falling in love was absolutely not in the cards.

Previous boyfriends weren't fans of my friendship with Austin and time and time again, it proved to be an awkward conversation. But either way, although earlier than I would have preferred, I felt like I needed to explain my relationship with Austin to Greyson.

Without going into too many details, I explained that Austin was Harden Packard's son who coincidentally sat next to me on the school bus on our first day of kindergarten. I told him we became instant best friends and how he practically became part of our family when his dad's basketball career skyrocketed, mainly to ensure some stability in his young life.

I insisted, a million times, that things between us had always been strictly platonic and was adamant that, if anything romantic happened between us now, it would feel like incest, at least mentally. Hesitant to make eye contact, I felt a weight lift from my shoulders as he nodded and smiled.

"Now would be a good time to say something," I urged, laughing.

"Is it weird that I had his dad's poster on my wall growing up?" he asked.

"You and every other boy born between 1992 and 1997," I smirked. "Wait, it's gone now though, right?"

We both laughed but I wasn't joking.

"Yes," he chuckled. "It's probably in storage somewhere!"

"Okay good!"

"Why?" he asked.

"If it was still by your bed, I'd probably never go to your apartment," I laughed.

For the most part, I ignored the NBA's influence on my life, including over the past eighteen years of friendship with the son of an NBA superstar. So now, nearly one thousand miles from home, I didn't want to sleep in a room where there were any reminders of my best friend's mostly absent father.

"So, you're not mad?" I asked Greyson.

"Why would I be?" he questioned. "It's not like I thought you had some lifelong Rapunzel quarantine before we met. I knew you'd have guy friends."

I smiled at him, grateful that he seemed to be relatively openminded about the whole thing.

"One thing though?" he asked.

"Yeah, anything."

"Do I get to meet him?"

"Austin or his dad?" I laughed, legitimately not sure who he was referring to. "Let's file both as a maybe for now."

The movie we were halfway watching ended during our tenser-than-I-would-have-preferred conversation.

"Valentine's Day is over," Greyson said, looking at his phone, as the credits rolled on repeat. "Want to go to the bar?"

"Can we rain check?" I asked. "I'm kind of tired."

"Of course," he replied. "What are you doing tomorrow? Want to hang out?"

"Yeah, text me in the morning."

With that, he gave me one more kiss and headed out hopefully back to his apartment, but I knew that was probably unlikely.

After he left, I was annoyed that I said no to the bar, finding myself wondering what he was doing, defeating the intention of going to bed early.

Had he gone home, deciding to call it an early night? Was he at the bar flirting with other girls and buying them drinks, the same way we had met just a few months ago?

Either way, I spent the next hour thinking about him and his caramel eyes.

At one point, when I definitely should have been asleep, I found myself comparing my halfway-relationship with Greyson to a halfway-relationship during the last few months of college. I'd been hanging out with this one guy for a few weeks and although we knew things weren't going anywhere after graduation, it was easier to avoid even the slightest mention of that conversation. So, that's what we did.

But I felt like things were different with Greyson. I was scared of how quickly my feelings were progressing but I just kept thinking about how intently he listened when I talked, always appearing genuinely interested in any conversation, silly or serious, as if he were hanging onto every word passing my lips.

I knew, unlike during college, a conversation about our halfway-relationship was one I couldn't avoid, making a pact with myself to have the always-dreaded feelings talk with Greyson the following day.

Twelve hours later, there was a knock on my apartment door. Opening it, I was greeted by Greyson and a dozen white roses.

Wrapping my arms around his neck and whispering "thank you," I was met by his lips on mine.

Walking to the kitchen, with Greyson right behind me, I grabbed a vase from the top cabinet, placed the roses in lukewarm water, and set them on the counter.

Glancing at Greyson, I couldn't ignore this kind gesture. Although a small act, picking up flowers, whether from a florist or the local bodega, was so meaningful.

"They're beautiful," I gushed, giving him another kiss. "Can we talk about something for a second?"

"Uh oh," he said. "Is everything okay?"

"Yeah," I laughed. "Why wouldn't it be?

"My mom taught me when a girl says 'can we talk?' it's never for a good reason!"

I laughed because I taught Wyatt and Austin the same thing, but in this particular instance, I had just chosen the wrong words.

"No, it's good," I chuckled. "Or at least I hope it is!"

"Okay, shoot," he said, hesitating.

"Where do you see this going?

"Us?" he asked.

"Yes, crazy," I laughed. "Us."

"Well," he paused.

I started overthinking everything.

Did I push the question too soon? Was I feeling this more than he was? Did he only see this as a "just for fun" thing? Did I misread the signs?

"Never mind," I insisted. "We don't have to talk about it."

"Babe, calm down, it's fine," he said, grabbing my hand, giving it a quick squeeze. "I had a whole speech planned out for later this afternoon."

"A speech?" I asked, confused.

"I really like you, Maeve. A lot." He said. "I think there's a lot of potential and I want to see where it could go."

I felt myself turning red.

"I saw this being a lot more romantic," he laughed. "But, will you be my girlfriend?"

I said yes immediately, glad we were on the same page.

"Now that the nerve-wracking part of the day is over, want to get out of here?" he asked.

"Where are we going?"

"It's a secret," he smirked.

I had lived in New York long enough to know everyone had a 'secret' spot. Mine was an open courtyard on West 42nd Street, directly between the Avenue of the Americas and Broadway. But, at least in my opinion, most 'secret spots' were tacky hole-in-the-wall bars that should have stayed unknown. Walking out of my apartment building, I hoped Greyson's spot was more like mine and less like a bar.

"There's one condition on this trip, though," he said.

"Oh yeah? What's that?"

"I know you don't like it, but we have to go through Times Square."

"I guess one walk in Times Square won't kill me," I laughed, secretly smiling that he remembered one of our first conversations.

I would never forget the first time I experienced Times Square. It was my first day in New York City and my eyes darted in every direction, trying to take in as many of my new surroundings, as quickly as possible. I had seen photos and videos of the world-famous tourist destination but they didn't do it justice. I knew people referred to the area as the 'Crossroads of the World,' but it wasn't until I was there for the first time that I realized just how many restaurants, coffee shops, newsstands, street performers, and tourists were squished in such a small space.

There was an almost unimaginable mixture of people crammed together, people of all shapes and sizes, on sidewalks and in crosswalks. There were businessmen who looked like they spent my entire life savings on a single dinner and people dressed as cartoon characters, looking to exchange knockoff Disney World-type photos for some extra cash. There were homeless people and panhandlers in the same half-block as business executives, showing the clear divide in New York's social structure. There were New York City's famous yellow taxis, blacked out SUVs likely carrying celebrities, men on bicycles peddling passengers, limo chauffeurs waiting for clients, and tourists crammed onto double-decker tour buses.

But, as months passed, the Times Square streets lost some of their magic and now, instead of looking up at the oversized billboards, I avoided the area as much as possible.

As we got closer to wherever we were headed, Greyson said this was the place he went whenever things became too much to handle.

"Is this your way of saying I'm a lot to handle?" I questioned, laughing. "Letting your true feelings out now that we're officially dating?"

"I hope you're a lot to handle," he smirked, squeezing my hand tighter. "But no, I wanted to show you my favorite place in the city."

Turning a corner, my instincts kicked in. Everything about the area screamed dangerous. It was the kind of place my parents warned me to stay away from but I was going into the day with an open mind.

"I know it's not much," Greyson said, stopping in front of a building.

I looked up, trying to figure out if we were in front of an office building or an abandoned warehouse. Based on appearance, either was a fair guess.

"Are we allowed to be here?" I asked.

"My uncle brought me here for the first time when I was thirteen. His wife's family has owned the building for like five generations," he explained, pulling a key out of his jacket pocket. "He died of lung cancer a few years later but told me the fifth floor was accessible whenever I wanted. So, I try to come at least once a month."

My jaw dropped when the elevator doors opened on the building's top floor. I quickly found myself admiring everything from the exposed brick walls and floor-to-ceiling windows to the floorboards and concrete pillars scattered throughout the oversized room.

"Greyson," I gasped. "This place is incredible."

"Right?"

Grabbing my hand, he brought me to the large windows on the far side of the room. They were massive panes of glass that overlooked the Hudson River.

"See that?" he asked as we stared outside. "I just stand here when I need a reminder that the world is bigger than whatever is going on in my life."

"Thank you for showing me this," I said, genuinely appreciative.

"I planned on asking you to be my girlfriend here but someone had to jump the gun a bit!" he laughed, nudging me. "But I have an idea."

I was intrigued.

"What if we spruce up that corner a bit?" he asked. "It has the best view of the river and it could be our spot whenever we need to get away from the craziness for a minute."

I loved the idea. I knew he could tell by how quickly my lips landed on his.

Our kisses were interrupted by a ringing phone again, but this time, it was his.

"Hang on a sec, babe? It's work," he said, rolling his eyes.

Not wanting to listen in on a call I probably wouldn't understand, I walked back to the windows at the far end of the room, mesmerized by the river. I knew it wasn't safe to swim in this part of the Hudson but, the way the sun reflected off its choppy waters, I had to admit that it looked refreshing.

A few minutes later, I felt Greyson behind me.

"I'm really sorry," he said, placing a kiss on top of my head. "Something happened and they need me to go into the office for a little while."

"On a Saturday afternoon?" I asked, disappointed that our day was coming to an end.

"I know, I'm really sorry. I called you a car already."

"Don't be sorry, your work is important, but I can take the subway back," I insisted.

"No way!" he exclaimed. "If they're making me go to work on a weekend, they can pay for your car!"

I wasn't going to argue that.

"I'll call you later, okay?" he said, kissing my forehead once more.

Halfway back to my apartment, I realized I never called Austin back after ignoring his call the night before.

Pulling my phone out of my pocket, I composed a quick text.

Sorry I never called back, it's been a crazy 24 hours! Call me later!

He texted back almost immediately.

No problem. Going to dinner with Missy tonight lol call you after.

I rolled my eyes, silently judging my best friend's decision.

Not bothering to respond to Austin, knowing it was in my best interest to keep my opinion to myself, I was relieved to see the town car was pulling onto my block.

Walking into the building, I was surprised to see Ralph at his post. It was after five o'clock on a Saturday afternoon, he should have gone home for the weekend.

"Ralph, why aren't you home with Miss Ruth?" I asked.

"Who was that boy who walked in with roses and walked out with you?" he countered.

"A friend," I smirked. "He's a nice boy, I promise."

"He better be!" he laughed. "Remember, thirty-five years of finding the best spots to hide a body!"

Ralph didn't talk much about his time in the police department, but I knew he worked in the homicide division before retiring, leading me to believe he likely knew where to dispose of a body in every borough.

"You know, I brought white roses to Miss Ruth on our first date nearly fifty-five years ago," he said.

"I'll let him know he's a few dates behind schedule!"

"Be careful," he smirked. "You might be telling the same story in fifty-four years, Miss Fitzpatrick."

"I'll make sure you get an invite to the wedding, Ralph."

Chapter Nine

When I first started working at Sampson West, I was warned that March, May, and September were the firm's busiest months. I heard the warning over and over again during my first few weeks, missing March and May, but I didn't remember September being any more stressful than August or October.

But, trying to stay at least somewhat prepared, I was ready to be thrown into the first as soon as the calendar flipped to March. Or at least I thought I was.

The first two weeks of March were the most stressed I had ever been, and I was the daughter of a man who was deployed four times within ten years. But even the stress of deployment after deployment seemed simple compared to my first March working at Sampson West.

The firm was hosting seventeen events in thirty-one days, each requiring an unfathomable amount of preparation. Community relations, and events, were Declan's responsibility so as his assistant, I had to do everything he didn't have time for and everything he didn't want to do. And for a reason I legitimately could not understand, there wasn't a paper trail. The firm put on these events year after year and nobody kept notes. When I asked a Senior Account Executive where I could find the information, he simply said, "I think the person before you just knew," which would have been a fine answer if the person before me was still here and still planning the events. Instead, I was being thrown into the fire blind.

One afternoon, I got so annoyed by the lack of organization and communication between staff members that I sent an email to Maribel, the head of Human Resources, asking if we could schedule a meeting. She answered immediately, asking if I wanted to grab coffee across the street in an hour.

Forty-five minutes later, I emailed Declan, letting him know I was running out for a meeting but would be back before the end of the workday. The last thing I needed was for him to come out of his office, see I wasn't at my desk, and dock an hour or two from my earned time off. I also, conveniently, didn't mention who I was meeting with. Declan had been in such a wretched mood lately, screaming about everything almost all the time, I didn't want to give him another reason to yell at me.

Arriving at the coffee shop first, I ordered a decaf tea for Maribel and an iced caramel macchiato for myself.

Maribel was possibly the sweetest woman I had ever met. She was a few years older than my mom and had successfully raised five kids on her own – which made her 'no caffeine' thing a complete shock. She was the closest thing I had to a mom in New York City and I found myself venting to her almost as often as I called my mom crying and complaining.

Maribel walked through the shop's doors almost immediately after I found a table.

"Mija, what's wrong?" she asked.

If we hadn't been employed by the same company, we'd have nothing in common, but she was, without question, my closest friend at Sampson West.

"Everyone in that building is driving me insane," I vented, pointing across the street.

"Declan?"

"Declan, the executives, and the clients. It's like everyone is teaming up, trying to make my day as complicated as ever," I continued. "Do you know Declan asked me to do one thing at 10:00 a.m., it was sent back to him at 10:15 a.m., and he was at my desk yelling that I was wrong by 10:45 a.m.? Then he got even more mad when I showed him his original email request."

"That's just how he is," she insisted. "Especially in March."

"How many days until April?" I asked.

"How's everything else, not at work, going?" She asked, purposely changing the subject.

That was one thing I admired about Maribel. She genuinely cared about people. She never went a day without asking how I was doing. She knew my drama, my ideas, and my aspirations.

"Greyson's been working nonstop, I've barely talked to Austin since he started dating Missy again, it's been over a week since I heard from my dad, and it's only Tuesday," I said, my lip starting to quiver.

Before I knew it, a tear slid down my cheek.

"Oh mija, it's okay."

I tried so hard to not cry in public but that was a feat easier said than done, especially during times like March at Sampson West, when things became too much to handle.

"Can I ask something? Not to be rude but I think it might help," she said.

I nodded.

"Have you ever considered talking to someone?"

"Like a therapist?" I asked.

She nodded.

"I went once when I was twelve. It didn't end well."

"In your hometown?" she asked.

I nodded.

"You should probably try someone you don't know," she said. "Give it another chance. Do some research and let me know if you need any help. My kids and I still go regularly."

She had a fair point. Going to therapy in Gulfpoint was like broadcasting your issues in the middle of town square.

"I will, thank you."

With that, her phone rang.

"It's Declan," she said, rolling her eyes.

I found comfort in knowing the sweetest woman ever felt the same way I did about our boss.

Hanging up the phone after a minute, she said she had to go.

"Stay here for a minute and get yourself collected," she insisted.

Taking a few deep breaths, I watched her cross the street toward 1207 Park Avenue.

Ten minutes later, I was back at my desk with zero desire to do any work.

The longer I sat there, staring into space, the more I realized Maribel might have been right. There was a lot going on in my life and it probably wouldn't hurt to talk to an unbiased outsider.

Opening the Internet on my cell phone, I started searching for nearby therapists, immediately overwhelmed by the options. Filtering the search to show only therapists in Midtown who took my insurance, the search results went from 610 pages to 126. It was a start, but still felt like I was shooting an arrow in the dark. There were so many focuses to choose from. Should I choose one who specialized in anxiety or career counseling or family or life coaching or relationships or stress? Did any exist who dealt with a little bit of all of that?

Today had already been an emotionally draining day, but I knew if I was going to follow through with this therapy thing, I would need everyone I cared about to be supportive of my decision.

I knew my parents would urge me to do whatever I thought was best for myself and that Wyatt was too caught up in his own life to worry about what I was doing in my free time. I was most concerned about what Austin and Greyson would say, more so because I had a feeling they would be my most talked-about subjects.

After a while of searching, I noticed it was past seven o'clock. I texted Greyson.

Hey, can we go to the warehouse?

He called me immediately.

"Babe, are you okay?" he asked as soon as I answered the phone.

The sound of his voice had me choked up again.

"Shhh, don't cry!" he said. "I can be at the warehouse in twenty minutes, come any time after that."

Hanging up, I left my desk a mess and went outside, hailing a cab.

With rush-hour traffic, it would take at least twenty-five minutes to arrive at the warehouse.

After giving the cab driver the address, I dialed Austin's number.

We hadn't talked much since I found out he was dating Missy McHale again. I wasn't mad they were sleeping together again – at the end of the day, he could do whatever or *whoever* he wanted – I was mad that I found out from Wyatt instead of Austin.

I didn't have energy to be petty today so, when Austin answered the phone, I acted like there was no tension between us.

"Fitz, how are you?" he answered.

"Honest or safe answer?" I asked.

We started asking each other 'honest or safe' in high school. 'Safe' was the socially accepted answer, like a cliché "I'm good" response to an acquaintance. 'Honest' was reserved for best friend to best friend, true feelings only, conversations.

"One hundred and ten percent honest," he replied.

I paused for a moment.

"Maeve?" he asked again.

I knew he was being serious when he called me by my actual name, not Fitz.

"I'm not doing great," I admitted. "I actually called for your advice."

"Are you pregnant?" he asked. "Did you kill someone? Do I need to kill someone?"

"No, no, and no," I replied. "But it's kind of serious."

"I'm listening," he said.

"Okay, but I also need one hundred and ten percent honesty."

"Always."

I scoffed, knowing he was nearly zero percent honest recently about his relationship with Missy.

"I know, I'm sorry, we'll talk about that in a minute," he said. "More importantly, what's going on with you?"

"I think I'm going to start going to therapy."

"Really?" he asked.

"Do you think that's a bad idea?"

"Not at all, I think it's a really good idea."

"Yeah?"

"Absolutely. You need someone other than your mom, Wyatt, Greyson, and me to vent to. What if you want to vent about us?"

I laughed. That was the exact argument I was going to make if he disagreed with my decision.

"Wait, that was your something serious?" he asked.

"Yeah."

"You're so dramatic," he laughed. "With that buildup, I thought it was going to be something way more scandalous."

"I'll leave the scandal to your new girlfriend," I replied.

"Touché, Fitz, touché. Let's talk about that for a second."

"I'm listening."

"First off, I'm sorry. You shouldn't have found out from Wyatt but, in my defense, he shouldn't have told you."

I scoffed again.

"I'm not making excuses," he said. "I just wasn't ready to tell you because I'm still not sure it's going anywhere. Plus, how long did it take you to tell me about Greyson?"

Fair point. I didn't mention Greyson's name until we had been hanging out for over a month.

"Apology accepted," I said, smiling.

Fights between Austin and I never lasted long. Any extended argument usually got blamed on a 'learning curve,' keeping in mind that we were still figuring out how to have stories, inside jokes, and memories that didn't include each other.

Noticing the taxi getting closer the warehouse, I told Austin I had to get going.

"Talk soon, Fitz," he said. "Love you."

"Love you too," I replied.

I was glad we made up and that he was on board with therapy.

"That your boyfriend?" the cab driver asked.

Shaking my head, in no mood for small talk with a stranger, I was grateful that we were pulling up to the warehouse.

"Thank you," I said, shutting the cab door behind me.

Standing in the lobby waiting for the elevator, I was surprised to see so many people in the building. Our first time here, Greyson mentioned that floors two through four housed a dozen companies, four on each floor, but I'd never been in the building during a workweek.

I was met by glares from the other two girls in the elevator as I pressed the button for the fifth floor.

"Nobody's allowed on that floor," one of them said with an evident snide. "The elevator won't even stop there."

I didn't answer or look in their direction.

They got off on the third floor and I rode the rest of the way up in silence.

When the doors opened on the fifth floor, Greyson was standing in the vestibule, waiting.

"Maeve, what's wrong?" he asked, pulling me in for a hug.

"Today's just one of those days," I said with an attempted, slight smile.

I was feeling a little better after my conversation with Austin, but I still had therapy and work on my mind.

"Good or bad news first?" I asked.

"Good, always."

"Austin and I made up."

"I didn't know you were fighting?" he asked, confused.

Greyson had been working nonstop, leaving us only enough time for a few texts scattered throughout the day. He stayed at my apartment most nights but a majority of our time was spent sleeping or not talking. I guess I forgot to tell him about the Austin and Missy drama.

"That part's not important because we're good now," I laughed. "But, can I ask you something?"

"Of course, what's up?"

"What would you think if I started going to therapy?" I asked.

"Do you think it will help?"

"Maybe," I said.

"Then I think you should try it. Anything to make your days easier, babe."

"Might as well, right?" I said before kissing him.

Seconds later, his phone alarm blared.

"Shit," he said. "I have to get back to work, my hour break is almost up."

"Okay," I said, defeated.

I knew we probably wouldn't have much time to spend together at the warehouse but I didn't realize it would go by this fast.

We walked out of the building together, he hailed a cab, and I walked toward the subway.

"I'll text you tonight before I come over," he said. "It shouldn't be too late."

Back on the Upper East Side, I passed a sidewalk flower sale on my walk back to my apartment. Thinking back to all of the times my mom came home with flower bouquets or how Gulfpoint Greenery and Florist made weekly deliveries to our house, I remembered thinking my mom just liked the way the flowers looked but, after re-reading the letter from my dad a few weeks ago, I realized there may have been more tough days than she made known.

Looking at the flowers on display, I figured today qualified as a tough day so I purchased two bouquets and headed toward my apartment building.

Making a rare stop in the mail room, off the lobby, I noticed a letter in my mailbox with an overseas return address.

Rushing upstairs, I couldn't get inside my apartment quickly enough, ripping the envelope open before taking off my shoes.

Dear Mae,

I'm sorry it's taken me a while to respond. We were off-base for a few weeks so I'm not quite sure when your latest letter came in. I know it's been a while since we last exchanged handwritten letters but, out of the two of us, I didn't think you'd be the one to

forget to write the date at the top! If you want to blame it on being rushed in the airport, I won't tell anyone!

I know I can't stop you from growing up but please promise that you'll put your happiness before all else, no matter how tough things get or how conflicted you feel about a situation. You always need to come first. I know you well enough to know you're going to get impatient but remember, you're always right where you're supposed to be. Please don't rush the next step of growing up.

It's a tough world out there, Mae. Things probably seem a bit blurry in the 'real world,' especially in a city where everyone is trying to 'make it.' Remember, some will succeed, and some will fail. Some will get up after they fall, and some will never recover from their stumbles. Get up, Maeve.

Be you. Be the girl who changes someone's life. Be the girl who finds inspiration that fuels your fire. I hope, as you continue on this new journey, you continue to be inspired by the space between where you are and where you want to be. Keep your worry and doubt at a minimum and your faith at a maximum.

You aren't the definition of the past or the limits of the present. You are the potential of the future, Mae.

As you continue to grow, remember that I will always believe in you and, no matter how rough things might get, remember that I'm extremely proud of the person you have become.

I love you more than you know.

Love,

Dad.

Tears rolled down my cheeks as I reached the letter's end. It was exactly what I needed to read after a day like this.

Looking at the clock, I knew I couldn't call my dad, it was the middle of the night where he was. Instead, I called my mom. Now realizing it was already after nine o'clock, I knew there was a one hundred percent chance that she was already asleep on the couch, a fact confirmed by the grogginess in her voice as she answered the phone.

"Maeve, is everything okay?" she asked.

"Yeah, mama, I'm sorry. Want me to call you back tomorrow?"

"No honey, don't be silly! What's going on?"

"It's been a really long day," I said, knowing I was only a few seconds away from more tears.

"What happened?" she asked, now fully awake.

"Work was terrible, I think I'm going to start going to therapy, Austin and I made up, and I got a letter from Dad."

The tears were back.

"First off, don't cry," she said. "I'm glad you and Austin are better, and I think therapy is good. Work will always be work so you can't let yourself get so worked up about that. What'd your dad say?"

"That he was proud of who I've become," I said, still sniffling.

"He's a smart guy," she laughed.

Chapter Ten

By mid-March, I could throw a Declan Danvers-approved event with my eyes closed. I knew which vendors he preferred and which to avoid. I knew what should be included on the menus and what decorations were "too cheesy for Sampson West's reputation." I could decipher his mood of the day by his shoe choice – brown meant 'decent but proceed with caution' and black meant 'steer clear.' Most importantly, I learned his pre-party jitters disappeared once the first guests arrived and, if I made it to that point, I could breathe easily for the remainder of the event.

Over the past few weeks, with a lot of help, I planned and attended dinner parties, movie premieres, networking events, brunches, luncheons, and red-carpet soirees.

I never knew so much effort or energy was necessary for book releases or movie premieres, but it didn't take long to learn the peaks and pits of each event.

Premieres and red-carpet soirees came with an exorbitant amount of added stress, jugging which celebrities were scheduled to appear but never showed up and dealing with PR backlash after one ended up splashed on the front page of every tabloid. Dancing on the bar at the after-party after a few too many drinks was never a good look. Networking events, no matter where or when, were always the worst. Dinner parties and brunches required extensive planning, almost down to the minute, but I always enjoyed chatting with billionaires over chardonnay or mimosas.

By the end of the month, there was no question that luncheons were my favorite type of event to plan *and* attend, requiring only four things to be considered a success: finger foods, light entertainment, a reputable venue, and a purpose people would leave work for. The venue where we hosted a majority of our luncheons specialized in such events, leaving not much for us to do. We didn't have to worry about anyone being overserved because, unlike during every other event we hosted throughout the month, limited alcohol was expected at luncheons. Guests were kind and didn't expect much, grateful to get out of their offices for a while. But my favorite part of luncheons, without question, was the set end times. There was no need to wonder if it was too early to leave.

Somehow, possibly only by the skin of my teeth, I made it through my first March at Sampson West. Every event happened with very few hiccups, Declan didn't fire me, and I was hopeful that sleepless nights and extended workdays had come to an end – at least until May.

On the last Friday of the month, unsurprisingly, I woke up to a group text from Declan. But its message wasn't what I was expecting.

> **Thanks for all of your time and effort this month. Enjoy today as a paid day off. See you Monday. Declan.**

I reread the message six times before comprehending it.

A Friday off? An unexpected three-day weekend? And I was getting paid for it?

In that moment, and maybe only for a moment, the stress of the last few weeks was worth it.

Not wanting to rub any of the tired from my eyes, I put my phone on the nightstand, rolled over, and fell back to sleep.

An hour later, I was shaken awake by a very concerned Greyson.

"Babe, it's after 8!" he exclaimed. "You're going to be late for work!"

"I don't have to go today," I said, completely groggy.

"It's Friday, you just have to get through one more day," he laughed.

Shaking my head, I showed him Declan's text.

"A full day off?!" he asked.

Nodding, I pulled the covers back over me.

"I'm so jealous," he said, kissing my forehead. "I'll be quiet getting ready. I'll see you after work."

I didn't reopen my eyes for three hours, clearly needing more rest than I realized.

After catching up on social media. I didn't know what to do. I had been running around like crazy for weeks, leaving no time to do anything normal, like grocery shopping or chores, but I didn't want to do those today.

No longer running on fumes, I wanted to spend the day venturing around the city.

"Playing hooky?" Ralph asked as I walked out of the building.

"Rare day off," I laughed.

"It's beautiful out there, enjoy it!"

He was right. The weather was perfect, completely unexpected for the end of March. The sun was shining, it was nearly seventy degrees, and there was a calm breeze. People were gathering on sidewalks and in parks. Preschool-aged kids were screeching on playgrounds and in sandboxes. Businessmen and businesswomen were eating lunch on outdoor patios instead of at their cubicles. Everything in the city seemed so alive. *This* was why I moved to New York City.

With nothing but time, I window-shopped for an hour before heading into Macy's. It was just me, the city's biggest department store, and a credit card waiting to be swiped. I tried on a lot of shoes, some dresses that weren't early spring appropriate, at least six pairs of jeans, and a few sweaters that seemed like necessities.

Settling on one of the dresses, two sweaters, a pair of shoes, a crossbody clutch, and a leather jacket, I made my way to the cash register, hoping that I wasn't spending more money than was in my bank account.

The cashier was an older woman with white hair and a Southern accent, a sweet reminder of home. She made little comments about the clothes I was buying, insisting they would look great on me, leaving me more confident about my purchases as I swiped my credit card.

Walking out of the store, my phone buzzed and a text from Wyatt appeared on the screen.

Hey. Call me when you're not busy?

I walked a few blocks to my spot before hitting the phone icon, waiting for him to answer.

"Slow day at the office?" he asked answering the phone.

"Actually, rare day not at the office," I laughed. "Aren't you supposed to be in class?"

"No, it's past twelve o'clock."

Right. Seniors at Gulfpoint High got to leave school at noon on Fridays, one of those things that was always just a thing. Rumors swirled every year, usually in late summer, that the administration was changing the rules and would now require seniors to attend school for the full day all week. And every year, nothing changed.

"You're not at the beach?" I asked.

Wyatt and his friends spent Friday afternoons surfing, just like Austin and I used to spend Friday afternoons at Gulfpoint Town Park with our friends.

"I'm going there in a minute," he said. "But I stopped home first."

"Mom there?"

"No, she's at work," he said. "That's why I'm calling you."

"What happened?" I asked, getting slightly concerned.

"I got into the University of Georgia," he said.

"Wyatt! That's awesome, congratulations!"

The University of Georgia had always been Wyatt's dream school. From the time he started playing football, he wanted to be a Georgia Bulldog. He talked to their recruiters and coaches, planned weekend visits, and studied for University of Georgia-caliber grades.

It was a known thing in the Fitzpatrick family that if Wyatt got into the University of Georgia, Wyatt would go to the University of Georgia.

"Thanks."

"Why don't you sound more excited?" I asked.

"I've been thinking about the University of Florida lately," he said.

"You want to be a Gator now instead?" I asked, dumbfounded.

"I don't know," he hesitated. "It's like $20,000 less a year."

"Don't let the money be a deciding factor," I insisted. "Mom and Dad have enough set aside. Plus, scholarships are a thing."

"I know, but do you think it's too far away from Mom?" he asked. "You know, with you in New York and Dad deployed?"

"Wy, not at all. I call Mom every day, Dad won't be in Iraq forever, and we all know Mom will kill you if she hears you're basing any decisions on her potential well-being."

"I just don't know which decision is the right one."

"You're not going to know right away. You just have to list out pros and cons and pick whichever you think is best."

"When did you know that you made the right choice?" he asked.

I didn't know how to answer that. I attended Collinswood University, a small school three hours from Gulfpoint, and even now, almost a year after graduation, I still wasn't sure I chose the right school. I made the most of my time at Collinswood but I still had "what if" questions floating through my head about other schools.

Personally, I thought Wyatt should stick with the University of Georgia. It was six hours from Gulfpoint, compared to University of Florida's one hour, and I believed there was more opportunity for growth in Athens than Gainesville. But that wasn't my decision to make.

"I think you just figure it out one day," I said. "Did you tell Austin?"

"Yeah, he said I should go to Georgia because everyone from Gulfpoint goes to Gainesville."

"They do," I agreed.

At least twenty kids in every Gulfpoint graduating class went to the University of Florida, a majority of them never expanding their friendship circle much beyond the people they knew from high school.

The friendships I made in college, even the temporary ones, played such a crucial role in my growth, opening me to so many different lifestyles and viewpoints.

There was the group of girls I shared a major with. We worked on countless projects together, but only saw each other outside the classroom long enough to insist we had to "get lunch and catch up" – two things that never happened. There was the boy I sat next to in English Lit freshman year. He didn't talk much but was always willing to explain the works of Chaucer, Austen, and Shakespeare. We may not have been best friends, but I never would have passed English Lit without him. There were the girls I became 'best friends' with week after week while waiting in the bathroom line during a night out, only to lose them after the cops busted the house or the bartender announced last call. And there were the frat guys more concerned with Rush Week than Finals Week, a lead I followed one semester and quickly regretted.

I didn't know who Wyatt would be at school, but as much as I didn't want to see him surrounded by the Gulfpoint mentality for the next four years, I knew it was on him to figure it out. He couldn't base his decision on anyone else's opinions or experiences.

"I'll wear red and black or orange and blue, Wy," I reminded him.

"You're the best," he said. "I gotta go, thank you."

"Anytime, love you."

"Love you too," he said as the phone clicked off.

Heading back to my apartment, with at least an hour until Greyson was finished at work, I was running out of ways to keep myself occupied.

Digging through my purse, I found a "free pass" for a nearby gym. Pulling out my phone and checking the gym's class schedule – there was a first time for everything – I noticed a spin class was starting in a half hour. I didn't see any harm in attending. How hard could it be to pedal a stationary bike for an hour?

I learned, very quickly, that pedaling a stationary bike for an hour was very hard. The class dragged on and by the end, my legs felt like jelly.

Getting back into the locker room, I noticed a missed call from Greyson.

"Sorry, I was at the gym," I said, calling him back.

"This is Maeve, right? My girlfriend?" he asked, hysterically laughing.

"Didn't know I was dating a comic," I replied, deadpan, not playing into his antics.

He continued laughing.

"I'm getting ready to leave work but some of the guys from college asked if I wanted to go to an indie band performance at Zone tonight," he said.

"Are you going?" I asked.

"Can I?"

"Of course," I laughed, not sure why he was asking.

"Will you come with me?" he asked.

"Really?"

"Yeah," he insisted. "I want you to meet my friends."

"I'm in," I said. "I just need some time to look a little more presentable and a little less sweaty."

"I'm sure you look fine," he said, laughing. "Meet you there at 8?"

"Perfect," I replied. "See you later."

I took a shower, did my hair and makeup, and pulled a black tank top, my new leather jacket, and a pair of jeans out of my closet, all in less than an hour, making it potentially the quickest I had ever gotten ready for a night out.

I was greeted by brisk air as I traded the stillness of my building's lobby for the bustle of Manhattan's streets. Deciding it was too cold to walk to the club, I hailed a cab, getting to Zone before Greyson and his friends.

There were people everywhere, the line to get in wrapped around the block, and girls seemed to be wearing less and less as we got closer to the club's entrance. Standing outside, waiting for Greyson and his friends to show up, I felt incredibly overdressed.

A few minutes later, Greyson showed up with three guys who introduced themselves as Emilio, Trey, and Ace. I recognized their names from his stories but shortly after meeting them, I put two and two together – they were Greyson's college roommates.

Emilio knew the bouncer and promoter so we didn't have to wait in line, leaving me grateful for connections because my leather jacket was for looks, not warmth.

As the four of us waited for the bartender to pour our drinks, I scanned the club. Back home, a night out was spent at a dive bar or in someone's basement, but Zone was unlike anything I had ever experienced, everything I expected in a big-city hotspot. Darkness invaded the oversized room, the only light coming from multicolored strobes flashing in mesmerizing patterns. Girls wearing barely-there clothes walked around with oversized bottles, groups of guys stood around the dance floor edges, looking for their girl of the night, and loud music played from speakers scattered throughout the room. With the exception of a drunk girl crying in the corner, everyone seemed at ease, as if they left their worries at the door.

Listening to Greyson and his friends reminisce on their college days, I felt a twinge of jealousy. Although I left most of my high school friends in Gulfpoint, I was pretty good at staying in touch with my college friends after moving to New York.

I lived with the same six girls from sophomore year until graduation. They were one-time strangers who became my closest friends. They were genuine and were there whenever I needed them. They were there freshman year when I needed friends. They were there when I needed someone to hold my hair back when a night of drinking became too much to handle, and when I needed someone to join my procrastination attempts. They saw me at my best and at my worst. They knew when I needed a night out and when I needed a movie marathon. They were by my side with ice cream when I got my heart "broken" by some frat guy and they were there to be wingmen when my eye was on *another* frat guy. They were there to drink margaritas on Taco Tuesdays and to binge-watch trashy reality TV shows on Sunday afternoons.

Unfortunately, none of them lived close to New York City so we couldn't go to Manhattan nightclubs together. Instead, our happy hours happened over video chat.

About twenty minutes after the band started playing, Trey let us know he had a "very important meeting" to get to. It was nearing 10:00 p.m. on Friday so I assumed this 'meeting' was more of a meet-up with a potential suitor.

I smirked at Greyson.

"Remember when that was us?" I asked.

"Except his has no long-term potential," he laughed.

"And you knew I did?" I asked, letting the alcohol do the talking.

"From the very first day we met," he insisted.

My heart skipped a beat.

Watching Greyson watch the band's performance, I realized that my feelings for him were becoming serious. Unable to play it coy any longer, I had to admit, at least to myself, that I was falling hard for the boy with the caramel eyes.

Chapter Eleven

My phone calendar dinged with a reminder at one o'clock on April 1.
Therapy – 6:30 PM.

Unfortunately, unlike most of my day, this wasn't an April Fool's joke. My first therapy session was scheduled for after work.

With the help of Maribel in New York and my mom in Gulfpoint, we found a therapist three blocks from Sampson West who took my insurance and had pretty decent online reviews.

Reviews aside, I was still nervous.

I hadn't spoken to a therapist since I was twelve. The woman I talked to was the mother of one of my classmates who told her son a watered-down version of what we spoke about. I shouldn't have been surprised that doctor-patient confidentiality hadn't quite caught on in Gulfpoint. When my mom confronted the woman about her lack of privacy, she insisted she told her son so he'd understand that I was going through a rough time. Telling a twelve-year-old boy to be extra nice to one of their young girl classmates was a guaranteed way to get that girl bullied.

Thankfully, I got over the small-town whispers pretty quickly, not giving them the power to impact my mood, the decisions I made, or the way I lived my life. But even though I tried to ignore them, the whispers still existed and, after a bad experience with Gulfpoint's only therapist, I found myself navigating them alone.

I knew this New York therapist wouldn't tell anyone what we spoke about, assuming she saw dozens of clients a day, but I still found myself apprehensive about the appointment. At one point in the afternoon, for the first time ever, I caught myself wishing the workday would slow down. But, of course, Declan had a ton of work he needed help with, making the afternoon fly by.

Not wanting to be late for my appointment, I left work at exactly six o'clock, completely miscalculating how quickly I could walk three blocks. Sidewalks were jammed with the post-work rush and I still made it to the address on her website with twenty minutes to spare. The weather was terrible, a cold and windy rain made it nearly impossible to be outside for any longer than necessary. Unable to hang around outside, pretending to be waiting for someone or scrolling on my phone to look busy, I walked into the building and found Cecilia Williams' office almost immediately. The 'take some extra time' gods were not on my side.

Walking into the office, I was expecting an oversized, packed waiting room with a lot of chairs and magazines to read, similar to every other doctor's office I had ever been to. Instead, I found the opposite. The waiting area was really small, landscape photos and framed diplomas hung on the beige walls. There were only five chairs in the room, leaving me hoping that Cecilia Williams was really good at scheduling, never having too many people in the office at one time, and that I had not misread her online reviews.

Letting the receptionist know I was here for my 6:30 p.m. appointment and apologizing for being so early, she told me to have a seat and that I would probably be seen early, because the patient scheduled before me hadn't shown for his appointment. I wasn't sure she was supposed to share that information but, either way, it wasn't helping my prejudgments of Cecilia and therapy.

A few minutes later, an older woman walked out of the back room, calling my name.

"I'm Cecilia," she said as I walked toward her, sticking out her hand. "Nice to meet you!"

"Nice to meet you too," I replied, shaking her hand. "I'm Maeve."

"Come on in and have a seat."

I don't know what I expected from her office, but I was surprised to see there wasn't a couch. There were three armchairs, a coffee table, a desk, and a bunch of landscape photos that matched the ones in the waiting area.

Sitting in one of the chairs, Cecilia sat across from me.

"Why don't you tell me a little about yourself?" she asked.

Ice breakers had always been my least favorite part of college classes, internship and job interviews, networking events, and conversations with strangers. No matter the day or the situation, it was like I forgot every fact about myself as soon as I heard those words.

"Ummm," I hesitated, not sure what to say.

"I'll go first," she chuckled. "My name is Cecilia Williams, but please just call me Cecilia. I live in Brooklyn and when I'm not working, I'm usually painting or taking care of my garden."

Following her lead, I started talking.

"I'm Maeve Fitzpatrick, I'm twenty-two, and moved to New York City a few months ago from a small town on Florida's Gulf Coast."

"Welcome," she said. "I won't ask too many questions after today. This is your time to talk but let's start things off easy. How did you end up here?"

"In New York or a spot where I need a therapist?" I asked.

"A lot of people go to therapy for a lot of reasons," she insisted. "Let's start with New York."

"I wanted a change. I didn't want to move back into my parents' house after college graduation," I explained. "After a conversation with my dad about being stagnant, I figured why not move to the biggest city I could find."

"Is it a decision you're happy with?" she asked.

"I think so, but I was hesitant to make the move up here. I wasn't sure I was ready to be alone so many miles from home."

"Alone in a crowded place, the joys of moving to a big city," she laughed.

"There are definitely some days when it's harder than I expected."

"It'd be the same in reverse," she said. "That's what I did."

I looked at her, waiting for a more detailed explanation.

"I lived in New York City, not caring about anyone else's business, and then moved upstate to live with my aunt after getting pregnant at seventeen," she said. "I was thrown into a small town as a pregnant, black teenager at a time when teen pregnancy and being black were looked down upon on their own. The combination made me a complete outcast."

"I can't imagine," I said. "I had a tough enough time being the kid with the dad in Iraq."

"Military?" she asked.

"Staff Sergeant in the Army," I replied.

"My dad was in the Army, as well," she said. "I wouldn't have made it through deployments without my friends and family."

"Me neither. My friends back home have always been really supportive."

"What about your friends in New York?" she asked.

"I have a few, mostly my boyfriend and his friends though, so I'm not sure they qualify."

"Anyone can count as a friend if you have a good time with them."

"We have a good time but, with the exception of my boyfriend, they don't know about my dad or his job."

"Tell me about this boyfriend," she said.

"His name's Greyson. A girl I work with is a mutual friend, she introduced us one night. We haven't been dating long but I think things are going well," I said. "He just asked me to spend Easter with his family."

"Will you?" she asked.

"I guess, I don't have enough time off from work to go back home."

"Do you want to meet his family?"

"Yeah, I like him, and it seems like the next step, but I've never had to meet a family before."

"Never?" she asked.

"I grew up in a small town. I *knew* everyone's family. And I never made it to the 'meet the family' stage with anyone in college," I laughed.

I started thinking about my college love life, a time that included plenty of hookups, some more consistent than others. Some guys stayed in rotation while others were short-lived flings, but each taught me something about myself.

There was the guy who got way too attached way too quickly, the guy who expected me to talk to him from the time his eyes opened every morning until they closed every night, and the guy who blew up my phone with texts, photos, and social media notifications. They taught me that clingy wasn't, and never would be, my type. There was the guy who expected me to answer every message immediately, the guy who wanted to know what I was doing at almost all hours of the day, and the guy who constantly tried to guilt trip me, constantly playing the 'you hurt my feelings' card. They made me realize that controlling was right up there with clingy. There was the guy who hadn't showered before meeting me, the guy obsessed with his horoscope, the guy who didn't like dogs, the guy who thought $2 beers were 'too expensive,' and the guy who wanted to be a dad by his next birthday. They taught me it was okay to have a niche, but it was also okay to avoid certain niches.

"Are you nervous to meet them?" Cecilia asked, pulling me from my thoughts.

"Terrified," I replied.

This thing with Greyson started as a simple no-strings-attached hookup. I didn't go into it looking for a relationship and, although

I liked the direction things were heading, I had to wonder if we were moving too fast.

"We're running out of time," she said. "But do me a favor?"

I nodded.

"Go into it with an open mind. Remember, these people are responsible for raising the guy you like, so they can't be that bad, right?"

She was right, but with a tendency to be overdramatic, I hadn't thought of it like that. I knew my nerves would calm down, but a reminder from a stranger never hurt.

Thanking Cecilia for her time, she said she'd like to see me in a month, so before leaving the office, I made an appointment for May 1, assuming talking to Cecilia ahead of another busy month at work was for the best.

The rain stopped by the time my appointment ended but the air was still bitter, so I didn't want to spend extra time outside. The nineteen-block subway ride back to my apartment was jammed with people. Standing on the subway was normal, and usually safer than sitting on a seat that had likely been peed on earlier in the day, but tonight, we were packed in like cattle headed to slaughter. Thankfully, and unknowingly, I got on an express train, cutting my ride time in half.

Getting back to my apartment, knowing Greyson was at a dinner party for work, I sent him a quick text.

Just got home from therapy, wasn't as bad as I expected!

I was surprised when he responded almost immediately.

That's great, babe! Can't wait to hear about it after this dumb dinner. I'll call you when I'm out.

Reading his text, I realized I still hadn't eaten dinner. Walking over to my fridge, I opened the door, hoping something would appear from mid-air. I hadn't been to the grocery store in weeks, choosing to live off takeout and leftovers, but both seemed like too much effort tonight.

Closing the refrigerator door, the Ground Rules letter caught my attention, specifically the 'write everything down' rule. It had been a while since I'd written but I figured it would be helpful to myself if I documented my therapy process and journey.

Giving up on dinner, I went to my desk and pulled my notebook out of the top drawer.

Opening its cover, I was met by my New Year's letter. It had only been a few months but it felt like forever ago that I wrote the twenty-three resolutions.

Reading over the list, I was surprised at how many things had already been crossed off.

I spent more time with and stayed in touch with the people who mattered back in Gulfpoint. I started sending and receiving handwritten letters again. I asked for more money at work and, although unsuccessful, intended to do the same again soon. I volunteered and met new people. I finally cleared out the clutter in my childhood bedroom, went somewhere I'd never been, saw live music, and started going to therapy.

I had another nine months to cross the remaining fourteen items off my list and going to bed that night, I felt incredibly optimistic.

Chapter Twelve

Before I knew it, it was the second Saturday of April and I was in a rental car with Greyson, headed toward Crescent Peak, Massachusetts, to meet his family. Nearly halfway into our trip, somewhere in Connecticut, I got lost in my thoughts as I watched raindrops race across the passenger window, some combining and some dodging the others.

I had opened up to the idea of meeting Greyson's family, ignoring the internal argument that it was too soon, but it was weird knowing this was the first holiday that I wouldn't be spending with my family. It was the first Easter I wouldn't have brunch at The Skillet, the first Easter I wouldn't lose to Wyatt and Austin in a million games of the always unfair two-on-one boys vs. girl basketball, and the first Easter my mom wouldn't hand me a twenty-dollar bill, a tradition that started when she got tired of hiding baskets.

I started wondering if Greyson's family had Easter traditions. Did they focus on the super-religious aspects of the resurrection or was it just a relaxing Sunday spent with family? Did they eat a full dinner at 4:00 p.m. or was it a 'pick as you please' eat-all-day kind of holiday? Did they get along or would I be thrown into some tense family drama?

By the time we crossed the Massachusetts border, Greyson still hadn't given me any warnings or any insight of what to expect.

"Why are we stopping?" I asked as we pulled into a rest stop. "The GPS said we're only like a half-hour from Crescent Peak."

"My parents are going to be so excited when we get there that there won't be any time to eat and then it'll be well before dinnertime and you'll get cranky and that's not good for anyone," he laughed.

I had to laugh, too. He wasn't wrong. It was common knowledge that I got an attitude whenever I got overly hungry.

There were only two food options at the rest stop and Greyson insisted we needed something with more sustenance than ice cream so I settled on chicken nuggets and fries from McDonald's, an American classic combination I usually saved for post-bar munchies or mid-afternoon hangovers.

"Are you ready?" Greyson asked as we sat at a table for two.

"To meet your parents?" I asked. "I think so."

"You're meeting more than just my parents," he laughed.

"How many people?" I questioned, getting nervous.

"Family? Anywhere between ten and thirty depending on who comes over tomorrow. Neighbors? I have no idea, but Crescent Peak is a small town, so probably a lot."

I assumed we'd be spending the holiday with more than just his parents, but I didn't realize I'd be introduced to so many people.

Then, I started to feel bad. Was I a terrible person for not being ready to introduce Greyson to my parents, extended family, and neighbors? Did he like me more than I liked him?

Thankfully, those thoughts were short-lived.

"Anything I need to know?" I asked.

"My aunts will probably ask a million questions, I don't bring girls home very often. My uncles will probably be smoking cigars in the backyard the whole time," he laughed. "Most of my cousins are younger and either obsessed with sports or Barbies, so just ask about that."

"And your parents?"

"They prefer sports over Barbies," he cracked up.

"No seriously," I said, trying not to laugh at his nonsense.

"They're going to love you, I promise," he insisted, grabbing my hand from across the table, giving it a squeeze.

Forty minutes later, we pulled into a quiet street lined with colonial homes. The trees and bushes in every yard were starting to bud. In a lot of ways, the street reminded me of the one I grew up on, only with oak and pine trees instead of palm. A minute later, we pulled into a driveway, about halfway down the street.

"This is where you grew up?" I asked.

"It's not much," he said. "But it's home."

"Greyson, it's beautiful, and huge!"

The home's exterior was entirely brick. Three white-siding turrets popped against the gray roof, contrasting against the black shutters and brick chimney. Two oversized hedges stood on either side of the black front door.

"Let's go inside," he said. "We can get our bags later."

Opening the car door, I followed him into the house.

"Mom? Dad?" he yelled, opening the front door.

"Terry! They're here!" I heard a woman's voice yell from an unseen part of the home.

A few seconds later, Greyson's parents appeared in the foyer, pulling their only child in for a tight embrace.

"Mom and Dad, this is Maeve. Maeve, these are my parents, Terry and Natalie."

"It's so nice to meet you, Mr. and Mrs. Raske," I said, sticking out my hand.

"Mrs. Raske is my mother-in-law, sweetie," Greyson's mom said, pulling me in for a hug. "Please call me Natalie."

She was a petite blonde who looked like she spent her days in Pilates and at sample sales.

Greyson was a spitting image of his father, tall and built but not overly muscular. He seemed more stoic than his wife, but equally as pleasant.

We followed them into the living room, Greyson and I sitting on one couch and his parents on the other. We chatted for a while about everything from how I grew up to how things were going for both of us in the city. I gave them the SparkNotes version of my life in Gulfpoint, my parents, Wyatt, and Austin. They asked a lot of questions about my job, Natalie eager to hear which celebrities I had met and Terry more intrigued by the business side of things.

During a lull in conversation, Greyson went to the car to grab our bags before showing me the upstairs of his childhood home.

Walking into his bedroom, I stopped in my tracks.

"I thought you said that was gone?" I asked, pointing to a photo on his dresser.

"The poster's gone. That's a signed photo of the basketball greats of the early 2000s, totally different!" he insisted.

"When's the next train to New York City?" I laughed.

"What's wrong with it?" he rebutted.

"I already wasn't having sex with you tonight because we're at your parents' house, but I hope you know that now there's no chance."

"Wait, what?!" he asked, exasperated.

"I'm not having Harden Packard watch me with my boyfriend," I stated, unable to understand why there would be any confusion about that.

"But it's just a photo and he's not the only one in it and it's not even facing my bed!" he tried to argue.

"Rules are rules," I insisted, making my way back downstairs.

Although I knew he wasn't going to give up the argument without a fight, I was surprised but grateful that Greyson followed me down to the kitchen.

"Mom, what are we doing for dinner tonight?" Greyson asked.

"Probably takeout? Maybe a restaurant?" she said.

"Not yet though, right?"

She shook her head.

"I'm going to show Maeve around Crescent Peak."

"Have a good time," she said as he led me toward the garage.

"You moved the rental car inside?" I asked. "Wait, how? I have the keys."

"No, we're taking my pride and joy," he laughed, opening the door.

Parked inside the garage was a four-door black pickup truck with tinted windows and black rims. I always pegged Greyson for a pickup truck kind of guy, but black on black surprised me, at least until we started driving around town. Everyone had black on black pickup trucks.

"Did the car dealerships have the same sale in this town?" I laughed.

"I was the first to turn seventeen and the first to get it. Everyone copied me!" he insisted.

"Sure," I joked. "So, where are we headed?"

"You'll see," he smirked.

He showed me downtown, his high school, Main Street, the candy shop he walked to after school on Fridays, the intersection where he got his first speeding ticket, the open field where they threw their underaged parties, and the mountain where they used to go snowboarding.

Turning down a dirt road, I turned toward Greyson.

"Is this where you kill me?" I asked, kind of joking but also kind of concerned.

"No, I'd be the first one questioned!" he laughed. "It wouldn't take long for the police to put two and two together."

Fair point, I thought.

He was the only reason I was in Crescent Peak, the nexus between a small-town girl from Florida and a small town in Massachusetts.

"What is this place?" I asked as we parked in front of a water tower, surrounded by trees, seemingly miles from the rest of the world.

"My spot," he smirked. "No parents, no basketball photos. Just me and you and, right now, too many clothes."

Before I knew it, his lips were on mine and we were climbing over the backseat. Within seconds, our clothes were strewn all over his truck's floor. We got as creative as we could in the crammed backseat of a pickup truck. For a while, we just laid there, tracing lines all over each other's bodies, and enjoying each other's company. I felt like I was back in high school, sneaking around with secret boyfriends.

After a few minutes of enjoyable silence, Greyson's phone dinged.

"My mom wants to know if we'll meet them in town for dinner."

"Can I please put clothes on before you start talking about your mom?" I asked, laughing and grabbing my pants from the floor.

Laughing along, Greyson waited for me to get my jeans and bra on before speaking again.

"So, do I tell her yes?" he asked.

"We're not going to leave them hanging," I laughed. "Tell them yes."

"Okay. I want to show you something else first," he said after typing a response and putting his phone in the cupholder. "But we have to hurry."

"This place has the best sunset view in the entire town," he said, a few minutes later, pulling into a park of ball fields.

"Are these the fields you played on growing up?" I asked.

"I threw a no-hitter here when I was twelve."

"Highlight of your career?" I laughed.

"Actually, kind of," he laughed. "We won the conference and the girl I had a crush on came to every game."

"To see you?"

"I thought so, but looking back, she was probably only there because her twin brother played on my team," he laughed.

"Is it an unresolved crush? Do I have to worry about her stealing you?"

"Nope, found out during high school that she likes girls."

"So, you didn't bring her to the water tower?" I asked, unable to control my laughter.

"I hate you," he smirked. "Just watch the sunset so we can go meet up with my parents."

The sunset was mesmerizing. The sky filled with yellows and oranges before transitioning to pinks and purples. I didn't have the heart to tell him it was nothing compared to Gulfpoint's beach sunsets, but I couldn't deny it was nicer than any I had seen in New York City.

Dinner was nothing extraordinary. We went to a seafood place and Greyson insisted I needed to get the clam chowder. Even though I grew up at the beach, I was never much of a seafood girl. I'd eat shrimp and fried calamari but avoided almost every other under-the-sea option. But I wasn't going to be a picky eater during my first meal with Greyson's parents. So, I ordered the clam chowder and was pleasantly surprised. I knew New England was famous for its clam chowder, and although it wasn't the best meal, it didn't disappoint.

We chatted with his parents over drinks, dinner, and dessert. They asked Greyson more about work and, although I was still learning the ins and outs of analytics, I knew enough to ask the right questions and give the right input at the appropriate time.

At one point, I asked his parents how they met. Natalie said they met in high school. Terry was a senior and she was a freshman when they coincidentally sat next to each other in study hall. The story surprised me, not because I didn't believe in high school sweethearts, but because I couldn't believe Natalie was only three years younger than Terry.

As we were leaving the restaurant, Greyson mentioned that he was surprised we didn't run into anyone he knew. From what I had been told, Crescent Peak was around the same size as Gulfpoint and I knew I'd be equally surprised to go out to dinner back home without seeing a familiar face or two.

"We'll see plenty at church tomorrow," he said as we got into the car.

"I can wear sweatpants, right?" I asked.

"Most of the shops in town are probably closed, but there's got to be somewhere we can find a church outfit. I'll text one of my old friends," he said, eyes widening as he looked at the clock, getting more frazzled with every word.

"Babe, stop!" I laughed. "I brought like four dresses!"

"Have I mentioned I hate you?" he questioned, huffing.

"No, you don't!" I laughed some more.

Out of respect for his parents, although they insisted it wasn't necessary, Greyson and I slept in separate rooms on Saturday night, it was the best decision we ever made. The guest room bed was the most comfortable I had ever lain on. It had been months since I slept anywhere that wasn't surrounded by city noises. Being in the countryside was so refreshing.

By the time I woke up on Sunday, I considered searching for jobs in Crescent Peak and trading my boyfriend for his family.

A few hours later, without participating in any egg hunts thus far, Greyson and I were following his parents to Easter mass. I never saw or heard Greyson talk about being religious but on our drive, he explained his parents were very loyal contributors to their local Catholic church. I wasn't the best at attending mass. My mom never missed a week and, growing up, we sat through the drawn-out services almost every Sunday. But as Wyatt and I grew up, my mom started going by herself. I had a tough time spending Sunday morning listening to a preacher spew from a book of beliefs I wasn't sure I believed in.

But, because Greyson was also Catholic, I knew I had some idea of what to expect during mass. Or so I thought.

Sometime between that morning and the last time I went to church, someone changed the words to every prayer I once knew. Some got longer, some got shorter, and some sounded like completely new prayers. I wasn't privy to the workings of Catholicism but I didn't think prayers could just be changed. Who made the decision? Did they send an email every time they added or took away a word? How were parishioners notified? I made a mental note to ask Greyson after mass, far away from his parents.

About halfway through mass, not paying much attention to the priest, I got distracted by a wooden door in the front corner of the church, reminding me of a similar one back home. Growing up, anyone brave enough to open the door and go down the creakiest staircase was met by an alleyway that, as kids, we thought nobody knew about. That myth was debunked a few years later, but that didn't stop our fun. As halfway-rebellious teenagers, my friends and I would meet in the alleyway before mass for a shot or two of whatever we could find in our parents' liquor cabinets – making zoning out a lot easier. Plus, it didn't take long to convince ourselves that the shots were no different than the wine offered during Communion. I remembered video chatting with my dad one Sunday afternoon and telling him about our trips to Pub Jesus, knowing he couldn't ground me from six-thousand miles away – or so seventeen-year-old Maeve Fitzpatrick thought. After our talk, my dad told my mom and we learned the hard way that it was possible to get grounded by someone halfway across the globe. For the first, and only, time in our lives, Austin and I were grounded for an entire weekend.

I zoned out during the second half of my first, and hopefully only, mass in Crescent Peak, praying nobody noticed. If they did, they didn't say anything.

After the priest walked into the vestibule, it was time for everyone's favorite part of church in a small town, catching up with people in every pew, even though they did the same last Sunday or sometime during the week. Back home, the half-hour after mass was when everyone put on their best act, doing their part to prove they were part of the perfect family. I was an outsider in Crescent Peak, but things seemed to work the same way around here. Within the first five minutes of this probably unnecessary catch-up session, I met Greyson's kindergarten teacher, first babysitter, varsity baseball coach, and pediatrician, proving Crescent Peak was, as I had assumed, similar to Gulfpoint.

Greyson's extended family had already arrived by the time we got back to his house. Nearly a dozen young children were running around his front yard and their moms stood on the sidewalk, only halfway keeping an eye on the kids.

Getting out of the car, I was introduced to his uncles before they disappeared to the backyard. His aunts reminded me of his mom and appeared welcoming. Then, Greyson made a quick, general announcement to his cousins, referring to me as his girlfriend, a word that made a majority of them cringe or squeal.

The weather was beautiful, the kind you could only dream of for the beginning of April, so most of the day was spent outside. The kids ran around the entire time and I flew relatively under the radar, at least until I got cornered by three of his aunts after dinner, each asking a million questions. Natalie came over at one point to tell her sisters and sister-in-law to cut me some slack.

At that point in our conversation, I learned Greyson didn't just "not bring girls home very often" but I was the first girl he brought home, a role I hadn't been prepared to play.

When one of his aunts asked about my family, I saw it as the perfect out.

"I actually have to call my mom and brother before they eat," I said, excusing myself from the conversation. "Thanks for the reminder!"

Walking away from the group, I dialed my home phone and Austin answered the line.

"Fitz!" he exclaimed. "Happy Easter!"

"Happy Easter, bud," I laughed. "Taking my spot at the dinner table this year?"

"Does that mean I get two servings of your mom's corn casserole?" he asked.

"You'd do that even if I was there," I reminded him, getting jealous, willing to do anything for even the smallest sliver of Susanna Fitzpatrick's homemade corn casserole.

Like almost every conversation with Austin, I wanted to hear all about what was going on in Gulfpoint, and, apparently, our small town was still "as boring as ever" – his words, not mine.

Even though I knew nothing exciting was happening in Gulfpoint, I still felt like I was missing out on something important. And, more than anything, I missed my mom.

"Want to talk to your mom?" he asked.

"Yes please. Call me this week, okay?"

"Of course, probably tomorrow," he laughed.

With that, he handed the landline to my mom and I almost broke down hearing her voice.

"How's Greyson's family?" she asked.

"They're nice," I said. "But it's not the same as being home with you guys."

"I know, you'll be back home soon though."

"Hopefully! But guess what? I think you'll be proud of me."

"I always am but why now?"

"I went to church today," I laughed. "I didn't know or remember any of the prayers, but you can't win them all, right?"

"My little angel," she said, sarcasm dripping in her tone. "Hey sweetie, the timer's going off, so I'll call you tomorrow, but Wyatt wants to say hi."

"Okay, love you Mama."

"Love you too, honey."

Wyatt picked up the phone next, immediately rambling about nothing, trying to get me caught up on everything happening in his life, which seemed a lot more exciting than Austin's. Baseball season was in full swing, graduation was approaching, and he had committed to the University of Georgia.

"Maeve, do you remember Mabel Adams?"

"How could I forget?" I laughed.

Mabel Adams was Wyatt's ex-girlfriend. They dated for a year-and-a-half, practically a lifetime in high school terms. She was an awful person, thriving on dramatics more than Missy, and adding nothing but stress to Wyatt's life.

"Well, she's going to Georgia, too."

"Georgia State?" I asked.

"No, University of Georgia. In Athens. The same place I'm going."

I gasped.

"It's a big school," I insisted. "Maybe you won't see her there."

"You think she's not going to call me? Especially in the middle of the night?"

"You don't have to answer," I reminded him.

"I'm eighteen and she's my ex-girlfriend, we both know I'm going to answer."

I laughed. He was absolutely going to answer, she was absolutely going to hurt him again, and I was absolutely going to be there to answer his calls.

"Listen Wy, I've been away from Greyson's family for a while so I'm going to get going," I said. "Call me after your game tomorrow."

"Okay, bye."

With that, before I even said goodbye, the phone clicked.

Returning to Greyson's family, it didn't take long for him to realize I was uncomfortable. I was trying to be a team player and Greyson's family was beyond welcoming, but they were equally overwhelming. I was used to being part of a large family, but I had never been the outsider at a family gathering. I didn't understand their inside jokes or their mid-conversation laughs. I didn't get their references or their "remember when's" and, as much as Greyson tried to explain them, I knew it would never be the same as being there.

"You're doing great," he whispered, grabbing my hand under the table and giving it a reassuring squeeze.

Chapter Thirteen

I t rained for a majority of the last few weeks of April so most of my time was spent inside.

For two straight weeks, Greyson and I watched two movies a night and in a single weekend, binge-watched an entire five-season series from start to finish. By the time the weather warmed up, I was sure my couch had permanent butt indentations.

When May rolled around, the sun got its act together, but I couldn't enjoy any of it because, of course, it was another "busy month" at Sampson West. I was at work more than my apartment and although I expected my days to get busier as the month progressed, I got more annoyed that I hadn't fully appreciated the movie marathons a few weeks earlier.

May was busier than March. There were the usual dinner parties, movie premieres, networking events, brunches, luncheons, and red-carpet soirees, but we *also* had store openings, product releases, press conferences, and video shoots to plan and attend.

Week after week, I was shuffling between the office, film sets, stores, and venues.

I knew a long weekend was waiting at the end of the month but that couldn't come soon enough.

I woke up every morning hoping for a few more minutes of sleep, fully aware that I wouldn't have a second to breathe until getting back into bed way too many hours later.

I should have been excited that it was Friday, but days of the week didn't matter during busy months at Sampson West. Hours meshed into each other, days became one, and I went through most conversations in a daze.

A year ago, I was thriving during my last few weeks of college. Days were spent staring into space at the library, evenings meant bouncing between happy hours, and nighttime hours were reserved for dancing in crowded bars and packed frat houses. This year, things were a lot different. I had one, or multiple, events to attend daily but instead of drinking my way through the days, I remained sober, exhausted, and cranky.

The second Sunday of May was the first, and only, day my schedule was completely clear. There wasn't a work brunch to attend, conference call to dial into, or post-work daily report email to send. With Greyson back in Crescent Peak for the weekend, I had the day to myself and I had no intention of doing anything other than watching TV.

Midway through the fourth episode of some trashy reality show, my computer rang, and my little brother's name appeared on the screen. Accepting the video call, I knew he was procrastinating on homework, likely telling our mom he was going to his room to "focus" which, in the Fitzpatrick family, translated to "procrastinate."

"How are things at home?" I asked my him.

"It's been raining for like a week," he said. "Three of my games have been rained out since Monday and they don't think we'll have time to make them up because of graduation."

Springtime rain in Florida was a guarantee and our high school administration always acted like the wet weather would put the spring sports season in jeopardy. I was convinced they said that so they'd look like the heroes when they found room on the calendar to make up almost every rained-out game, the way they did year after year.

"They always say that and they always find a way to fit them in," I insisted. "Don't worry."

"I'm not yet," he said. "But listen, I called for a reason."

"I'm not shipping alcohol to you," I said. "Just ask Austin to get you some."

"It's actually not alcohol this time," he laughed. "Well, not quite."

"What's going on?" I asked.

"Remember that party at the Riverwalk Hotel a few months ago?"

"The one Austin and I convinced you not to attend?" I asked. He nodded.

"Yeah, I remember it," I said. "Why?"

"Well this kid I know went and he hooked up with Bev McGunn and now she's a little pregnant," he sputtered, barely taking a breath between words.

"Wyatt! You better not be talking about yourself!" I exclaimed. "Also, you can't be a little pregnant. You either are or you aren't."

"It's not me, I swear!" he promised. "I didn't go to that party!"

"Who was it then?"

"Griffin Kingsley," he said.

"Didn't he go to juvie?" I asked. "I'm sure Bev's dad was thrilled about that."

Bev McGunn's dad was a pastor in Gulfpoint and, if I thought my family lived under a microscope, that scrutiny was multiplied by twenty for the McGunns.

"No, that was his brother," he said. "Griffin's probably not far behind but hasn't been yet."

"So, the oldest McGunn girl from my grade went to rehab and now the one in yours is going to be a teen mom?" I asked. "Looks like things aren't picture perfect for the pastor's family."

"Things are never as they seem in Gulfpoint," he laughed.

Getting back to the office on Monday, after sleeping as many hours as possible on Sunday night, I was surprised to see an email from Declan at the top of my inbox.

> **Maeve,**
> **Please come to my office at 9:30 a.m. for a chat.**
> **Declan.**

I got nauseous immediately. There were no major blunders at recent events and I'd been working extra hours lately but I was still nervous, convinced I was getting fired.

Asking my cubicle-mates if they got an email from Declan, I got even more nervous as each one said no. I almost started packing up my belongings before going into his office.

"Come in," Declan said as I knocked on his door.

Walking into his office, I was surprised to see Maribel sitting across from his desk. Trying not to assume the worst, I was taken back by how much stuff was scattered throughout the not-so-big room. I didn't know how he could run an entire department in a successful publishing firm in such a cluttered space, but that wasn't my choice to make.

"How's your morning going, Maeve?" he asked, seemingly refreshed.

"Not bad," I replied, assuming he also treated yesterday as a legitimate day of rest. "Just getting ready for another busy day."

"That's actually what we want to talk to you about," he said.

Uh oh. This was it. I was getting fired.

"Oh, okay," I said, waiting for him to hand me a pink slip.

"How do you think May's events are going?" he asked.

I had been employed by Sampson West for nearly a year and I still had a hard time reading Declan. When I first started, I spoke when spoken to, but never went out of my way to interact with him. A few months ago, we started making conversation with each other, with the exception of busy months when a majority of our meetings came in the form of an email or a quick pass-by in the hallway. But even as I got to know more about him, I still couldn't figure out our dynamic.

Still unsure of the reasoning behind this meeting, I wanted to play it safe, offering a generic response.

"So far, so good. Everyone seems to be doing their part and the guests all seem to be enjoying themselves, no?" I said.

"I agree," he said, shocking me. "Remember that conversation we had a few months ago about your salary? And how I said I'd do my best to find you some extra cash for every paycheck?"

I remembered the conversation, but I also remembered it going very differently. He insisted it was impossible to modify the already-set budget for the year and I walked out of his office ready to hand in my two weeks' notice. Even though he was wearing brown shoes today, I didn't feel like correcting him, nodding instead.

"Well," he said. "I really appreciate everything you've been doing, so I found room in this year's budget to add about twenty-percent to your annual salary."

"That's great, Declan," I said. "Thank you!"

An extra five-hundred dollars a month wasn't much, especially by New York standards, but I hoped it would alleviate some of the stress of paying bills.

"Please keep this in private," he warned as I walked out of his office.

When I got back to my cubicle, everyone asked if I still had a job.

"Yeah," I laughed, playing it off. "He just had a few questions about today's press conference."

Looking at my watch, I realized I had to leave the office in ten minutes if I wanted to be on time to set up for the 11:00 a.m. event. We were announcing Sampson West's collaboration with one of the country's largest and most successful production companies. This partnership, which would adapt some of our best-selling books to film, was going to be great. It would open doors for our writers, giving them the opportunity to share their stories to a larger audience.

We teased the announcement on social media for weeks. Different outlets were speculating, based on our digital campaigns, but we made it all the way to the announcement without anyone leaking the news, an incredible feat, especially in this industry.

The event was as successful as we could have hoped and based on immediate response, people were watching, and they were excited. Fans were speculating which novels would become feature films, actors were anxious to see which roles they could audition for, and the entire staff of Sampson West was relieved to see another event was over, marking one step closer to June.

After the event, as everyone was filing out of the ballroom, I accidentally ran into one of our guests, more focused on reading tweets than where I was walking.

"I'm so sorry," I said before gasping, realizing who I walked into.

With a single glance, I knew it was Judson Sanders, the man behind the entertainment industry's biggest events.

"Don't worry about it," he said, looking at my staff all-access credentials. "Do you work for Sampson West?"

"Yes, sir." I responded, still mortified.

Judson Sanders was the man to know in the entertainment industry and, due to carelessness, I scuffed his shoes, shoes that probably cost more than my entire salary.

"You guys did a great job today," he said.

"Thank you," I replied. "Thank you for coming."

"Absolutely. Enjoy the rest of your day."

"You too!"

With that, he was gone, and I was internally freaking out. Judson Sanders was event royalty and he complimented our event!

I sent a group text to my coworkers immediately, assuming they'd be as excited as I was, confirmed by how quickly the responses came.

Getting back to the office, Declan was so impressed by the event, he sent the entire staff an email, thanking us for our hard work, and complimented everyone in person. Everyone was on a high.

Around 6:00 p.m., Declan emailed everyone who worked the press conference, excusing us from tonight's unrelated dinner party. In the same email, he changed tomorrow's staff meeting from 10:00 a.m. to 2:00 p.m., opening the office at noon. It felt like my lucky day. I even considered buying a lottery ticket.

Greyson and I got back to the apartment at the same time.

He spent most of his time at my place, especially while I was at work, insisting he didn't want to be at his apartment with his roommates and their girlfriends. I didn't mind. I liked knowing he'd be there when I got back, whether that be at 8:00 p.m. or 2:00 a.m. I spent all day surrounded by people, some strangers and some acquaintances, but it was nice ending every day with my favorite person in New York City.

"Babe, what are you doing back already?" he asked.

"Declan let us leave early," I said. "Want to grab dinner?"

"Yeah, let me just shower first," he replied. "It was cardio day."

While he was in the shower, I noticed Greyson's phone on the kitchen counter, unable to ignore its constant dinging. Greyson Raske didn't grasp the concept of different tones for different types of notifications. His text message tone was the same as his emails and his phone calls. It quickly became my biggest pet peeve.

As the dinging continued, I looked at his lock screen, making sure he wasn't missing a phone call from his parents. There wasn't an incoming call but there were a lot of notifications. Most were sports updates and work emails but a text from a girl named Amelia caught my attention.

Thanks for last night. I needed that.

What did that even mean? Who was this girl? Was he cheating on me? Did I need to worry? Greyson said he was at a work event last night, was he lying? Had he been lying about other things, too?

Between my raise and meeting Judson Sanders, I should have still been riding my high of the day. Instead, I was stressed because all signs from the text message pointed to Greyson cheating on me.

I wanted to call Austin, like I did when anything went wrong, but, as mad as I was at Greyson, I didn't want him dead. Fully aware that Austin would be on the next New York-bound flight, I instead placed Greyson's phone back on the counter, sat on the couch, and scrolled through my social media profiles, trying to distract myself.

When Greyson got out of the shower, I put my acting skills to the test, telling him I thought I was getting my period and wasn't feeling great, asking if we could take a rain check on dinner.

I'd been on birth control for years, purposely not getting my period in months, and I felt fine. I just couldn't look at him. I didn't want to fight tonight but I needed some time to myself.

"Want me to stay and make dinner?" he asked.

Absolutely not.

"I'm okay, I'm just going to shower and go to sleep."

"Okay," he said. "Call or text if you need anything, babe."

With that, he left, and I broke down.

This was why I didn't open up to people. This was why I didn't let myself be vulnerable. This was why I chose flings over relationships. They always ended with me getting hurt.

Chapter Fourteen

As May continued, I threw myself into my work. Spending most of my time at the office or at events made it easier to avoid Greyson. He wasn't staying at my place as much and, when we did hang out, I didn't mention the text message from Amelia. Instead, I let my frustration build. It was a coping mechanism Cecilia probably wouldn't approve of, but it worked.

I made it through the rest of the month without confronting him and Memorial Day weekend was in sight. Wyatt was graduating from high school, so I was headed back to Gulfpoint for the long weekend. Greyson was in a friend's wedding on Cape Cod so I had at least four days ahead that wouldn't include a confrontation about his potential sidepiece.

Midday on the Thursday of Memorial Day weekend, I arrived at LaGuardia Airport, along with almost every other person who lived in the New York City area. I thought I had arrived at the airport with plenty of time, but the TSA lines were the longest I'd ever seen, and I almost missed my flight. Apparently, I was not the only one with the bright idea of leaving the city for the extended weekend.

Group B was already boarding by the time I reached the gate. Barely making the flight, I settled in my seat and caught my breath. I thought I was in relatively decent shape but rushing through a crowded airport with a carry-on and backpack was a workout of another caliber.

As the plane taxied, listening to the safety demonstration, I prepared for my favorite part of every flight. Very few moments compared to the force, sounds, and sights that accompanied an airplane's departure. Takeoff was a reminder that the world was bigger than any worries that formed in my mind. For a brief moment, I was allowed to give up control, something I struggled with in almost every other area of my life.

I spent this flight the same way I spent every other, unsuccessfully flipping through channels on the static seat-back television before giving up, pretending I was going to read a book, and eventually taking a nap.

Although this trip home wasn't a surprise, Austin still picked me up from the airport. Even though we talked every day, the past four-and-a-half months were the longest we went without seeing each other in person, in the past eighteen years.

"How are things? he asked as we pulled out of the airport. "How's Greyson?"

"Not bad, he's in Cape Cod this weekend," I said.

I didn't get into details of our current situation because I still didn't know what, if anything, was happening between Amelia and Greyson. I didn't find any obvious red flags on his social media profiles, so I kept this one quiet from my best friend, for Greyson's sake. Austin had never been as forgiving as me, so I didn't want him to be angry, especially if there was even the slightest possibility of Greyson and me working things out.

"How's Missy?" I asked, trying to get the subject away from my relationship.

"Eh, that's more fun than serious," he said.

I didn't ask about her or their pseudo-relationship much. I knew it wouldn't last long and knew he only paid her mind to keep himself occupied. Austin didn't do long-term serious relationships, partially because his parents hadn't been the best example to follow. I knew he wanted to settle down and start a family eventually but, like most boys our age, he wanted to spend his early twenties playing the field.

"Your mom said I need to find a nice girl to bring home," he said.

"She's usually right," I reminded him.

"Usually?" he laughed. "More like 99 percent of the time!"

She was right when she told us nobody would remember embarrassing moments in elementary school, just like she was right when she told us, "that person isn't a real friend" in high school, and when she told us, "have fun, but not too much fun" during college.

"She's actually having a bonfire on Coral Manors Beach tomorrow night," he said.

"My mom? On graduation night?" I asked, knowing he wasn't talking about her anymore.

"No, crazy," he laughed. "Missy. And you're coming!"

"Are you sure that's a good idea?" I asked, now laughing alongside him.

"It'll be fun. Plus, don't you want to see everyone if you're back in town for the weekend?" he asked, knowing my answer.

With the exception of my friendship with Austin, I had always been a relatively closed-off person. After leaving for college, I realized I didn't have much in common with my peers from back home and I found myself justifying why it was okay to outgrow the people and places I knew for the first eighteen years of my life. That mindset continued through college and, every time I returned home, I stayed in touch with fewer people, putting significantly less effort into maintaining superficial friendships. I continued to be polite when I ran into them downtown, but I didn't feel the need to get invested in the small-town drama they never outgrew.

But, reluctantly, I agreed to go to the beach bonfire with Austin.

With that settled, we continued driving toward Gulfpoint High School for Awards Night. Every year, on the night before graduation, Gulfpoint High held an award ceremony for the graduating seniors. The intention was that, by presenting awards and scholarships ahead of graduation, the actual commencement ceremony wouldn't drag on. That was never the case. I went to at least six Gulfpoint graduations and each seemed longer than the one before.

Walking into Gulfpoint High School was like stepping into a time machine. With a single glance, it seemed very little changed in the past five years. Due to a nauseating increase in school shootings throughout the country, they added a security vestibule inside the main entrance but, other than that, everything in the lobby and auditorium looked exactly the same.

I wondered if they fixed the leaking skylight in the gym or the hole in the weight-room wall that appeared one day, coincidentally the same size as a dumbbell. I wondered if the ceiling in the junior science classroom still had a burn mark from the one afternoon when a chemistry experiment went wrong.

Watching the ceremony, I thought back to the fun my classmates and I had within these walls, wondering what kind of stories and memories this year's graduating class would carry with them for the next five years and beyond.

When the ceremony ended, we got takeout from Bailey's BBQ and spent a quiet night at home. After watching our third movie, I couldn't ignore that my mom had been acting really weird all night. I knew I hadn't been as great about calling her, but she knew how busy I was. I didn't know exactly what was wrong, but something was.

"Does Mom seem weird tonight?" I asked Wyatt and Austin after she went to bed.

They shook their heads.

"She's probably just stressed about Wyatt graduating," Austin laughed. "That's her baby."

I hoped that was the only thing she was worried about.

"Probably," I said. "I'm going to bed but I'll see you guys in the morning."

"Night, Maeve," they said at the same time.

The next morning, I woke up feeling so refreshed, not realizing how much I missed my own bed and waking up in Gulfpoint.

Looking at the clock, I knew the boys weren't awake yet and I heard my mom on the phone in her office. Noticing the sun was out and assuming the temperature and humidity weren't too high yet, I put on shorts and a tee-shirt, left a note for my mom, and went for a run.

By the time I got downtown, I was reminded that Gulfpoint took holidays and celebrations very seriously. Running down Main Street, I saw that there were 'Congratulations Seniors' banners and balloons hung all over town and American flags proudly displayed on every corner and storefront, making no exceptions for Memorial Day and graduation weekend.

Every flag and banner passed made me think of my family and how lost I would be without them. Although my dad wasn't with us this weekend, I was grateful for every family vacation, for those random Tuesday nights when all of us were home, for the holidays spent together, and for spontaneous adventures. But, especially on a day like today when it was impossible to ignore that frequent deployments meant missed events, resentment accompanied that gratefulness. I resented myself for becoming annoyed with Wyatt and Austin, for the times I insisted my parents were "ruining my life," and for every time I had ever been angry with them. But, most of all, I resented my dad's career for making him miss family milestones.

An hour later, exhausted, I ran into my driveway, noticing an unfamiliar car parked next to Wyatt's. Assuming it was one of his friends, probably over to pregame before graduation, I thought nothing of it.

Walking into the house, I stopped in my tracks and burst into tears.

"What are you doing here?!" I yelled, unable to catch my breath.

My dad was standing in the kitchen.

I couldn't believe it and I couldn't run to him fast enough.

Practically jumping into his arms, I continued to sob.

"Hi sweetie," he said, laughing.

I hadn't seen him in over a year and now, wrapped in his arms again, I was in complete shock. I had absolutely no idea that he was coming home.

"Did you guys know about this?" I asked, turning toward my mom and the boys when I was finally able to speak.

They all smirked.

"Is this why you were acting weird, Mom?"

"It was a hard secret to keep!" she laughed.

I couldn't believe the three of them kept such a monumental secret. But more than that, I couldn't believe my dad was home and would be able to see Wyatt graduate.

The actual commencement ceremony went exactly as expected. The principal spoke forever, delivering what sounded like the same exact speech from my graduation five years ago. The valedictorian gave a really nice speech about growing up with strangers who quickly became forever-friends, a sentiment shared by most students who passed through the halls of the Gulfpoint school district, no matter what year they graduated. But, as nice as her speech was, the entire ceremony dragged on for far too long.

Three hours after graduation, as Austin and I walked from his house to the Coral Manors bonfire pit, I second-guessed my decision to attend tonight's fire. I wanted to stay home, but with Wyatt at the PTO-planned all-night party, Austin made a fair point that my parents probably wanted a night alone after being apart for over a year. As much as I didn't want to be at this party, I didn't want to hear my parents together even more.

The party was the same as every get-together we threw and attended during high school and college breaks. Dozens of my classmates were scattered around the firepit, some cliques keeping to themselves while others gathered around the keg and beer pong table.

I must have trudged through a dozen of the always awkward "it's so good to see you, what have you been doing?" conversations during my first hour at the beach. They were all more-or-less the same, likely genuine but equally unmemorable. When I explained I was living in New York City and working in the publishing industry, the same look appeared on everyone's face, one of confusion with a sprinkle of judgment. Most people I spoke to couldn't understand that I made the decision to escape our small-town bubble.

A short while later, as I was grabbing my third or fourth drink of the night, I was approached by Hickman Hays. Hickman and I had only been kind-of friends during school. He was a friend-of-a-friend of some of my friends, but we didn't run in the same circles. I was slightly taken aback when he wanted to chat by the keg.

"I'm surprised you're here," he said.

I looked at him, confused. I knew I didn't put much effort into maintaining friendships and that the two of us hadn't spoken since high school graduation but during high school, there was rarely a Gulfpoint party that I didn't attend.

"Why?" I asked. "I like a good party."

"Not at the party," he laughed. "I mean I'm surprised you're in Gulfpoint. I always assumed you'd move to some faraway city after college."

"I did," I said. "I live in New York, I'm just back in town for the weekend."

"Oh," he replied, standing awkwardly.

Neither of us was sure what to say next. I hoped he would have gotten the hint and walked away before I had to but, like a million times before, Austin saved the day.

"Fitz, you okay?" he asked.

"Yeah, why?" I replied, more confused than I'd been during my conversation with Hickman.

"Sawyer is here."

"Okay?" I laughed.

"You're okay with that?"

"We dated a million years ago," I reminded him.

Sawyer was my middle school boyfriend. We "dated" for about a month and a hug was the furthest we'd gone. Nearly ten years later, I had no hard feelings, or any feelings of any kind, toward Sawyer.

Austin knew there was no bad blood between Sawyer and me, so I didn't understand why he felt it necessary to share that news.

"Would you rather talk to me, him, or Hickman Hays?" Austin laughed.

"I hate you!" I laughed, pushing him away. "Go find Missy!"

As the night went on and the drinks kept flowing, I continued mingling with people I hadn't seen in years. As I caught up with former classmates and friends, I was surprised how many were still dealing with the same high school drama: girls had the same rivals and were crying over the same guys. The boys were still messaging the same girls, seemingly forgetting that everyone talked in towns as small as Gulfpoint.

Listening to everyone, I realized almost everything around here remained the same, except me.

Chapter Fifteen

A year ago, almost immediately after moving to New York, I realized most things in the city were a far cry from the life I lived and loved in Florida. I was okay with living on my own most days, but my first day back in New York after Memorial Day Weekend was a very different story. This time, I had a really hard time leaving Gulfpoint, likely because my dad was back home, and for the first time since moving away, I didn't have another trip back scheduled.

Before leaving for the airport, I asked my parents if I could move back home for a while, wanting nothing more than to enjoy some time with my whole family before Wyatt left for college.

My mom insisted their door would always be open but reminded me that I made a commitment to Sampson West, New York City, and my apartment lease, commitments that needed to be honored. I knew she was right, but it wasn't what I wanted to hear. Adding insult to injury, my dad reiterated her sentiments, reminding me of a conversation we had a few years ago when he made me promise that I'd never settle for a mundane life. And although I didn't want to admit defeat, I knew that an ordinary life was the undeniable result of abandoning New York City and returning to Gulfpoint.

But still, the one-time dreams-turned-reality were starting to feel more like nightmares. I came to New York with an unwavering sense of confidence and I had every intention of being independent and courageous but tonight, as a result of unnecessarily getting lost in my own mind, I felt unusually pessimistic about the way things were turning out.

Ready to throw in the towel, I dialed my mom's cell phone number, hoping she hadn't already gone to bed.

"Hey sweetie," she said, answering the call. "How are you?"

I broke down immediately after hearing her voice.

"What's wrong, honey?" she asked, worry evident in her tone.

"I don't know if I can do this, Mama," I cried.

"Stop right now!" she said, cutting me off. "I've seen you be strong a million times. This is no different."

"It feels different," I sniffled.

"Okay," she said. "I'll make you a deal."

"Yeah?" I asked, intrigued.

"You can move home, but you'll have to work at one of the shops on Main Street until you find another job. You're not just going to come back to town to hang out and live off us again."

I knew what she was doing. She knew there was no way I'd agree to those terms. After working at a dress shop on Elm Street one summer, I promised myself that I would never work in retail again. The weeks spent in that overpriced dress shop were the worst of my life. Tourists weren't shopping for cocktail dresses in a beach town, the owner was a miserable person, and, at nineteen, sitting in an empty shop while my friends were at the beach was worst case scenario.

So, there was a zero percent chance I would take my mom up on that offer.

"No thanks," I told her. "Thanks though?"

"New York doesn't seem that bad now, huh?" she laughed.

"I guess not," I laughed, my tears subsiding.

"Maybe you should find a hobby," she suggested.

"A hobby?" I asked. "Like what?"

"There are a lot of options. You could draw or paint or start training for a marathon, or plant vegetables," she said. "Just something small so all of your free time isn't spent overthinking."

"I'm probably not going to go to train for a marathon," I insisted. "I only run so I can eat junk food and drink margaritas, not to go extended distances or just for fun."

"Yeah, that probably wasn't my best suggestion," she laughed. "Think about it though."

"I will, thanks," I said. "I'll call you tomorrow, okay?"

"Love you, sweetie. Goodnight."

"Love you too, Mama."

I went to bed that night thinking of our conversation, too tired to start researching hobbies, but not opposed to finding a way to fill my weekends.

Work the next day was unusually quiet. Most people with seniority took an extra-long extended Memorial Day weekend, and people at the office were mentally still on vacation, me included.

With no supervisors looking over shoulders and no meetings scheduled, I spent my day scrolling through social media, clicking on random YouTube videos, and planning out my schedule for the week. There was no productive work completed during the entirety of the workday.

Looking at my calendar, I realized I had therapy after work. I tried to schedule sessions for the first of the month, figuring I needed therapy on the same day eighteen-hundred dollars moved from my bank account to my landlord's, but Cecilia had a conflict this month, forcing June's session to happen a few days early.

I also needed to decide which night I was going to meet up with Greyson. He texted me last night after I fell asleep, letting me know he was back in the city, asking if he could come over.

I didn't answer when I woke up, but sitting at my desk, with nothing else to do, I typed a response.

> **Sorry, I passed out early last night. Guess I'm still worn out from the weekend!**

He responded over an hour later.

> **No problem! How was home? Didn't hear from you much.**

A year ago, I would have been petty and would have waited at least an hour to respond but I wasn't in the mood to play games, so I replied right away.

> **It was great. Sorry about that, time got away from me between Wyatt's graduation and my dad surprising us.**

I didn't feel the need to give him too many details of my weekend over text, especially because I thought I was still at least somewhat mad at him.

This time, he responded almost immediately.

> **Your dad came home?! Let's get together tonight. I want to hear all about it!**

He knew my dad came home. He was one of the firsts to "like" the photos online but I assumed this text was his way of reminding me that I hadn't called him all weekend.

Trying my hardest to not be petty, I replied.

Waiting to hear if I have to go to a dinner for Declan. I'll text you as soon as I know.

Declan wouldn't be back in town until tomorrow but Greyson didn't need to know that. There was no dinner planned but the potential work event excuse gave me extra time to decide if I wanted to see him tonight.

I was amazed at how fast hours passed while scrolling through social media instead of working. Before I knew it, it was seven o'clock and time to head to Cecilia's office.

When I got to Cecilia's, she wanted to know about home. I told her about my dad's surprise, Wyatt's graduation, the beach bonfire, and my unexpected homesickness. She chose to focus on the latter.

"Did you get homesick during college?" she asked.

"Only after move-in day of freshman year," I said. "That was the worst."

I walked her through the worst day of my college career, explaining how I tried so hard to postpone move-in day and how my parents insisted that wasn't allowed. Instead, they packed the car, drove to Collinswood University, decorated my dorm room, brought me out to lunch, and said goodbye in the parking lot near my building.

Cecilia responded with the most cliché therapist question.

"How did that make you feel?"

"Scared, anxious, and traumatized," I rattled off. "As I watched them drive away, I knew there was no turning back. I was there and they were gone."

"How did you respond?"

"I resented them for weeks. They left me standing alone in a parking lot. My mom insisted saying goodbye was like ripping off a bandage, the longer you take, the more it hurts."

"Looking back, do you agree with her?" she asked.

"I guess. I learned to like living on campus. As the years passed and graduation approached, I got emotional about college being in my rearview mirror. Before I knew it, I was the one pulling out of the parking lot. Again, there was no turning back but that time, Collinswood was there and I was gone."

"How does that compare to now?" she continued to question.

"What do you mean?" I asked.

"Is this homesickness the same as then?"

"I don't think so," I said, starting to ramble. "Right before I started college, my parents consistently reminded me that my new classmates were in the same position as me. That really helped me get through the hard days. For the most part, I'm on my own in New York City and, much to my dismay, there is no real-world orientation."

"Unfortunately not," she said. "But there wouldn't be a rule book for this stuff even if you were back home."

I nodded, assuming she was right, solely based on the fact that she had a lot more years of experience in the whole adulting thing.

"You said you're on your own in New York?" she asked. "Why's that? What about your boyfriend and your friends? How are things going with them?"

"The boyfriend thing isn't going too great right now," I laughed.

"How come?"

"I think he's sleeping with someone else."

I almost choked trying to get the words out, realizing it was the first time I said it out loud.

"Have you asked him about it?" she asked.

"No."

"When did you find out?"

"I don't know if I really have found out," I said, kind of laughing but more so trying not to cry. "But I got suspicious a couple of weeks ago."

"And you haven't said anything?"

"I don't know how or what to say. What if he isn't? Or worse, what if he is?"

"Either way, you won't know unless you ask."

"I know," I said.

And I did know. As much as I might have wanted to, I knew I couldn't avoid him or the conversation forever.

"Our time is almost up," she said. "But I want you to consider asking him and have some sort of answer or resolution by the end of the week, okay?"

I nodded, thanked her for her time, and left the office in a somewhat better mood than I arrived.

Taking a page from my mother's playbook, I knew my best bet would be to just rip off the bandage, so I texted Greyson on my walk to the subway.

> Hey, didn't have to go to that work thing tonight. Want to come over for dinner and to talk?

He hadn't answered by the time I got to the platform so, thanks to a complete lack of cell phone service underground, I second-guessed myself for the entirety of the nineteen-block subway ride.

There still wasn't a text by the time I got above ground.

My phone dinged as soon as I walked into my apartment.

Sounds good. I can be there in an hour, is that okay?

That gave me enough time to figure out dinner and have it delivered because, even after partially convincing myself, and the world, that I could be a semi-self-sufficient adult, I still couldn't cook to save my life.

I sent my reply while thinking of what restaurant to order from.

Perfect, see you then.

Deciding on Sal's, a steakhouse down the block that we went to regularly, I ordered our usual before settling on the couch to wait for Greyson and our dinner.

After refreshing my social media apps three times with no updates, I thought about the hobby conversation I had with my mom the night before. I still wasn't completely on board, but I needed to occupy my mind with something other than the dark clouds surrounding my imminent conversation with Greyson.

The more I thought about hobbies, the more I didn't completely hate the idea. I only knew one person who would give solid input, whether it was the input I wanted or not, so I texted Austin, looking for his opinion.

Mom says I need a hobby. Any ideas?

The typing-bubbles appeared before I could exit the conversation screen.

Porn.

I double-checked the name at the top of the screen, making sure I texted the first person. Then, my phone buzzed with text message after text message in a matter of seconds.

> **JUST KIDDING!**
> **Maeve Fitzpatrick, don't even think about doing porn!**
> **Imagine if your dad or brother saw it?! Or me?!**
> **I'm serious Fitz, don't do it!**
> **Hello???**

I almost couldn't type a response because I was laughing so hard.

> **Seriously Austin?! I was never even considering porn! You're**
> **insane! Why wouldn't you suggest photography or painting like**
> **a normal person?!**

When I didn't get an immediate response, I had a feeling he was laughing as much as I was. I should have known I was going to get some out-of-the-box response from my best friend, but even I wasn't expecting this.

I was also a bit taken back by how many texts he sent about making sure I didn't consider a hobby or career in porn. I was all about freedom of expression but participating in porn couldn't have been lower on the list of things I was willing to do.

My phone dinged again.

> **Do photography. That's a better idea – clothed!**

A few seconds later, the intercom in my apartment made a noise. Ralph knew Greyson was allowed right through, so I knew it wasn't him.

"Miss Fitzpatrick," Ralph's voice crackled through the voice box. "Did you order dinner? I think it's here."

"Oh great! I'll be down in a minute," I responded before heading to the lobby, tipping the delivery driver, and returning to my apartment.

A few minutes later, there was a knock on my door.

Like always, Greyson was right on time.

As I opened the door, he pulled me in for a hug and kissed my cheek.

"I missed you, babe," he whispered into my hair.

Back in his arms, I realized just how much I had missed him, and for the first time in a week, I found myself hoping that my Amelia suspicions were incorrect.

"I missed you too," I said. "I got dinner from Sal's."

"A steak dinner?" he asked, eyes widening. "Wait, is this a breakup dinner?"

"I hope not, but I do have a question," I replied.

"Yeah, anything, what's up?"

There probably would have been something in the real-world orientation rule book about not asking accusatory questions before dinner, but I didn't want to pretend everything was okay during the meal just to have my heart broken after clearing the table. So, I was going to try to put a kibosh on the elephant in the room before we ate.

"Who's Amelia?" I asked.

"Ace's girlfriend," he answered with no hesitation. "Why?"

I was immediately embarrassed. I had only met Ace at Zone, months ago, and we didn't talk relationships, and if Greyson had mentioned Amelia in the past, I hadn't been paying attention.

"So, you guys aren't sleeping together?" I asked, with no intention of beating around the bush.

"What? Absolutely not!" he exclaimed. "Where did you get that idea?"

"I saw a text where she 'thanked you for last night.'"

"A few weeks ago?" he asked.

I nodded.

"It's not what you think at all, I promise," he said, as we sat at the high-top table that barely fit in my small kitchen. "Let me explain over dinner."

Uncovering the food, I still didn't have much of an appetite, knowing I wouldn't be able to eat until I knew the Greyson and Amelia backstory.

Noticing my hesitation, he took a sip of his beer, and started to explain.

"Amelia's best friend from high school is a girl I dated for like five minutes in college. One weekend, she came up to visit and was freaking out about being a third wheel at a frat party," he laughed. "So, I introduced her to Ace, getting wingman points from him and not-quite-boyfriend brownie points from the girl. She and I didn't last through fall semester, but Ace and Amelia have been dating since."

"So, what was the text about?" I asked, starting to feel humiliated.

"She called that day to see why Ace was acting so weird," he explained. "So, I talked her off the metaphorical ledge without letting it spill that he's getting ready to propose."

"Wow, I'm an asshole," I said. "I'm really sorry."

I couldn't believe how quickly I overreacted or how off-base I was with my assumptions.

"Wait, is that why you've been avoiding my calls?" he asked, starting to laugh.

"You're not mad?" I countered.

"Babe, just ask me next time, I'll tell you exactly what's going on!"

"Or we could just not have a 'next time' in this conversation?" I chuckled, hoping he'd see at least a little bit of humor in this situation.

Chapter Sixteen

Before moving to New York, I had heard of the city coming together through tragedies and triumphs, but I didn't expect almost every company to join forces for Summer Fridays.

I didn't know when the city decided non-essential businesses should only operate Mondays through Thursdays between Memorial Day and Labor Day, but I was grateful that they did. Having a three-day weekend for fifteen consecutive weeks was a godsend, especially when three-digit "feels like" temperatures took over the Northeast.

Most people at Sampson West spent their extended weekends at the Hamptons or in the Catskills. I had heard countless horror stories every Monday about traffic, but the number in my bank account made weekly getaways impossible.

I was still getting used to life in the city last summer, only taking one weekend trip to the Jersey Shore. But I had different plans this summer, I didn't know where I would go, but I wanted to leave Manhattan at least one weekend every month.

My travel plans hadn't been solidified by the middle of June, so I made the decision to spend the second weekend of the month with Greyson. Although he understood where I was coming from, and we moved passed the Amelia situation, I still felt bad about overreacting. Thankfully, we were on the same page about spending the weekend together, so there was no conflict when I asked if he wanted to go to dinner on Thursday night.

After being unable to choose between our usual restaurants, we ended up at a new Asian fusion spot a few blocks from Bryant Park. I was always hesitant to try new restaurants, back home and in New York, within their first few weeks of opening. Selfishly, just in case the food was terrible, I wanted other people to try it first. But Greyson's co-worker said this place was good, so we took his word for it, a decision we both regretted after taking our first bite.

We looked at each other and burst into laughter. Greyson ordered the Miso Chilean Sea Bass, his co-worker's recommendation, and I chose the Mango Chicken, thinking I was playing it safe. I wasn't. It was disgusting.

"Is yours as bad as mine?" I asked.

"Probably, but I don't want to try it," he laughed. "Can we just not eat it?"

"You have to move the food around, so it looks like you ate some," I laughed.

"How do you know that?" he asked, amazed.

"My mom is a great baker, but she can't cook," I giggled. "It works every time."

"Lucky! My parents always made me eat everything on my plate."

It was easy to forget that Greyson and I grew up with very different lifestyles. I couldn't see Terry and Natalie Raske putting up with sneaking out, skipping classes, and pushing the envelope – three things Wyatt, Austin, and I mastered at a very young age.

"Most nights, it was my mom versus Austin, Wyatt, and I," I explained. "She lost that battle almost every time."

"Did you guys give her a hard time?" he asked.

"All the time, about everything."

In hindsight, we made hard times even harder, especially while my dad was deployed or on base, but we were teenagers and she rarely scolded us for innocent defiance.

"I actually talked to her the other day about finding a hobby," I told him.

"You or her?"

"Me."

"Oh yeah?"

"She thinks it will keep me out of my own head," I explained.

"I agree," he laughed. "I'll try some with you."

"Yeah?"

"Why not? It could be fun," he smirked.

"You aren't going to suggest porn like Austin did, right?"

His eyes widened.

"Would you be into that?" he asked.

"Absolutely not!" I exclaimed.

"Okay, good," he said, looking relieved, "I don't like to share what's mine."

I kicked him gently under the table.

"I'm just saying!" he exclaimed, raising his arms in innocence.

Greyson stayed over that night for the first time in weeks and my nerves acted like it was the first time I ever shared a bed with a boy.

In the middle of watching a movie, Greyson turned toward me and asked what I was doing next weekend.

"Just hanging out here, why? Planning on hanging out two weekends in a row?" I laughed.

"You aren't going home?" he asked. "It's Father's Day."

I shook my head.

My dad wasn't home for Father's Day last year so this year should have been a big deal, and it would be, but unfortunately, due to exorbitant pricing on plane tickets, I would have to make my appearance on FaceTime instead of face-to-face.

"Oh," he said. "I was going to go home. It's my mom's birthday on Saturday then obviously Father's Day on Sunday. But I can stay here if you are."

"Absolutely not! You're going home," I laughed. "I can find plenty of ways to entertain myself for a weekend."

"Are you sure?" he asked, hesitating. "Do you want to come with me?"

Not with a pity invite like that.

"No, it's totally fine, I promise! You should enjoy time with them," I insisted.

I was still overwhelmed from Easter weekend and that had only been a little longer than a day. I wasn't ready for anywhere between forty-eight and seventy-two hours with the Raske family.

Thankfully, the movie started to get good, so our conversation came to an end. It seemed like I was in the clear on another trip to Crescent Peak, Massachusetts, at least for now.

I fell asleep shortly after midnight, during our third movie, only to be woken up by Greyson's snoring eight hours later.

Deciding to let him sleep a bit longer, I went into the living room, trying to make as little noise as possible.

With some time to myself, I searched the Internet for ideas of different hobbies, determined to find something I might be at least slightly interested in. Every website showed similar lists, some ideas with potential and others that seemed far-fetched. I couldn't see myself antiquing or perfecting my family tree through genealogy. From past experience, I'd be staying away from astrology and running. I considered gardening and meditation, but there was nowhere to garden in New York City and I didn't know if I had the necessary patience for meditation. Reading through list after list, I thought painting, calligraphy, and photography seemed like my best options.

Today's forecast was too nice to spend inside, so outdoor photography seemed like the winner. I'd ask Greyson if he wanted to join when he woke up, hoping he'd say yes because now I had my mind set on spending the day venturing around the city.

A half-hour later, my bedroom door flung open.

"Oh my god, babe!" he exclaimed. "Thank god you're still here!"

"It's Friday," I laughed, pausing the movie I started.

"I woke up and freaked out because I thought you thought it wasn't Friday and I didn't know if you knew we didn't have to work today," he rambled, each word making me laugh more.

"I always know when it's a Summer Friday," I insisted as he plopped next to me on the couch.

"I should have known," he laughed. "So, what are we tackling today?"

"I was thinking photography around the city," I said.

"Let's do it! I'll go shower quick then I'll be ready to go!"

While Greyson was getting ready, I found what looked like a reliable camera shop online and it was only a few blocks from my apartment. Dialing the phone number on their website, an older man answered the phone. I asked if they had any cheap-but-high-quality cameras, already charged and ready to use, in stock. When he said yes, I asked if he could put one on hold, promising I'd be there within the hour to pay for it.

Forty-five minutes later, I walked into the film shop as Greyson headed into the café across the street, insisting we'd need caffeine to get through the day. I wasn't going to argue with that.

The man in the shop, the same I had spoken to earlier, was incredibly pleasant. He wanted to have a conversation about everything, asking me what I planned on taking photos of, offering tips and insights on this specific camera, and sharing some of the best places to shoot in the city.

I thought he would have chatted for hours if given the chance, assuming not too many people visited a camera shop in today's digital world. When he explained that his family opened the shop thirty-five years ago and he had been running it since, I made a mental note to stop in every so often, wanting to do my part to support a local, family-owned business in a neighborhood full of retail giants.

Noticing Greyson waiting outside, I thanked the shop owner for his help and met my boyfriend on the sidewalk, taking a minute to appreciate how good he looked today. His blue shirt and white shorts popped against his newly tanned skin, leaving me excited to see how that would progress as the summer months brought more heat and more sun to the city.

"What do you want to take pictures of first?" he asked, his voice pulling me out of my trance.

"Portraits of strangers," I said. "The Internet said those are the most telling."

Even though it was one of my least favorite places in the city, we decided to start in Times Square, knowing we'd find people of all types and assuming at least some would let us take their photo.

When we reached the city's central hub, we couldn't ignore how quiet it was compared to normal days, until we realized everyone was either on their way to the beach or the mountains or stuck working. People from the suburbs hadn't come into the city for the day yet, like they did most weekends, aware that most people fled the boroughs Friday through Sunday. There were always tourists around, and although they seemed more bearable during daylight hours – not distracted by Times Square's lights – language barriers and reluctance to talk to New Yorkers made it unlikely that they'd be willing to participate in my photography.

Somewhat surprisingly, I found nearly a dozen people who agreed to have their photo taken during our first half-hour in Times Square.

Every person had their own look and vibe, but I was most surprised by the stories told in their eyes. Some looked sad while others beamed with joy.

There was a woman, older than my mom, with an oversized turquoise necklace that popped against her all-black outfit. She reminded me of an elementary school librarian, likely, and stereotypically, due to the book in her hand that looked like it had been read a million times.

There was a man in an olive-green jacket with furrowed eyes and a crease at the top of his nose. He appeared well-traveled and well-educated, most likely by the streets instead of books. He was the most skeptical of the miniature photoshoot, asking half-a-dozen times what I wanted in return, not quite believing me when I insisted photography was just a newfound hobby.

There were twin girls, who couldn't have been older than eight, in matching magenta dresses and pigtails, held together with white bows. One seemed more reserved than her sister, but their smiles were wide, and their eyes were bright, neither tainted by the harsh realities of life. On the contrary, there was a girl around my age with purple hair and tattoos scattered on her arms. She looked stressed, a commonality among the generation that was the gap between the industrial age and the internet age.

There was a couple beaming, telling Greyson and me that they were visiting New York for the first time and had just gotten engaged moments earlier. Her eyes were red from tears of joy, I hoped, and his smile was plastered from ear to ear. With subtle touches here and there, his arm wrapped around her shoulder, her hand with new jewelry placed on his stomach, they couldn't keep their hands off each other.

Just as unable to keep their bodies apart was an elderly couple, their eyes wrinkled with experience. Her bright orange top and matching shoes popped against his khakis and white shirt. His tie was the same orange. To an outsider, like myself, their playful banter was proof of a life full of laughter, one I strived for.

171

After taking a bunch of photos, Greyson and I passed an advertisement for the city's largest Fourth of July fireworks show.

Last year, Wyatt and Austin flew up for the Fourth and we started to watch the show on television until the delay between the bangs outside my window and the noise from the TV became almost infuriating. Midway through the show, I remembered Ralph said something about the view from the top floor of my building so we watched the rest from what I expected would be a crowded rooftop but ended up being quite the opposite.

I'd turn twenty-three on July 4th this year and, wanting to spend the day with Greyson, I asked if we could go to the show together, preferably with seats right along the river.

"Actually," he said. "I was wondering if you'd want to spend the Fourth in Nantucket with my family and me."

I hesitated.

I just said no to spending Father's Day with the Raske family and I knew Greyson would stop inviting me if I said no too many times in a row. I'd never been to Nantucket, but I knew it was a small island off the coast of Massachusetts. I also knew islands in the summertime meant beaches and I saw nothing wrong with spending my twenty-third birthday at the beach, the same way I spent the first twenty-one.

So, I said yes, and his face lit up.

The next night I was in my apartment, waiting for Greyson to get back with the takeout we ordered when my phone rang. Wyatt's name and contact photo, a shot from years ago, appeared on the screen.

"Hey bud!" I said, instantly met by music blaring, followed by uncontrollable laughter.

"Maeve, it was Austin's idea," my little brother screamed, unable to control himself, laughing through every word.

"Hi Fitz," I heard my best friend say.

"Hi guys," I laughed. "I miss you!"

"We miss you, too. That's why we're calling!"

"And the real reason?" I asked.

Most of the time, Wyatt and Austin only called together when one of them needed something, usually asking me to convince our parents to let them participate in some sort of shenanigans.

"Why do you assume we need something?" Wyatt asked.

"Don't you?" I countered.

"Just ask her, dude," Austin said, confirming what I already knew.

"What's going on, Wyatt?" I asked.

"Everyone's going to Cancun for the Fourth and I need to go, too. Mom and Dad let you go, right?"

Celebrating America's birthday in Cancun was a tradition for Gulfpoint's teenagers, taking the weekend before or after the holiday to drink legally on Mexican beaches.

"Dad still doesn't know I went and if you tell him, I'll kill you," I threatened. "But I went after freshman year of college, not before."

"Will you just talk to mom for me?" he asked.

"Call me when you get home and I'll talk to her," I said.

"She's standing right here," he laughed. "Hang on."

I shouldn't have been surprised that he had her nearby before dialing my number, leaving me no time to think about what I wanted to say.

"Hi, Mama," I said.

"Hey sweetie. What's your brother trying to do now?" she laughed.

"Is he giving you a hard time?" I asked.

"I swear you and Austin combined were easier to deal with. And your dad is just giving into whatever the boys want these days."

"Dad's on board with Mexico?"

"On board?" she exclaimed. "It was his idea!"

I was shocked.

"What? Just the thought of me going was the end of the world!" I exclaimed, laughing about the secret we've kept for so many years. "I think he'd still have a heart attack if he knew I went!"

"That's why he doesn't know and won't find out," she laughed. "What are your thoughts on Wyatt going?"

"He just did his entire senior year without Dad at home," I reminded her, knowing she didn't need to be reminded of my dad's absence. "It wasn't easy, but he stayed on track. He deserves some fun."

"I suppose," she said.

I knew she was close to saying yes.

"Did Wyatt pay you to say that?" she asked.

"No," I laughed. "He just sprung it on me like five minutes ago, but if it works, I might have to charge him!"

"You make a good point," she said. "I'll tell him to thank you."

"You're letting him go?" I asked.

"I guess I am," she laughed before getting serious. "Hey, honey? Can we switch to video chat?"

"Sure, is everything okay?"

"Yeah, hold on."

A second later, my mom and dad were both on the screen and my mom called the boys into the room.

After handing the phone to Austin, my parents sat on the couch they only used to deliver news.

"What's going on?" I asked.

"Your dad has something to tell you," our mom said.

"Are you getting deployed again?" Wyatt asked, instantly sounding defeated.

I tried not to show that my emotions mirrored his. Our dad had just gotten home. I didn't know the rules of the United States Army, but I didn't think it was possible to get redeployed so quickly.

"Actually, quite the opposite," our dad laughed.

My ears perked.

"What?" Austin asked.

"I'm not going back, I just got approved for retirement."

"Seriously?" I asked, starting to cry.

Although I knew retirement was approaching, I knew not to get my hopes up because of the uncertainty of the United States Army. But with a confirmed approved request, there would be no more nightmares of IEDs or worries of welcoming him back to America in a wooden box. There would be no more missed holidays or weeks without talking. There would be a significant decrease in stress for all of us and, for the first time in a really long time, I could breathe easy.

Chapter Seventeen

W hen Greyson and I planned our weekend in Nantucket, he insisted it would be in our best interest to take the SunStreak ferry from Manhattan's Eastside Terminal to Nantucket's Steamship Authority Terminal. I'd never been, so I took his word for it, not asking any questions, and only somewhat hesitating before entering my credit card information for a $330 roundtrip ticket. For that price, and with a name like SunStreak, I assumed the ferry was the quickest way to get from Manhattan to the island. I was shocked when we got on the boat around 4:00 p.m. and the captain said we wouldn't be arriving in Nantucket until shortly after ten o'clock.

Over six hours on a boat? Almost instantly, I was terrified of getting seasick. Back home, we spent almost every weekend on the boat, tubing, drinking, and having a good time, but after a few attempts, it became a known fact that I got incredibly nauseous every time we tried to go deep-sea fishing. A known fact that I never told Greyson because I didn't think we'd be spending much time out at sea while living in New York City.

I spent the first hour of the ferry ride rushing from my seat to the restroom, convinced I was going to vomit. I never did, but quickly remembered that almost throwing up was one hundred times worse than *actually* throwing up.

A short while later, noticing my frequent trips to the bathroom and the paleness that replaced my face's tanned skin, an older woman offered me a water bottle, some Dramamine, and a can of ginger ale, insisting the combination would ease any seasickness. Desperate for relief, I ignored everything my parents taught me about accepting medication from strangers. Popping the pills immediately, I washed them down with the water before sipping the ginger ale.

Greyson was a trooper through all of it, rubbing my back between bathroom breaks, wiping my tears as I got more frustrated, and letting me lay my head on his lap while I waited for the medicine to kick in.

With the pain finally subsiding, I closed my eyes, not opening them again until we arrived in Nantucket.

Our trip was off to a great start.

Seasickness aside, my first impression of the notoriously preppy island was dark. It was nearly 10:30 p.m. by the time we got a taxi and the town's streets weren't well-lit, leaving not much opportunity to take in the surroundings.

"We can explore town tomorrow," Greyson laughed. "Plus, I hear sightseeing is more fun at twenty-three."

I nudged him from across the cab, well aware that he was purposely giving me a hard time. He knew birthdays were my favorite, but he also knew I was nervous about turning twenty-three.

In my mind, twenty-three felt very 'adult.' I felt like I had free reign from eighteen to twenty-two. I could blame mistakes and bad decisions on being in college or just getting out of college but now, kids my age were getting married and having babies on purpose.

A decade ago, I thought it was realistic to be married by my twenty-third birthday but now, I was just trying to figure out if things between Greyson and I were serious enough to introduce him to my parents.

Marriage seemed very outside my realm of possibility.

As our drive continued, cars and streetlights seemed fewer and further between. A few minutes after driving through town, we pulled into a driveway.

"Don't run over any of the hydrangeas," Greyson laughed, talking to the cab driver. "My mom would kill me, or she might find you and kill you."

I only caught a glimpse of the flowers he spoke of, noticing a lot of blues, purples, and pinks illuminated by the taxi's headlights.

"Your mom doesn't seem like she'd hurt a fly," I laughed as we got out of the cab.

"You haven't seen her get defensive over her hydrangeas yet," he insisted, leading me into the house. "You tired?"

"I think I got a second wind," I said, shaking my head.

"Let me give you a quick tour then."

We started in the kitchen. Its white cabinets and marble countertops reminded me of my childhood home. Based on first impression, Natalie clearly put a lot of effort into making this house feel like a home.

"This stove has been used maybe five times in the last ten years," Greyson laughed. "My mom doesn't believe in cooking at this house. For her, Nantucket is vacation and cooking on vacation might as well be one of the seven deadly sins."

The more I learned about Greyson's mom, the more I believed she and my mom would have been really great friends if they didn't live on opposite ends of the East Coast.

"So, you guys do takeout or go out for every meal?" I asked.

"Or my dad makes something on the grill. We're allowed to use the appliances but my mom refuses to participate," he laughed.

"That might be my new goal in life," I smirked, knowing my repertoire of edible meals was at a bare minimum. "Although I might sign up for a cooking class or two so I can learn to make something other than macaroni and cheese."

"We'll find one to take together," Greyson said, grabbing my hand, giving it a squeeze, and leading me to a room off the kitchen. "If it rains or it's a movie night, this is where we hang out."

An oversized television hung on a stone fireplace and the room's white couches matched the accent wall, which popped against three navy blue walls. I could picture myself curling up on these cushions after a full day at the beach or during a summer rainstorm, but knowing Greyson, there wouldn't be much time for lounging around this weekend. Even though I hadn't seen anything other than the kitchen and living room, I was already trying to figure out how to convince him to let us spend another weekend here.

"My parents' room, the laundry room, a bathroom, and the office are down that hallway," he said, pointing as we stood at the bottom of the stairs.

"Is this where I'm sleeping?" I asked after climbing two flights of stairs and entering a room with four beds built into the walls, assuming his parents wouldn't want us in the same room.

"No, we're in our twenties, you've already met my parents, and we've been dating long enough," he laughed. "We can share a bed. I'm sure my parents assume we do in the city, or they should."

I agreed but didn't want to be the one to bring it up.

I was fine with sleeping in separate rooms when I met them for the first time, but that was nearly three months ago. I had every intention of being respectful but, although I didn't mention it to Greyson, I thought they'd be more suspicious if our relationship hadn't seemed to progress since Easter.

Walking through the bunk bed galley, we entered a room with a few couches, a television, a bar, a ping pong table, and a pool table.

"What's this?" I asked. "Your hang out spot?"

"Growing up, my mom didn't like video games on the downstairs TV or my friends and I hanging out so close to the pantry, so one summer, my dad turned the home gym into this for us," he explained. "We also host a sick beer pong and flip cup tournament every summer."

"Drinking games definitely take priority over working out," I laughed.

"The gym's still here," he said. "It just got moved. It's on the second floor now with three guest rooms and the library."

"Is that where your room is?" I asked.

"Trying to get into my bed already, Fitzpatrick?" he winked.

"Just trying to get the full tour, Raske," I smirked.

"My room's this way, come on," Greyson said, leading me back through the galley and opening the door across the hall.

His bedroom was so far from the nautical, homey feel of the rest of the house. The dark gray walls didn't box everything in, but the space definitely wasn't as open and airy as the other rooms I saw.

"This is where the magic happens," he laughed, his hand gestures mirroring the celebrity home tour television show our generation grew up watching.

It was the epitome of a boy's bedroom. Shelves were lined with video games, and sport photos were displayed throughout the room. Thankfully, there weren't any posters or photos of Harden Packard.

"No basketball stars?" I laughed. "Maybe there will be some magic for you this weekend."

"Of course there will be, it's your birthday," he smirked before changing his tune. "Only if you want, though."

"Later," I responded, placing a kiss on his cheek.

"Follow me," Greyson said, heading toward the stairs.

Back downstairs, we walked outside to a patio off the kitchen and Greyson lit the firepit.

"What do we have planned for tomorrow?" I asked, knowing I'd go along with whatever he said.

"You're going to meet so many of my friends from back home. The Fourth on Nantucket has been our tradition forever," he explained. "Years ago, we promised we'd always spend America's birthday back in town and it's a promise we haven't broken yet."

"And now it's my birthday too," I smirked.

"It's after midnight, babe, happy birthday!" he said, looking at his watch before giving me a kiss. "Feel any older?"

"Not yet, I don't think that's how that works," I laughed. "But I am starting to feel a bit relaxed."

"That's the magic of Nantucket," he insisted. "Still nauseous?" I shook my head.

"My cousin wore these wristbands to help with nausea when she was pregnant," I told him. "Maybe we could stop at a drug store before the trip back to the city?"

"Do you think you're pregnant?" he asked, tensing up and eyes widening. "I thought it was just seasickness? We've been careful!"

"I'm definitely not pregnant, I promise!" I exclaimed. "The wristbands just hit the pressure point that makes you not nauseous anymore or something like that."

A noticeable wave of relief washed over his face. There wasn't a question that a baby wasn't in the plans for either of us right now.

"The best sunrise on the island happens right through there," Greyson said, pointing into the distance, clearly trying to change the subject.

"I'm going to wake up tomorrow to see it," I said after a brief pause.

"Really?" he asked.

"My dad always called really early on birthdays if he was deployed or on base, so I always watched the sunrise right before or after the call," I explained.

"Well then we better get to bed right now," he laughed. "Set your alarm for five o'clock at the latest if you want the best view."

Four hours after we fell asleep, my phone's alarm blared, and I second guessed how much I actually wanted to watch the sunrise. After a few minutes of internal debate, I knew I'd regret it if I didn't get out of bed, especially now that I was awake. Greyson didn't budge when my alarm rang or when I moved so I decided to let him sleep.

Walking downstairs and back out to the patio, I left the door wide open, afraid to get locked out of the house in a place I didn't know, especially with Greyson in a deep sleep. I didn't want his neighbors calling the cops because I was sitting outside of the house or, even worse, I didn't want to be stuck outside when his parents arrived.

Heading in the general direction Greyson had pointed last night, or at least what I thought was the right direction, I hoped I'd be able to find the spot he was talking about.

Less than one hundred yards from the patio, I came to a gate that opened directly onto the beach and I immediately knew I was in the right place. I made it just in time, mesmerized by the yellows and oranges that took over the sky.

I took some time to myself, thinking about everything that happened at twenty-two and everything that was possible for twenty-three. I grew a lot, mentally and emotionally, in the past twelve months and I had a notable optimism about the next twelve.

A few minutes later, climbing back into bed, I curled into Greyson and fell asleep, waking up three hours later when his parents arrived.

"Happy birthday, Maeve," they both said when I walked downstairs.

"Thank you!" I smiled.

"I hope we didn't wake you," Natalie said.

"Not at all, don't worry," I insisted, not wanting them to feel bad. "I've been up, I watched the sunrise this morning."

"On purpose?" Greyson's dad asked.

I nodded, laughing.

"How was it?" he asked.

"Beautiful," I smiled.

"Did you have a place like this to escape to back home?" Natalie asked.

"Every day is an escape when you live at the beach," I laughed.

Greyson's parents were as nice as I remembered.

Thinking back to the conversation I had with Cecilia a few months ago about them being responsible for raising one of my favorite people, I couldn't remember why I had been so nervous about this weekend.

"What do you have planned for today, Grey?" Terry asked. "Want to take the boat out?"

"No boats, Dad," he laughed. "Maeve had a rough bout of seasickness from the ferry yesterday."

"Oh, sweetie!" Natalie exclaimed. "Are you alright?"

I nodded, laughing.

"She's good but I'm going to keep her on solid ground today," he insisted, still laughing. "I'm going to show her around town then we'll meet up with everyone at the beach and go out tonight."

"Sounds like a full birthday," Terry laughed.

I nodded.

More than anything, I glad I fell back to sleep after the sunrise. It sounded like I was going to need all the rest I could get.

"Did Greyson show you the upstairs library, honey?" Natalie asked.

"Not yet."

"Follow me," she insisted.

I was speechless as I walked into the oversized room. There must have been eight hundred books on these shelves.

"Have fun," she laughed. "Look around and borrow whatever you want."

"Are you sure?" I asked.

"Absolutely! They're just sitting in here collecting dust," she said, leaving the room.

Scanning the shelves, I couldn't believe what I saw. There may have been more options in the Raske family library than Gulfpoint Public Library. There were first editions and autographed copies, titles I hadn't heard of and American classics, and every genre imaginable.

What felt like only minutes later, the door cracked open.

"There you are," Greyson laughed. "Will you be ready to get going soon?"

"Do we have to?" I asked, somewhat joking. "I could spend all day in here."

"We'll come back again," he promised. "But my friends are going to be mad if they don't get to meet you."

Chapter Eighteen

An hour later, on my tour, I fell in love with the small island almost immediately. In town, Greyson insisted most of the shops were closed for the holiday, so there wouldn't be much for me to see before we needed to get to the beach.

From the people in seersucker and pastels to the cobblestone streets, high-end boutiques and steepled churches, I could see myself visiting this place over and over again. If there were a few more dollars in my bank account, I could spend hours browsing through boutique after boutique. Unfortunately, my rent was paid a few days ago, so on this trip to Nantucket, I could only afford to window shop.

Main Street Nantucket on the Fourth of July reminded me of downtown Gulfpoint on Memorial Day weekend. Everything, and everyone, was decked out in red, white, and blue. American flags hung outside every shop and everyone appeared to agree that the only focus of the day was celebration. That had always been one of my favorite things about sharing a birthday with the United

States of America. As a young kid, I convinced myself that everyone had the day off to celebrate me and, although I knew otherwise as I got older, my inner child still believed it every year when July 4 rolled around.

"There's not much else to see," Greyson insisted. "Ready to go to the beach?"

I nodded, following him away from the center of town, toward the beach.

"My friends are really excited to meet you," he said. "So, you have no reason to be nervous."

"I wasn't nervous at all but now I might start to be," I laughed. "What have you told them?"

"Just the basics so they knew I wasn't dating a serial killer."

"Have you done that in the past?"

"Yeah, of course," he rolled his eyes.

I didn't have time to ask more questions because we were approaching a large group on the sand and, based on Greyson's smile, I knew these were the people we were meeting.

Within our first five minutes on the beach, I must have met a dozen of Greyson's friends. He mentioned a few weeks ago that a lot of them had summer homes in Nantucket, but I assumed that meant three or four, not twelve or fifteen.

Although I couldn't remember everyone's name, they were all incredibly welcoming. Nobody treated me like an outsider, and once they realized it was my birthday, drinks started flowing at an unprecedented rate, especially for so shortly after lunchtime.

I knew we had plans to go out that night so I had to pace myself, or at least try to, but that was a task easier said than done. I tried to slowly sip on the beer in my hand but I had a tough time saying 'no' to shots and cold beers. It was hot outside, the Fourth of July, my birthday, and I didn't want Greyson's friends to think I was rude for turning down drinks.

The afternoon continued much of the same way, but with some water bottles added to the drink consumption cycle.

Between this and incredibly competitive games of beach volleyball, Greyson's friends shared stories from growing up and from high school, giving me additional insight into his life before me. I heard how they skipped school, got drunk before football games, pulled harmless pranks on teachers, and spent weekends cruising around town. In a lot of ways, their stories reminded me of growing up in Gulfpoint, leaving me to wonder if life was the same in every small town.

Talking to a group of girls, some were his friends from home and the others were girlfriends of his guy friends, I asked about his past relationships.

"Have you guys gotten along with his past girlfriends?" I asked.

"You're the only one we've met since high school," one said. "And we only knew about them because we were in school together."

"Really?" I asked, surprised.

I knew Greyson had girlfriends before me and I knew they hadn't met his extended family but why hadn't they met his friends?

"We honestly never thought he'd bring a girl here until they were engaged," she said, everyone else nodding in agreement. "Greyson Raske hasn't been the kind of guy to settle down, so he must really like you."

That freaked me out. Was he nearing that point? I couldn't have been further away. He almost had a panic attack last night at just the thought of a baby and now I was feeling the same way about getting engaged or married.

A few hours later, and one very necessary power nap later, Greyson and I grabbed a bite to eat before meeting up with his friends again at The Landing, the local dive bar.

Greyson explained this bar was where the locals went, priding itself on not being a tourist trap.

Unexpectedly, it was almost identical to Penny's Pub.

"Penny's back home is exactly like this," I laughed as we went inside.

"Makes sense," he said. "Isn't that your locals bar?"

"I guess so."

I lived in Gulfpoint for the overwhelming majority of my life and I knew it was very rare to see a tourist drinking there, but I never put two and two together that Penny's was our 'locals only' bar.

A few drinks in, I felt someone tap me on the shoulder.

"Maeve Fitzpatrick?"

Turning around, I couldn't believe it.

Sebastian Barrett lived down the street from me growing up, his house only three from mine on Del Ray Lane. He and Austin were friends through sports, but the two of us only knew each other in passing. We were in the same class every so often but I hadn't seen or heard from him since the summer after high school graduation.

"What are you doing here?" he asked, almost as surprised as I was.

"I moved to New York City last year and my boyfriend's family has a house here so we're in town for the weekend."

"I thought I heard you left Gulfpoint!"

"The rumors are true," I laughed. "Are you living around here?"

"No, I'm still in New York," he said. "I have a loft in Brooklyn."

Sebastian went to college somewhere in the Northeast and had an internship in New York every summer during school but I didn't realize he was still living in the city. I wish I knew that a year, or even six months ago, when I hoped day after day for even the smallest bit of Gulfpoint.

"New York's a bit different than home, right?" he asked, laughing.

I nodded, thinking back to my first twenty-four hours in New York City. My bags were unpacked, my closet was organized, and I was still in shock. In a matter of hours, for the first time in my life, I went from feeling like an oversized trout in a tiny puddle to a minnow drowning in an oversized ocean.

"A little change never hurt anyone, right?" I laughed. "What are you doing here?"

"It's one of my friend's bachelor party," he said, pointing to a group of guys near the bar.

"In Nantucket of all places?" I laughed.

"He's from Boston so we're staying at his family's house. We weren't going to turn down a free stay."

"I'll drink to that," I smirked.

"Hey, wait," he said as our glasses clinked. "Isn't it your birthday?"

"You remember that?" I laughed.

"Yours is one of those birthdays I don't think I'll ever forget," he laughed. "I think about you and your birthday parties every year on the Fourth of July."

Maeve Fitzpatrick birthday parties were notorious in Gulfpoint and the surrounding areas. During high school and college, we used my birthday as an excuse to throw the biggest parties and they never disappointed. Most of them started relatively lowkey, but always ended with a beach bonfire, excessive drinking, and fireworks.

Like most bars, our time at The Landing was spent dodging spilled drinks and sloppy dancers, making it far from the best place to catch up with an old friend.

"Let's grab lunch back in the city?" he asked, knowing we couldn't carry on a conversation over this music.

"Absolutely!"

"You still have the same number?"

I nodded.

"I'll text you," he said before returning to his friends.

A few minutes later, after a refill, I found Greyson.

"Can we go talk for a second?" he asked, grabbing my arm and leading me outside.

"What's wrong?" I asked.

I didn't want to fight on my birthday, but I had a feeling one was about to start.

"You could at least pretend to be interested in my friends. You checked your phone like a million times today."

"I like your friends a lot, but it's my birthday. My friends and family were wishing me a happy birthday, so I responded," I argued back. "It would have been rude to ignore them. Do you want to date someone without manners?"

"Fine, you didn't have to flirt with that guy right in front of me!"

"I wasn't flirting! We were catching up; I hadn't seen him in years!"

Now people on the sidewalk were starting to watch and I wasn't going to fight in front of an audience, so I walked back into the bar.

Moments later, with Greyson still outside, Sebastian and his friends showed up to our group with a round of shots and before I knew it, everything got blurry.

I felt bad and didn't want to pit Greyson's friends against him, but I was glad the girls were on my side, well aware that my boyfriend was being ridiculous in this particular situation.

"Emotions are just heightened for both of you because there's alcohol involved," they said. "Things will be better in the morning."

I went to bed that night hoping they would be right, but things were still tense when we woke up the morning. We put on what could have been an award-winning performance for his parents, but it wasn't a game I was willing to play all day.

We'd have to talk about last night before our trip back to the city, but it would have to wait until after brunch with his friends.

Brunch was awkward but thankfully, the boys sat at one end of the table and the girls at the other. I spent most of the time looking over the deck's railing, admiring the boats in the wharf and doing everything I could to avoid eye contact with my boyfriend. We locked eyes a few times, but I kept most of my focus on the conversation the girls were having about the latest celebrity drama.

Brunch didn't last too long because everyone wanted to beat the traffic rush back to their home cities.

"Let's go talk for a minute?" Greyson asked as we walked out of the restaurant after saying goodbye to everyone.

"What happened last night?" I asked as we sat on a bench, still not understanding why he freaked out.

"What was the deal with that guy?" he responded.

"This was my first birthday away from my family so yes, it was nice to see a tiny reminder of home," I told him.

"I thought you were okay with spending your birthday here," he said, getting defensive. "I wouldn't have invited you if I thought otherwise."

"That's not the point at all!" I insisted. "I wanted to be here and spend the weekend with you. I'm just saying it was a nice surprise to see someone from back home, especially unexpectedly."

"Unexpectedly?" he asked, pausing. "You didn't invite him?"

"What?!" I asked, confused. "You thought I invited a guy I haven't seen or spoken to since the summer after high school graduation to a bar that I was at, a million miles from home, with my boyfriend and his friends?"

"I don't know," he replied, hopefully beginning to understand how crazy that sounded.

"I didn't even know he still lived in New York, let alone that he would be in Nantucket this weekend," I laughed.

"You could have explained that last night!"

"You could have given me the chance to!"

He got silent for a minute and I assumed he was finally starting to understand.

"Did I overreact?" he asked.

"Completely," I insisted.

Greyson and I got along really well about ninety-five percent of the time, but I couldn't ignore that these little fights took a lot out of me.

Chapter Nineteen

We sat next to a man with a Labrador Retriever on the ferry ride back to the city a few weeks ago and Greyson hadn't stopped talking about the dog since.

Greyson never owned a dog and rolled his eyes every time I insisted they were a lot of work.

"You're the one responsible for literally keeping them alive," I told him over and over again. But my reminders didn't seem to make much of a difference.

Greyson spent his free time researching breeds, watching dog training videos online, and brainstorming names. He seemed really serious about adding a four-legged family member and I hoped that all of the responsibility wouldn't fall on me.

"You know we've done some work stuff with a dog shelter downtown, right? I'm sure they'd be okay with you and I volunteering there this weekend," I told him after days of nonstop dog conversation.

"Really?"

"Yeah, I'll text Calvin, the owner, today. Maybe it will show you how much work dogs are," I laughed.

"Or maybe I'll come home with one."

"No, no, no," I said. "That's not part of the plan!"

"It might be," he smirked.

Greyson and I met Calvin inside the shelter a few days later.

"Thank you so much for coming," he said, seeming just as appreciative as he had when I came to the shelter with everyone from work.

"I told you I'd be back," I laughed.

"I know Maeve's been here before but have you, young man?" Stefan asked Greyson.

"Stop flirting," Calvin said to his professional, and probably personal, partner. "He's clearly here with Maeve and for the pups."

I could tell Greyson was taken aback by his far-from-subtle advances. I purposely didn't warn him about Calvin and Stefan or their over-the-top personalities, finding slight joy in seeing him squirm.

"Can we split you lovebirds up?" Calvin asked.

I nodded, too excited to play with puppies to worry about my boyfriend.

"I have dibs on him," Stefan said, obviously taking a liking to Greyson.

"Do I have to be worried?" I asked, laughing at Stephan's harmless schoolboy crush and Greyson's internal battle of being polite and concerned.

"I'll take care of him, sweetie," Stefan said. "Don't worry."

"That's exactly what I'm worried about!" I exclaimed.

I followed Calvin and a few volunteers to the room of puppies while Greyson, Stefan, and the other volunteers went to the section of the shelter that housed the senior dogs.

I brought Greyson here to show him that dogs were a lot of work but leaving him in a room with Stefan and older dogs, I had a feeling I was about to lose the 'getting a dog right now isn't the best idea' battle.

Spending time in the room of puppies was everything I needed. Baby dogs, of all kinds, were running around the oversized room, playing with toys and fighting with each other. I wanted to take all of them home, but I had to be the stern one on this venture. I couldn't adopt a puppy if I just spent hours convincing Greyson that taking home a senior dog wasn't a good idea.

Thankfully, after fostering a bunch of puppies in the past, I knew how much work they were so it was easier to ignore the internal desire to bring one, or a few, back to my apartment.

"How has your day been so far?" I asked Greyson when we met up a few hours later.

"This might be my new favorite place," he laughed. "I'm bringing a dog from that room home with me."

"You can't just point at a dog and bring it home though," I laughed. "You need to do some research on each dog first."

"Like the breed and stuff?" he asked.

"Kind of but more like the particular dog. You have to be a good match and need compatible personalities."

"So, picking a dog is like picking a girlfriend?"

"I guess?" I laughed.

Opening the shelter's website, I read through some of their descriptions, trying to lead Greyson in the direction of a dog that could be a good match for his personality and lifestyle.

"This one's food aggressive," I told him, showing Marco's profile.

"What's wrong with that?" he asked. "You are too, sometimes." I gave his arm a playful smack.

"Food aggressive dogs are not the same as sometimes-hangry girlfriends," I insisted. "Although neither should be your first."

"Okay, he's out. Who's next?" he asked.

"Polo," I laughed. "But, he's not suitable for first time owners."

"What does that mean?"

"It means he's a lot to handle," I laughed.

"Again, so are you!"

"Can we stop comparing me to shelter dogs, please?" I asked.

"It's not my fault that their adoption bios could be mistaken for your dating app bio."

"Oh?" I smirked. "Should I sign up for a dating app? You can write my bio."

"That's not what I meant!" he insisted.

"Let's check out Ringo," I said, changing the subject. "His picture is cute."

"He was in that room."

"Did you play with him?"

"Yeah, he was really sweet. His eyes looked calm."

He was right. Ringo's eyes, like Greyson's, were the first thing I noticed.

"What does his bio say?"

Ringo is estimated to be between 8-10 years old and is looking

for his forever home. He was brought to the shelter when his longtime owner passed away after a brief battle with cancer, leaving behind a widow with early onset Alzheimer's who was unable to care for him. Ringo is fully vetted, housebroken, and crate trained. He is laid back but still loves toys, treats, and to play! He likes going for walks, playing fetch, and acting like an oversized lap dog. Please help Ringo find a loving home to live out his golden years.

"He sounds perfect," Greyson exclaimed.

"Which part of his bio are you going to compare me to?" I tested him.

"I probably shouldn't say the housebroken part, right?" he laughed.

I rolled my eyes.

"Just kidding, it's obviously the laid-back part," he said. "Because I have the most caring and supportive and easy-going girlfriend ever."

"Nice save," I said, sarcastically. "Is Ringo the winner?"

"I love him but I'm not a huge fan of his name. I could change it though, right?"

"Not really," I laughed. "He's like sixty in dog years. Imagine if someone tried to change your name after having it your whole life!"

"I guess you're right," he said.

"Usually am," I smirked.

I followed Greyson into the senior dog room and watching him interact with Ringo, I knew they would be a great pair and I knew it was only a matter of time before the four-legged friend became a permanent part of our lives. But I also knew Greyson's apartment wasn't dog-proofed so he wouldn't be able to come with us today.

An hour later, before leaving the shelter, I pulled Calvin and Stefan to the side, thanked them for letting us spend the day, and asked what kind of attention Ringo was receiving from other potential adopters.

"Most families are only interested in puppies," Stefan said. "Not the older guys."

"Are you thinking of adding Ringo to your family?" Calvin asked.

"Greyson's considering it but we have to talk about it some more," I explained, knowing this wasn't a battle I was going to win.

"Take a few days to think about it," Calvin said. "I'll put an 'adoption pending' sign on his cage."

"You can do that?" I asked.

It hadn't crossed my mind that you could put a hold on a dog.

"Honey!" Stefan exclaimed. "We can do whatever we want!"

"The perks of running the place," I laughed before saying my goodbyes.

Greyson and I stopped at a pizza place on our walk back to the subway.

One of my favorite things about our usually compatible personalities was the agreement that sometimes there was nothing better than a dollar slice. It was agreed upon, at least in our relationship, that New York City thrived because of places that specialized in slices of pizza that cost less than an hour at a parking meter.

I felt my phone buzz as we waited for our pizza.

Hey Maeve, it's Sebastian. You around to grab lunch tomorrow?

I knew it was wrong to lie to Greyson about where I was going, but it seemed equally unnecessary to start another fight over a harmless lunch between two old acquaintances, especially because I didn't think lunch would last longer than an hour.

"It's Declan asking if I can sit in for him at some lunch tomorrow," I told Greyson.

"On a Sunday? With such short notice?" he asked.

"You know how Declan is," I insisted. "He probably thought he'd make it home from the Hamptons in time."

"Well if it's work, you can't really say no, can you?"

"Rain check on whatever you had planned?" I asked.

I didn't know if Greyson planned on spending the day with me but, over the past few weeks, I realized he would make snide comments if I didn't assume we were spending weekends together.

"Some of my friends from home are in town this weekend so I thought we could meet up with them tonight," he said.

"I think I'm going to stay in. Hangovers suck even more at work events." I laughed. "But you should go!"

"Are you sure?"

"I'll probably go to bed pretty early anyway so just don't expect me to wait up."

"I'll probably just crash on the couch in their hotel room," he said. "Is that okay?"

"Absolutely!" I said, trying not to make it known that I was relieved.

With Greyson spending the nighttime, overnight, and morning hours with his friends from Crescent Peak, I wouldn't have to worry about maintaining my 'I'm going to a work event' lie.

We were never really close friends so there wasn't going to be much for us to catch up on. But we went to school together for thirteen years and we were what seemed like the only two people from our generation to make the Gulfpoint-to-New York City move so I wanted to meet up.

As soon as I got the go-ahead from Greyson to attend the 'work event,' I texted Sebastian back.

Sounds good, where are you thinking?

"It's a sign!" Greyson insisted, pointing at the pet shop across from the pizza place.

"A sign that taking care of pets is so much work that you won't have time to take care of your outside appearance?" I asked, referring to its desolate exterior.

"No! You know what I meant!" he laughed. "Can we go inside?"

"If you're going to get a dog, you're getting one from a shelter, not a pet store with dogs from puppy mills!" I insisted.

"I'm bringing Ringo home, but he needs treats and toys!"

"Let's go pick some out then," I laughed, realizing he was already halfway across the street.

The only employee in the store was a woman who appeared to be in her seventies or eighties. Her noticeable surprise when the door opened led me to assume not too many people visited the shop.

Greyson was disappointed to learn there were no puppies in the store, apparently not fulfilling his fix at the shelter, but realized that meant this shop didn't support puppy mills, making both of us want to buy Ringo's supplies from this particular store.

"What can I help you guys with?" the woman asked.

"I'm getting a new puppy," Greyson said, excitedly. "Well, he's a grown dog but he needs all of the usual dog stuff."

"Have you ever owned a dog?"

He shook his head.

"I have," I told her. "Don't worry, I know what he needs."

I didn't want her following us around the shop. Walking seemed to be troublesome for her and I didn't want Greyson and I to be responsible for causing any additional pain.

"Please don't hesitate to ask if you have any questions," she said.

"We will, I promise," Greyson replied before starting to explore the aisles.

"Okay, babe, what do we need?" he asked.

"Food and water bowls, a collar and leash, an ID tag, a crate and bed, a brush, poop bags, a lot of toys, and a lot more treats," I said, rattling off a list.

"All at once?" he asked, starting to laugh.

"I told you, dogs need a lot!"

"He's worth every penny," he laughed.

As we checked out, Greyson asked the woman behind the counter a bunch of questions about dogs, each question surprising me with how serious he sounded about this entire situation.

Maybe this wasn't such a bad idea.

Walking into Greyson's apartment a little while later, bags full of dog toys in hand, I quickly remembered why I didn't like spending much time there. It was dirty, cramped, full of roommates, and smelled like weeks' worth of unwashed dishes.

Greyson didn't have long before having to meet up with his friends so I got to leave the apartment as soon as I dropped the bags of Ringo's supplies.

Heading out of the apartment, I pulled out my phone and texted Calvin.

I think we're a go on Ringo!

He sent a thumb's up emoji and I went to bed that night knowing Greyson was getting a dog.

I met up with Sebastian the following day, around noon, at a pub not too far from the Brooklyn Bridge. It was more of a hike than I preferred on a normal day but I wasn't going to scoff at Sebastian's recommendation.

I was nervous lunch would be awkward, given our nowhere-near-best-friends acquaintanceship, but when I mentioned that to Austin, he said I had nothing to be worried about because Sebastian Barrett could carry a conversation with a wall.

Within five minutes of sitting down, I knew I needed to add another tick to the "Things Austin Packard has been right about" list, one that seemed to get longer with every passing day.

Things between Sebastian and me weren't the slightest bit awkward, both of us clearly outgrowing the 'I don't know how to have a real conversation with the opposite sex' phase seemingly engrained in every middle and high schooler.

I was so used to knowing nothing about anyone I met in New York that it was refreshing to sit and have a conversation with someone I didn't need to introduce myself to.

"When was the last time you were in Gulfpoint?" I asked after the waitress took our order.

"Winter break of our freshman year of college."

"Really?"

"Yeah, and only for like a week. I fled to my roommate's house when my parents told me they were getting divorced."

I knew his childhood house sold during the first spring we were away at school but I never asked my mom for details regarding the sale or the new neighbors. Sebastian was the youngest of four kids, so part of me assumed with all of their kids out of the house his parents were downsizing. It never crossed my mind that they split up.

I knew so many people with divorced parents, but Sebastian and I weren't close friends, so I didn't know what to say.

"I'm really sorry to hear that," I said, hoping it was generic enough but equally kind. "If it's any sort of consolation, not much has changed since then."

"I figured as much," he laughed. "Do you still go back?"

"Every chance I get," I said. "My brother just graduated from Gulfpoint High so I was in town for that."

"I miss it," he replied.

"Me too," I admitted. "All the time."

"Have you and Packard dated yet?" he asked.

I knew that was coming. It was a pretty common question during any catch-up sessions with people from Gulfpoint.

"Nope, never have and probably never will," I laughed. "He practically lives with my family."

"I don't believe that," Sebastian smirked. "I still have money on the two of you getting married."

"You can make that check out to Maeve Fitzpatrick," I laughed. "What about you? I don't see a ring on your finger."

"I thought you have a boyfriend?"

"I'm not talking about for me!" I smiled, glad things were going well between us.

"Packard isn't really my type," he laughed, making me laugh.

"Shocker," I smirked. "Any lucky lady in the picture?"

"Do you remember Tessa McGrady?"

"She graduated the year after us, right?"

"Yeah, she ended up going to Boston College, too," he said. "We ran into each other at a party her first semester and we've been dating since."

"No way! That's so cute! I guess it is possible to find love from our small town," I laughed. "Does she live in New York, too?"

"She did but she just got a new job and got transferred to Houston."

"Oh no, that sucks! How has long distance been?" I asked.

"The company I work for has an office in Houston. I made my schedule so I can spend at least two weeks a month working there," he explained. "So, all in all, long distance could be a lot worse."

"That doesn't sound too bad," I laughed.

"What do you do for work?" he asked.

"I'm an Administrative Assistant at this publishing company called Sampson West."

"No way?"

"You've heard of it?" I laughed.

"I interned there the summer before senior year."

"Seriously?"

Sebastian Barrett didn't strike me as the kind of guy interested in books or the publishing industry.

"Seriously," he laughed. "I interned for the IT department."

"You're lying! That's such a small world!"

"It really is!" he said. "Actually, the guy I interned for is practically running the company's community relations department now."

"Really?"

"Yeah, his name is Declan Danvers. Do you know him?"

"Know him?" I laughed. "I'm his assistant."

"That's so funny! You'll have to tell him I said hi."

"Absolutely! Are you still in IT?" I asked.

"Yep, I'm working for a guy named Judson Sanders. Ever hear of him?" He smirked.

He knew I'd heard of him. Everyone in the entertainment industry knew of Judson Sanders. Everyone in the entertainment industry had a Judson Sanders story or knew someone who had a Judson Sanders story. And everyone in the entertainment industry, myself included, dreamed of being part of Judson Sanders' team.

I couldn't believe Sebastian Barrett, the somewhat-nerdy kid I'd known for years, worked for the man behind the biggest events in the industry.

"You really work for Judson Sanders?" I asked.

"One thousand percent," he laughed. "Want me to give him a call?"

"I mean, kind of… But not really!"

"I was actually thinking about you and him the other day after hearing you're in New York," he said.

"Really? Why?"

"Are you still a writer?"

It was practically guaranteed if you saw me between freshman and senior year of high school, there was a good chance that two things were nearby – Austin Packard and a tattered notebook. I never went anywhere without a notebook.

"I don't think that part of me will ever fully go away," I laughed. "I don't always have a notebook in hand anymore but my wheels are always turning."

"We might have an opportunity for you."

"We?" I asked.

"Judson's usually looking for people to freelance, to write press releases and blog posts," he said. "I don't think there are any good positions right now but when one opens up, it could be a foot in the door."

That seemed too good to be true.

"We met for the quickest minute at a Sampson West press conference a few months ago when we announced our production company collaboration. I actually scuffed his shoes."

"You were there?" he asked. "So was I!

"And we didn't run into each other?" I laughed, amazed at how small the world could be sometimes.

"Nope, I guess not," he smiled. "My shoes escaped the event unscathed."

"Be careful," I warned. "There's still plenty of time today!"

He straightened up, joking acting concerned, before mentioning my brief meeting with Judson a few months back.

"You know, he'll probably remember you."

"No way," I insisted. "It was like a thirty-second interaction, max."

"Judson Sanders doesn't forget faces," he laughed. "That's how he's so good at what he does!"

"Would I still be able to keep my job at Sampson West if something with Judson opened up?" I asked, trying to think of this potential opportunity's logistics.

"Of course! Nobody can afford to live in New York on just a freelance, part-time salary," he laughed. "I'm trying to help you out a bit, not get you evicted!"

Fair point, I thought.

"Would you be interested?" he asked.

"Would I? Absolutely!"

"Perfect, just send me some work samples and I'll pass them along when something opens!"

These were the moments I dreamed of when I left Gulfpoint. I convinced myself that things would work in my favor if I moved to New York City and finally, after what felt like a million hurdles and hardships, I felt like things were finally getting near the point I wished for so many nights in a row.

Chapter Twenty

A few weeks after waiting, home inspections, references getting checked, and questions getting answered, Greyson was approved to adopt Ringo and we learned very quickly that he was the best dog ever. He was calm, loved to snuggle, and was attached to Greyson and me almost immediately. Very little time was spent feeling each other out or testing the waters. He fit into our dynamic almost perfectly by the end of our first day together.

Already knowing right from wrong, Ringo didn't need to be scolded like a puppy, but Greyson appropriately took on the role of alpha. That allowed me to be the good cop, a position appreciated by both Ringo and myself. I insisted I was Ringo's favorite and Greyson, although he refused to admit it, knew it was true.

Coincidentally, there was also a heatwave in New York City that week where I learned that the high nineties in New York felt very different than the high nineties in Gulfpoint. With the heat getting stuck between skyscrapers, and a lack of sea breeze, high nineties in New York City were nearly unbearable. I had a bunch of saved time off from work, with seemingly no plans to use most of it, so I took the week that Greyson brought Ringo home off, assuming he would need some help getting our new four-legged friend acclimated to his new home.

My lease said I couldn't own a dog but there was nothing in writing prohibiting dogs from visiting tenants so, with Ralph at his post, we bent the rules a bit, and ended up spending most of our time with Ringo at my apartment. There was more space for him to spread out, it was significantly cleaner than Greyson's, and I had no roommates to distract what Greyson referred to as "Ringo's acclimation process," which only consisted of giving him a treat every time he sat down, voluntarily or requested.

I tried to explain that Ringo would get fat if the constant treats continued, suggesting that Greyson only give them a few times a day. Based on his reaction to that suggestion, you'd think I recommended eliminating summer vacation to a group of elementary aged school children.

The only person possibly more excited than Greyson about Ringo was Wyatt. He would call and FaceTime us multiple times a day, desperate to catch even a glimpse of Manhattan's newest adopted resident.

One afternoon, he called while Greyson had Ringo out for a walk and it may as well have been the end of the world.

"Are you just using me for my boyfriend's dog or do you maybe want to chat with your sister?" I asked him.

"Well, I called for Ringo, but I have a few minutes to talk," he laughed.

Wyatt was leaving for college in a few days and I knew he was giving my parents a hard time about nearly everything. I remembered snapping at my parents very easily right before leaving for school for the first time, so I wanted to pick his brain a bit to see if he too, was rebelling on purpose.

"I hear you're fighting with Mom and Dad a lot," I said.

"Now they're talking about me behind my back?" he asked, getting annoyed.

"No, calm down. I asked them how you were holding up."

"I'm fine."

"You know, it's not easier to leave if you're mad at them."

"That's not what I'm trying to do."

"Yes, it is. I did the same thing," I reminded. "Trust me, it doesn't make a difference. All it means is that you'll regret being rude in five years when you realize you spent your last few days at home being mean to Mom and Dad."

"Is that what happened to you?" he asked.

"I wouldn't be having this conversation with you if it didn't," I insisted. "As your big sister, my main responsibility is to make sure you learn from my mistakes. So, can you just do me a favor and listen to me this one time?"

"I listen to you most of the time," he said, lying.

"We can pretend that's a little true but it's not," I laughed. "Just be nice to Mom and Dad and hang out with them before you leave."

"I will, I promise," he said. "I have to go, I'll call you later."

"Bye, Wy."

The line went dead before his response.

Waiting for Greyson and Ringo to return from their walk, I thought more about that conversation with my younger brother. I tried to lead him in the right direction over the years and I knew it was time for him to fly the coop and try life on his own but I knew I'd sleep easier at night believing at least a few lessons stuck with him.

A few days later, I was sitting on the living room floor, playing fetch with Ringo when my phone rang. Greyson, sitting closest to it, handed it to me with a look of disgust.

"Who is it?" I asked.

"Look for yourself," he said with such snide.

Sebastian's name was written across the top of the screen.

"He texted me the other day to see if I was still a writer and asked me to send him some samples so maybe it's about that," I said before walking into the other room and answering the phone, leaving out details of our lunch together after returning from Nantucket.

It wasn't a complete lie.

I really didn't know why he was calling today, we hadn't spoken since his quick "thank you" response to my email of work samples.

"Hey Maeve," Sebastian said as I answered the phone. "Are you busy today?"

"Hey. Not really, why?"

"Any chance you could meet Judson and I for lunch in Midtown in like an hour?"

In terms of outside appearance, I was in no shape to have lunch, or spend any amount of time, with Judson Sanders. I hadn't showered and had been wearing the same sweats for the past two days.

But mentally, I was completely prepared for this meeting.

"Yeah, of course," I replied. "Just send me the address."

"Great, see you soon," he said.

The line clicked before I had a chance to respond.

Almost immediately after we hung up, Sebastian texted me an address.

Typing it into Google, my nerves skyrocketed as soon as the page loaded.

Sebastian wanted me to meet him and Judson at The 45 Club, a prestigious restaurant notorious for some of the world's most famous business deals. It was speculated throughout the industry that executives from Disney, Apple, and Amazon, all chose the best tables at The 45 Club for finalizing deal negotiations.

I passed the restaurant a few times but had never been inside. You couldn't just walk in and expect a table. You needed a reservation and needed a spot on the waitlist to even be considered. Rumor had it the waiting list was already into next spring. I wasn't surprised that Judson Sanders was able to get, what I assumed was, a last-minute reservation.

Walking back into the living room, Greyson looked at me with bated breath.

"He asked if I could meet him and his boss for lunch," I said. "I'm going to take a quick shower."

"You're going?" he asked.

"A lunch offer with Judson Sanders isn't an offer you turn down."

"Is he a celebrity?"

Sometimes it was easy to forget that Greyson wasn't as in tune with the entertainment world.

"In the publishing and entertainment world, he may as well be Madonna," I insisted.

"Sebastian's going too?" he asked, clearly still not a fan of my former neighbor.

"He's the one introducing us so I think he has no choice but to be there," I laughed.

"Remind him that we're dating," he chuckled, even though I knew he wasn't kidding.

"And I'll remind you that he's dating a girl we went to high school with," I smirked, getting annoyed by his unnecessary jealousy.

After taking what may have been the fastest shower in human history, I got to the restaurant way earlier than necessary, not wanting a delayed train or midday foot traffic to be the reason for a less-than-ideal first impression. I also didn't want them to know I took a week off from work to hang out with a dog, purposely wearing an outfit that I wore to the office more than once.

The inside of The 45 Club was so far from what I expected to find at a restaurant in the center of New York City. From the street, it looked the same as every other high-rise, with scaffolding shielding the steel from eyesight but, walking through the double-doors was like being transported to a secluded oasis. Exposed brick lined the walls. Black steel hung across the ceiling and around strategically placed windows. Greenery and trees were placed throughout the room and the tables looked like they belonged at the most high-end picnic. It felt like I entered a courtyard in the countryside, a far cry from the outside streets of Midtown Manhattan.

With at least a few minutes to spare before the guys got to The 45 Club, I thought about how crazy this was. Although I wanted to believe everything Sebastian said about potentially working for Judson, I was so used to empty promises and didn't know what, if anything, would come from our conversation. So, after saying goodbye at lunch a few weeks ago, I assumed I'd never hear about working for Judson Sanders again. Now, less than a month later, I was set to meet him for a meal and conversation at one of the most desirable restaurants in New York City.

A half-hour later, running a bit late, Sebastian and Judson walked through the door, and the entire atmosphere of the restaurant changed. Everyone in the oversized space noticed his presence. Businessmen turned to stare at the same rate as the hostess and busboys. Nobody was safe from Judson Sanders' charm.

Every set of eyes followed Judson and Sebastian as they made their way to my table. I knew it was only a matter of seconds until everyone started whispering about me to their tablemates, likely wondering why I was the one meeting with the mogul. A small part of me expected Judson to take one look at me and turn around but, as they approached the table, he stuck his hand out.

"Maeve Fitzpatrick?" he asked as I stood up. "It's a pleasure to meet you."

"You as well," I said, shaking his hand. "Thank you for fitting me into your schedule."

Although I still had no idea what to expect from our meeting, I tried to act as confident as possible. But, confidence aside, I couldn't change the fact that Judson Sanders was arguably the biggest name in the most cutthroat industry and I was just some small-town girl from Florida.

But he already hired a boy from that same small town in Florida. I hoped that was a sign, praying the odds wouldn't be completely stacked against me.

"Have we met before?" he asked.

"Once," I said. "At a Sampson West press conference."

"When?" he asked. "I thought you looked familiar."

"Back in May," I replied. "Also, I'm still really sorry because I accidentally scuffed your shoes. I was looking at my phone and walking and ran right into your back!"

"Ah, yes, I remember. They were Ferragamo's," he laughed. "Don't worry, I have a dozen pairs. No harm, no foul!"

Of course, they were Ferragamo's and of course Judson was the kind of guy to own more pairs than there were days in the week.

"How are you liking New York?" Judson asked, surprising me with more small talk.

"I love it. Very few things make me smile as much as being surrounded by fast walkers, finding cell service while waiting on a subway platform, and getting the walk signal at every crosswalk," I said. "I feel like I was made for this city."

"I felt the same way when I first moved here," he said. "It's why New York continues to be one of my favorite cities in the world."

"You have offices all over, right?" I asked, already knowing the answer but also not wanting it to seem like I spent the past hour familiarizing myself with his accomplishments.

"New York, Los Angeles, Houston, Toronto, Miami, Paris, Milan, Berlin, Abu Dhabi, and Tokyo," he said.

Ten cities scattered throughout the world seemed insane, further proving Judson solidified his spot as the best in the business.

Almost immediately after ordering our meals, Judson got a call that he couldn't ignore, stepping away for a moment.

"How did you get a table here on such short notice?" I asked Sebastian with Judson out of earshot.

"Judson has a standing reservation every afternoon."

"Every afternoon?"

"Monday through Friday, at least. It's his favorite place to close deals," he said. "Plus, their menu is so extensive that he can have something different every day of the month."

"He must spend more on meals here in a month than I do on rent," I laughed.

"He just puts it all on a tab but honestly, I don't think it ever gets paid," Sebastian said. "See how full this place is right now?

I nodded.

"Most of these people are here because they know Judson comes for lunch every day. They want to go back to their respective offices with exclusive scoop on who Judson Sanders was meeting with."

"Seriously?"

"One hundred percent," he insisted. "So, based on what I've heard, Judson's meals are on the house in exchange for attracting so many other diners."

"Makes sense," I laughed. "Must be nice to have that kind of power in a city like this."

Thankfully, Sebastian and I had enough in common that we didn't struggle to fill the air while waiting for Judson's call to end. It was nice to catch up on life back home and fill him in on how our former classmates were doing and what they were doing with their lives.

Twenty minutes later, Judson returned to the table.

"I'm sorry about that," he said. "There was an issue setting up an event in Los Angeles. They always call during my lunch meetings."

I smiled, knowing Judson Sanders would never owe me any sort of apology and not quite knowing what to say back.

"Okay, let's get down to business," Judson laughed. "Sebastian has said some great things about you. When did you meet? At a bar one night during college?"

"I knew Sebastian before I knew how to tie shoes," I laughed. "We grew up together."

"You're from that cute little town in Florida, too?" he asked.

"You know about Gulfpoint?" I asked, shocked.

"I spent plenty of weekends there, usually with this guy," he said, pointing to Sebastian.

The surprises kept coming. Potentially more shocking than securing a meeting with Judson Sanders was finding out that he spent time in Gulfpoint, Florida.

"How'd you like it?"

"I stayed in the sweetest bed and breakfast, run by the sweetest old lady."

"Was her name Martha?" I asked.

"That's the one!" he exclaimed. "You know her?"

"Of course," I laughed. "Everyone knows everyone in Gulfpoint. But, the most important question, did you get ice cream from SaraBelle's?"

Sebastian's eyes widened.

"Shit, I forgot about SaraBelle's," he laughed.

"It's a Gulfpoint staple so I guess you'll just have to visit again to try it," I smirked toward Judson.

"Consider it done," he laughed.

I was surprised by how much Judson differed from my expectations. He seemed like a no-nonsense kind of guy, a trait I assumed was necessary given his accomplishments, but conversation flowed easily during our meeting.

"How long have you guys known each other?" I asked. "Since Sebastian started working for you?"

"Sebastian didn't tell you that he's my younger cousin?" Judson asked, laughing. "My dad is his mom's older brother!"

"No way!" I exclaimed.

"So, when I needed someone to handle the organization of my company's IT work, Sebastian was an obvious choice," Judson said.

As I listened to Judson talk, I had no question about the validity of his work ethic. I knew he was referred to as a dedicated and confident businessman by many but it was impossible to ignore his passion as he spoke about his endeavors. He was excited about everything from the 'wow factor' at the biggest parties to the smallest details at the smallest get-togethers.

What felt like a short while later, our waitress appeared at our table to let us know the restaurant was supposed to close soon to prepare for the dinner crowd. Looking at my watch, I was surprised to see it was already after 4:00 p.m., not realizing we had been talking for over two and a half hours.

She insisted we could stay seated but just wanted us to know that, if we didn't mind, they were going to prepare around us.

Looking between Judson, Sebastian, and the restaurant staff, I felt terrible. The employees still had an evening shift to work and they probably wanted to use the hour as a break, not to sit around and watch three people talk, no matter how famous one of them was.

"I actually have a dinner party to get to across town," Judson said. "You can just put the meal on my tab and thank Pierre for us."

"That's the chef," Sebastian whispered to me as the waitress handed Judson a slip to sign.

"Good to know," I whispered back with a laugh.

"It was great to meet you," Judson said as we walked out of the restaurant. "I'll be in touch soon."

"Great! And thank you again for the lunch!"

"My pleasure, get home safe."

He and Sebastian were on their way downtown as I headed north toward the high-numbered streets.

I called Greyson on my walk back to my building, hoping he calmed down a bit from earlier this afternoon.

"How did your lunch go?" he asked, answering the phone.

"I think Judson Sanders might hire me one day," I said, feeling incredibly optimistic.

"Seriously?"

"I told you it was a lunch worth attending," I laughed.

"But does that mean more time spent with that Sebastian kid?"

"Well, since I haven't gotten an offer yet, I'd say no, probably not."

With that, the conversation ended, and I continued to walk in silence, annoyed that Greyson's first reaction wasn't one of support.

Chapter Twenty-One

Sebastian-related jealousy aside, things between Greyson and I were going well as the summer months ended. We were spending a lot of time together, going on walks with Ringo, taking day trips to the shore, trying new restaurants, and keeping up with our usual movie night at least once a week. He even started joining in on my twice-weekly face mask applications. We shared meals and stories, aspirations and lessons learned, and got to know more about each other every day.

In past relationships, I would have bailed at the first sign of jealousy, blaming the guy's insecurity as the reason a relationship between us wouldn't last. But this time, even though there were tiffs, I came to learn my previous tendency to run was actually my own insecurity.

I didn't know how to be in relationships because I never allowed myself to be vulnerable but, as I knew from the beginning, things were different with Greyson Raske.

We had disagreements and arguments but I learned those were normal, at least to a certain extent, in healthy relationships with potential to grow. So, for the first time, I didn't want to run when things got tough between the two of us. When I told my mom, she insisted it was a sign that I was maturing, a statement that was probably right but still made me laugh.

Getting back from work one afternoon in mid-August, Greyson stopped me in the doorway. He practically moved into my apartment by the end of July, but it was rare that he was back from work before me.

"Woah," I said, startled. "What are you doing here already, babe?"

"Go put on some jeans and a tank top, we have plans tonight."

"We do?"

"Yep," he said, leading me toward the bedroom. "Hurry, we can't be late."

"There wasn't anything on the calendar when I checked this morning," I laughed.

Our work schedules were so hectic lately that it was nearly impossible to keep track of our own commitments, let alone the other person's, so we created a shared online calendar. Life was so much easier knowing we could check the other's availability while trying to schedule date nights, adventures around the city, and get-togethers with friends or co-workers.

When our friends found out we had this calendar, they insisted it was the next step in taking our relationship to a serious, potentially lifelong, place. It didn't take long for "check the calendar" to become a running joke, always met by group-wide laughter.

"It's a last-minute addition," Greyson said as I reached for my phone. "But, don't look because I didn't actually put it in the app."

"Shocker," I laughed.

As much as we tried to stay on the same page, Greyson became notoriously forgetful when it came to making sure important events were on the calendar. I learned to laugh about it very quickly but things always got awkward when we had to decide which events or reservations to skip because we were unknowingly double-booked.

"Will you at least tell me where we're going?" I asked.

"You said you want to learn how to cook, right?"

I remembered mentioning it in Nantucket but hadn't brought it up since. Between our jobs, adopting Ringo, and trying to juggle some semblance of a social life, it must have slipped my mind.

"Yeah, I should probably master more than just macaroni and cheese," I laughed.

"We're calling you a master at mac and cheese now?" he smirked. "Are you sure? Didn't you burn it last week?"

He had a fair point but I would continue to insist it was a one-time thing and it wasn't my fault. Ringo wanted to play tug-of-war at the same time the macaroni was almost finished. The game ended up going a lot longer and getting more intense than expected. I couldn't say no to Ringo. Greyson had brought him into my life so it wasn't too hard to convince myself that it was, in fact, Greyson's fault that the macaroni and cheese ended up burnt.

"I hate you," I laughed. "Are you teaching me how to cook? Let me remind you that you're no master in the kitchen either!"

"Some of the guys and I thought we'd go on a triple-date to a cooking class," he smiled. "But it starts in a half hour, so we really have to get going!"

"That's so sweet!" I exclaimed. "That sounds like fun."

"So, we're meeting Emilio, Trey, and their girls there."

"Are they established girlfriends or flings of the week?" I asked.

"Emilio's been dating his girlfriend for like a million years and Trey's bringing someone he matched with this week. Honestly, I don't even think they've met in person yet."

"Wonderful," I laughed.

From what I heard, Trey swiped right on nearly fifty girls a week and liked to keep as many of them as possible in rotation at one time. Greyson told me a million stories of Trey's dating life, but I only met three or four of the girls, usually accidentally and always only in passing.

I'd never met Emilio's girlfriend, so I didn't know if "for like a million years" meant actual years or if they got together only a few weeks or months ago.

I was curious as to why Ace and Amelia weren't joining the date but I hadn't heard anything about Ace in over a week. This group of guys tended to be pettier than middle school girls, constantly bickering like teenagers. I was never quite sure when they were friends and when they were fighting so it was easier to avoid the "why isn't Ace coming?" question.

We got to the class with a few minutes to spare and I was glad we did. A group of three girls showed up less than five minutes after class started and the instructor acted like it was the end of the world. She went on and on about how their chicken cacciatore wouldn't be put in the oven at the right time so they'd be delayed in starting their crème brulee, insisting she wouldn't give a refund if the product was subpar due to their tardiness. I felt terrible. The three girls, who were probably no older than us, looked mortified.

As the class continued, she continued to talk down to everyone, clearly not realizing nobody was here to become the next Michelin star chef. I didn't know where the boys found this class, or which one of them reserved our spot, but I had to believe this particular instructor didn't have too many positive reviews or returning students.

The boys also must have forgotten to look at the menu before selecting the class. There was approximately a zero percent chance that any of us would remake this meal after tonight. There were nearly fifteen ingredients in the entrée, plus another five in the dessert. Any meal with that many ingredients was nearly impossible to prepare in the closet-sized kitchen found in nearly every New York City apartment.

While waiting for our crème brulee to bake, Trey explained their friend group dynamic to his date, a blonde elementary school teacher who seemed nice and a little more put-together than his usual type. He told her how the four of them were college roommates who remained best friends over the years. I saw their conversation as an opening, asking where Ace was tonight, weighing the risks and going for it anyway.

"He's proposing to Amelia tonight," Emilio said. "We're meeting up with them after this if she says yes."

"You didn't think to tell me this?" I asked, turning to Greyson, laughing.

"Ace is proposing to Amelia tonight," he laughed. "We're meeting them at some rooftop bar if she says yes. And she better say yes because I went to like four different jewelers to help find the right ring."

"You helped pick out the ring?" I exclaimed. "And you didn't tell me?"

"I must have forgotten," he laughed.

I didn't understand the male brain. How does someone forget something like that?

When the Crème Brulee came out of the oven, we realized it didn't matter what time we got to class because our dessert was runny and we were in the room before the instructor introduced herself.

But we didn't have time to worry about our far-from-perfect dessert because the boys got a text at the same time, starting to laugh.

"What is it?" I asked Greyson.

He showed me his phone, a photo of Ace and Amelia, both smiling from ear-to-ear, taking up the entire screen. Amelia had a very noticeable rock on her finger.

New jewelry aside, I couldn't believe how beautiful Amelia was. We hadn't met yet. She was out of town or working every time I hung out with the guys and Ace was terrible at updating his social media profiles, so this was the first time I saw a photo of her. She looked like a supermodel and I was immediately self-conscious and glad I didn't know what she looked like during the 'suspicious text from Amelia fiasco' a few months ago. At the time, knowing my boyfriend was getting a 'thanks for last night' text from someone who looked like Amelia would have sent me into a complete downward spiral of overthinking compared to the considerably mini-spiral I actually went through.

"That's so exciting for them," I gushed. "So, I guess we're going to the bar tonight."

"They just got there so we should probably get going as soon as this drill sergeant dismisses the class," Emilio laughed.

Ten minutes later, there was no instruction or cooking happening but there also weren't any signs that the other groups were going to be the first to make a move toward the door. We didn't want to make Ace and Amelia wait too long so the six of us stood and gathered our stuff.

"Where are you going?" the instructor asked, taking on what sounded like a Russian accent for the first time.

"We have something we have to get to," Greyson said. "Thanks for the lesson!"

"A meal is not meant to be left right after finishing it!" she exclaimed. "You need time to digest and enjoy the flavors!

It was an exclamation that fell on deaf ears. We were already halfway out the door.

We had more fun on our walk from the class to the bar than during the entire cooking session. No longer separated by countertops or other people, we talked and laughed freely, not worried about disrupting others or getting yelled at by the crazy chef.

The walk took longer than I thought, leaving extra time to ask questions.

I learned Emilio and his girlfriend had been dating for nearly ten years, making Greyson's "like a million years" description fairly accurate. I also learned Trey was a police officer in the NYPD, a revelation that surprised me but made a lot of sense the more I thought about it, considering his crazy work schedule and clean-cut appearance.

A few minutes later, I realized we were near the film shop where Greyson and I purchased my camera earlier this summer. I hadn't been back since, making a mental note to stop in one day this week to visit with the shop's owner.

Continuing down the street, I didn't see the storefront but could have sworn this was the street the shop was on.

"Greyson, isn't this where the camera shop is? Shouldn't we have passed it by now?"

"It's not here anymore," Trey said. "You didn't hear?"

"What do you mean?" I asked. "The guy said he owned it for the last thirty-five years. How is it just not here now?"

"There was a robbery gone wrong the other night," he said. "The store owner was killed."

"What?" I exclaimed. "You're lying!"

"Unfortunately, I'm not. It was brutal and his family was devastated. It looks like it was a drug deal gone wrong."

"He was selling drugs?" I asked, still in shock.

"No, his grandson was. Apparently, he'd put a folded chair in the window display when he had product and, apparently, he forgot to move it the other day when he sold out," he explained. "So, a group came in, got angry when they realized the grandson or his drugs weren't at the shop. They murdered the owner and ransacked the place."

"No way! Did you guys catch them?"

"Not yet. We have some leads, but the security cameras hadn't been updated in years, so the video is too grainy to make out their faces."

I couldn't believe it. I meant to visit that man one hundred times over the past few weeks but got too busy or too caught up in my own life. And now, he was gone.

I spent the rest of our walk remembering his kind eyes and gentle demeanor.

Arriving at the rooftop bar, Ace and Amelia were waiting with excitement and a round of celebratory shots.

After being introduced to Amelia, I spent a lot more time than I thought admiring her ring. It was more beautiful in person than the photo I saw earlier. The diamond was impressive, bigger than I ever saw on anyone our age. I knew Ace had a job on Wall Street, but I didn't realize he earned enough to afford a ring of this caliber.

As our drinking continued, the boys shared stories from their time in college and their post-grad lives, laughing with each tale told. I'd heard most of them by now, but Trey's date seemed impressed and I knew, at least in a small way, the point of this storytelling session was to make Trey look good.

The whole table laughed when Emilio proposed a toast, reminding everyone that Ace was the last expected to settle down but somehow was the first engaged to be married. Greyson's friends from home told me the same in Nantucket, minus the engagement part, leaving me to wonder if that was a commonality for everyone in this core group of college friends.

During what felt like the thirtieth story from the boys, Amelia caught my attention from across the table, asking if we could go talk for a minute.

It wasn't prime "go out" time yet, at least by New York City's standards, so it was relatively easy to find a quiet corner of the bar.

"Thanks for coming tonight," she said.

"I wouldn't have missed it," I insisted. "Congratulations, again!"

"Thank you," she smiled. "Did you know this was happening?"

"I had no idea until like an hour before we got here," I laughed. "Greyson 'forgot' to tell me."

"He's a good guy, you know?"

"Greyson or Ace?" I asked.

"Well, both," she laughed. "But Greyson saved my life two years ago."

"He did?"

This was the first I had heard of any such thing.

"The worst thing imaginable happened and Greyson walked in at the right time."

"The worst thing being someone attacked you?" I asked, taken back.

"Yeah, that," she replied.

"It wasn't Ace, right?"

He didn't seem like that kind of guy but I knew the statistics. Most assaults, especially sexual, came from the guy who 'would never do that.'

I didn't know how I would react but I wanted clarification that this was a celebratory engagement, not a commitment to a relationship where she felt trapped.

"God, no! Ace is the best," she exclaimed.

"He seems like it. If you don't mind me asking, what happened?"

"We went to Mexico for spring break. The resort only had suites, so we shared a few to save some money," she explained. "One night, I got really drunk at the tiki bar by like eleven o'clock, so Ace brought me upstairs. I went to bed immediately and he went back downstairs to rejoin the group."

"You don't have to tell me if you don't want to," I said, noticing she was getting emotional and knowing it was her story to tell when, or if, she was ready.

"No, it's okay, I promise. It's easier talking to strangers about it," she insisted, taking a deep breath. "So, everyone came back after the bar closed. I guess Greyson had to go to the bathroom but someone else was in the hallway one so Ace said he could use the one in our bedroom as long as he stayed quiet."

I didn't say anything, giving her a minute to collect herself and her understandable emotions, letting her decide if she wanted to finish the story.

"I got startled out of my sleep when he opened the bedroom door. When that happened, I realized a mutual friend of a friend, who I didn't know well, was on top of me," she continued.

"Did Greyson see him?" I asked.

"No, as soon as my brain registered what was going on, I pushed myself away, shoved the guy, and told him to leave," she said. "I tried to ignore it but, as soon as Greyson came out of the bathroom, I completely broke down."

"Amelia, I'm so sorry."

I didn't know what else to say. I couldn't imagine how she felt, then or now.

"At first, he thought I was crying because I was drunkenly mad that he woke me up but once I explained what I thought happened, he has been nothing but supportive and attentive," she said. "I wouldn't be here today without your boyfriend."

Greyson and I may have argued and bickered occasionally, but I never questioned his heart or his kindness.

"I don't know how long it was going on or too many details of what happened before I woke up, so I don't know if it really counts as being raped," she said. "That's why I didn't go to the hospital or the police."

"Either way, whatever happened was wrong and wasn't your fault."

"It took a long time for me to believe that," she said. "It's hard to convince yourself that you aren't to blame, especially because it was my choice to drink as much as I did."

"But you didn't choose to have someone attack you while you were asleep," I reminded her, hoping I wasn't crossing any boundaries.

"That was the part that took the longest to learn. I think Greyson told me that a million times in the first few months," she laughed.

"I'm really sorry, Amelia," I repeated, knowing my words likely weren't making a difference. "You didn't have to tell me, but I appreciate you doing so."

"It's nice being able to talk about it every so often," she said. "It doesn't feel like I have a giant X plastered across my body. That's how I felt for the first year or so after it happened."

"Well, I'm here whenever you want to talk about it."

"Thank you," she said. "Also, Maeve?"

I nodded.

"I love Ace with my whole heart and whole being, but I literally wouldn't have survived this without Greyson," she said. "You have a good one, hold onto him."

I smiled. I wasn't planning on letting go anytime soon.

Chapter Twenty-Two

W yatt called me before the start of Labor Day Weekend to ask if I could come back to Florida for a few days.

I knew my younger brother was having a tough time adjusting to life at school, but I couldn't justify going back to Gulfpoint for this particular holiday weekend. September was still peak hurricane season in Florida, along with one of the busy months at Sampson West. I couldn't risk delayed flights resulting in missed work events so, as much as I would have loved to spend the extended weekend with my family, it made the most sense to stay in New York City.

Greyson and I invited some friends to a beer garden in my neighborhood on Saturday afternoon but, of course, we chose a bar that wasn't showing the Georgia/Florida game. The bartender insisted he couldn't change the channel because contractually, he had to play the 'local' games. He ignored my pleas as I explained that my younger brother went to the school that was playing in the game and didn't react when I offered an additional twenty percent tip on our tab.

Seemingly out of options, I was glued to my phone for a majority of the afternoon, religiously checking the score, and trying to keep up with text notifications from Austin and my parents, all of whom were at the stadium with Wyatt. Reading their messages, I felt terrible for missing the game so I was trying to figure out how I could, realistically and logistically, surprise Wyatt at Georgia's game against Kentucky later in the season.

When Saturday night rolled around, after a relatively uneventful day, Greyson and I traded the beer garden for an apartment rooftop party, hosted by one of his co-workers.

Austin called right as Greyson and I were getting to the party. Assuming he wanted to talk about Wyatt, I ignored my ringing phone, sent him a quick 'call you later' text, made a mental note to call him after the party or in the morning, and put my phone back in my pocket.

The party was relatively lowkey and went as expected. My time was spent socializing with strangers, making small talk with people whose names I couldn't remember, and standing silently by Greyson's side for conversations with his peers and superiors.

The more time I spent in Greyson's world, the more I realized I preferred hanging out with his college friends over work friends. Most of his colleagues had a sense of entitlement, commonly found in the Manhattan business world, as if they were too good to interact with outsiders. Knowing I didn't have much in common with most people at the party, I didn't have much to contribute to conversations. I smiled and nodded when appropriate but I didn't have much insight on stocks, analytics, or returns.

Unlike parties with his college friends, I hadn't spent enough time with any of these people to have the slightest idea about their personal lives, and they didn't know anything about mine, so those topics remained off limits.

By the time the party was winding down, I was exhausted. Even though I had been doing it for months, playing the girlfriend role at these events was a lot of work. I wanted nothing more than to get back to my apartment and veg on the couch for the remainder of the night.

Pulling my phone out to check the time, I realized it didn't ring once during the party. I never got a text back from Austin.

I knew Wyatt was going back to Gulfpoint with my parents and Austin for the remainder of the weekend, so I assumed they were out to dinner or venturing around town, an assumption that left me unconcerned that I hadn't heard from any of them in the last few hours.

But that lack of concern changed as soon as Greyson and I got down to the street and as soon as I realized I had no cell service for the duration of our time on the rooftop.

Notifications started appearing on my phone's lock screen faster than I could keep up with. I had nearly a dozen missed calls from Austin, a few more from Wyatt, and some from my parents. My mom and Austin had both sent 'call as soon as you can' texts over an hour ago.

I knew something was wrong. I sobered up immediately, any slight buzz vanishing.

I called Austin first. I assumed something happened to someone in my family and I didn't want to hear bad news directly from my mom. He didn't answer so I called twice more. Those also went unanswered.

Getting more nervous, I dialed my mom's number and waited for her to pick up. She didn't.

Dialing Wyatt's number, my phone started to ring.

It was my mom.

"Mom? What's going on? What's wrong? Is it Dad?" I asked, frazzled.

"Your dad's fine," she said. "Austin's mom was in an accident."

"Is she okay?"

"She's in ICU at Gulf Coast Medical and it doesn't look good," she said, getting choked up. "I'll keep you posted, okay?"

"I'm coming home."

"Are you sure you can?" she asked. "What about work?"

The Sampson West End of Summer Bash was the day after tomorrow and although I knew missing an event was almost equivalent to handing in a resignation letter, I didn't care. I just needed to get back to Gulfpoint, as soon as possible.

"I don't care about work. This is so much more important," I insisted. "I'll text you my flight info after I book it."

"Okay, sweetie, see you soon," she said before hanging up.

After filling Greyson in on what was going on, we rushed back to the apartment so I could grab my wallet, cell phone charger, and some necessities. I threw it all into a backpack before hailing a taxi toward the airport.

I bought a one-way ticket on my phone in the backseat of the cab and emailed Declan and Maribel to let them know I had a family emergency and was getting on a flight to Florida.

I didn't know how long I'd be in town or what I was going to do about work but that didn't matter. I just needed to be home.

My flight was scheduled to start boarding less than a half-hour after I got to the airport. Thankfully, because it was the middle of the night, the security line was nearly empty, a huge difference from the last time I was at LaGuardia, allowing me to make it to the gate with a few minutes to spare.

I texted my mom when I boarded, letting her know I was taking off soon and would take a cab from the airport directly to Gulf Coast Medical. She didn't respond before the pilot told everyone to turn off their phones. I hoped her silence was a sign that everything was fine and that she was back at our house, asleep.

It had been a long day, with no end in sight, so I wanted to sleep on the flight, but my mind was spinning a million miles a minute, making any hope of some shut eye a farfetched dream. Instead, I spent the entirety of the flight overthinking. I didn't want to jump to worst case scenario, but for my mom, the most optimistic person I knew, to say things weren't looking good, I had a feeling that worst case scenario was the reality we'd soon be facing.

More than anything, I was mad at myself for ignoring Austin's call on my walk into the party. It was one of the very few times, the only one in recent memory, that I didn't follow our 'answer before the third ring' rule, and the guilt was nearing the point of unbearable. Greyson and I were running late to the party but I shouldn't have ignored his call. He needed me and I should have been there for him, the same way he was there for me every time I needed him. The guilt ate me apart. I needed everything to be alright, solely for Austin's sake.

Landing at Gulf Coast International Airport, my phone buzzed with a text from my mom saying she was waiting outside of the terminal. That wasn't good. She should have been asleep, at home, because Austin's mom should have been out of the woods and discharged from the ICU by now.

With no bags to retrieve from the luggage carousel, I rushed outside to the terminal loop, desperate to see my mom. We both started to cry as soon as our eyes met and I ran to her for a hug. It was the tightest embrace, a million times tighter than when I showed up at her doorstep unexpectedly in January.

I still didn't know any details of the accident or of Candace Packard's condition, but with worst case scenario in the forefront of my mind, I couldn't stop crying.

"How's she doing?" I asked, terrified of the answer.

"She didn't make it," she cried. "She had no brain activity."

"No," I sobbed. "How's Austin?"

"Numb," she said.

I didn't know what to say. I didn't know how to react. I didn't know what happened to cause the accident but I wanted to scream and cry. I was angry and I wanted to be with Austin.

Greyson offered to come back to Florida with me, but I was glad that I didn't take him up on that. I didn't want him meeting my parents or seeing Gulfpoint for the first time when I was in town for my best friend's mom's funeral.

Looking over at the driver's seat, I felt terrible for my mom. She didn't always agree with Candace and Harden's parenting choices but she loved Austin like her own. She knew this would be hard for him to handle.

"What happened?" I asked, wanting to be at least a little prepared before seeing Austin.

"She was driving home from that bar in Sand Harbor and lost control of her car."

"Was anyone else hurt?" I asked.

It was bad enough that she was drinking and driving, although I wasn't surprised that was what killed her, but I knew Austin wouldn't be able to sleep at night if anyone else was injured or killed.

"No," my mom said with a sigh of relief. "Just her."

"Good," I replied before realizing what I said. "I mean no, not good, but at least no one else was involved. Did Austin get to see her?"

"I'm not sure," she said. "We'll be at his house in a minute so we'll find out."

Looking out the window, I couldn't believe how close we were to Coral Manors. I knew there wouldn't be much traffic at this hour of the morning, especially on a holiday weekend, but it felt like we just left the airport.

Austin and Wyatt came outside as soon as we pulled into the driveway and I couldn't open the car door fast enough, rushing into my best friend's arms.

"Austin, I'm so sorry," I cried.

He hugged me tighter, but his eyes were dry.

"How are you doing?" I asked.

"I'm fine," he said. "How was your flight?"

"A blur," I laughed. "Is there any coffee here?"

If I was dealing with anyone else, I wouldn't have asked them to get coffee at a time like this but I knew Austin better than anyone else and I knew he needed to keep himself occupied. I knew he would only talk about how he felt when he was ready.

For the next few hours, my parents sat in the office with Austin's dad, planning the wake and funeral arrangements. Austin's parents separated a few months ago and Harden didn't see the point of having a wake or funeral for Candace, preferring something private or family-only. He insisted a funeral, especially one open to the public, would attract the media. On the contrary, my parents insisted both a wake and funeral were necessary to give Austin an opportunity to say goodbye to his mother. They said it was what he deserved and would eventually result in proper closure.

Differences aside, the three of them always agreed that Austin came first. They planned a wake and a funeral.

Wanting to get Austin out of his house and away from funeral talk, even if just for a minute, Wyatt, Austin, and I went to breakfast at The Skillet, a diner not too far from Coral Manors.

Everything felt familiar as we walked through the doors of the family-owned restaurant. Sitting at a table near the diner's kitchen, I remembered why this was our go-to spot almost every weekend growing up. Older couples were enjoying a calm breakfast, high school kids were looking for a weekend hangover cure, and families were substituting normal milk-and-cereal meals with waffles and omelets. Like everything else in Gulfpoint, The Skillet felt like home.

Knowing we all needed to talk and think about something else, I asked Wyatt how things were going at school. I knew he was having a hard time with the transition but I wanted to know everything, especially how it compared to my time away. For me, freshman year was a blur as I tried to transition from a high school student into a semi-real adult. Sophomore year was when I moved into an off-campus house and had to learn real responsibility. Junior year was the worst as I struggled with heartache, lost friendships, and a difficult workload. Senior year was even more of a blur than freshman year as my final months and weeks on campus flew by.

From what Wyatt said at The Skillet, referencing uncertainty and hesitation about new friendships, I knew what he was dealing with was normal, even if it felt like the end of the world.

"Have you seen Mabel at school?" I asked, somewhat afraid of the answer.

"We've been hanging out a bit," he said, hesitating to share that news with me.

Even though I thought it was a terrible idea, that wasn't my lesson to learn.

I looked to Austin, curious to hear what he thought of Wyatt's decision. He laughed. Of course, he already knew and likely encouraged it. Like always, the boys stuck together.

The rest of the day continued in a blur. We went back to my house and put on a movie, trying to distract ourselves from everything going on, but I don't think any of us paid attention to a single minute of the film.

When my parents filled us in on the schedule of the next few days, I sent Declan and Maribel another email. I wanted to let them know the family emergency turned into a family death, reiterating that I wouldn't be at tomorrow's End of Summer Bash but hoped to be back at work by Wednesday. She sent back a message of support, but he still hadn't responded to my original email.

As the credits rolled on the movie, Austin asked if we could go outside to talk for a minute. I agreed, glad he was ready to do some sort of talking. The last thing I wanted was for him to shut me out because I knew, even if he wouldn't admit it to himself or anyone else, this loss was weighing heavy on his mind.

Grabbing his hand, I led him through my backyard, realizing roles were reversed from the third-grade version of ourselves, where I followed Austin Packard's every move. Now, I had to be the strong one. I had to be the brave face in a time of unexpected and unprecedented adversity.

We usually had heart-to-heart conversations at the bar in my backyard that we helped my dad build one spring, but today, we passed the high-top chairs, continuing to the gate at the far end of my parents' property line.

"We've had some good times out here, haven't we?" he laughed.

At ten years old, Austin realized he was tall enough to reach the gate's lock. The two of us would 'sneak out' of my backyard to a set of rocks that, in hindsight, were no further than fifty feet from the fence line. At the time, it seemed like the ultimate act of rebellion, but today the rocks seemed a lot smaller and a lot closer to the house than twelve years ago.

"How are you feeling about everything?" I asked as we settled on the rocks.

"I don't know," he answered. "How am I supposed to feel?"

"Your guess is as good as mine," I laughed, trying to lighten the mood.

"Do you know your dad thinks we're going to get married?" Austin asked, changing the subject.

"I thought you were planning on proposing to one of my college roommates?" I laughed.

Austin was in love with at least three of my roommates over the past few years. For a while, I became suspicious that his infatuation was the only reason he continued to visit me at school. Even now, more than a year since college graduation, I still wasn't convinced otherwise.

"I am," He smirked. "But I didn't just bring that up for no reason. Can I show you something I've had in my wallet for a while?"

"It's not the wrapped condom you found in seventh grade, right?" I asked, trying to get him to laugh.

"No, that got used shortly after finding it," he said without as much as a smile, as he reached into his wallet.

He handed me a folded piece of paper. I let out a barely audible gasp, realizing it was a letter from my dad.

"When did you get this?" I asked.

"Right after high school graduation," he said. "Just read it, you'll see why I kept it."

Unfolding the paper, I began to read.

> Dear Austin,
>
> I need to start this off by saying 'thank you.' Thank you for the way you look after Maeve and for the way you care for Wyatt as if he were your own little brother. Those two are my world and my days are easier knowing they have you to count on while I'm halfway across the globe. I hope you realize it's extremely comforting for Susanna and me to go to bed each night knowing our kids have someone like you in their lives.
>
> But besides offering my thanks, this letter is to let you know I've

seen the way you look at Maeve, it's the same way I've always looked at Susanna. Knowing I'll walk her down the aisle one day stresses me out, but things are a little easier when I remember that I'll be giving her to you. Yes, you have my blessing but please let her find herself before you ask the big question. Keep her in check. Be there on her good days and her not so good ones. Remind her that the world doesn't revolve around her, even if our worlds do. Let her spread her wings but, more importantly don't let go. She needs you and you need her.

Also, don't try to hide your tears as she walks down the aisle.

Love,

George

Coming to the letter's end, I got choked up. I knew Austin was the only friend my dad really took the time to get to know, a necessity when allowing someone to move into your house, but I didn't realize the two exchanged letters during deployments.

Forty-eight hours after finding out about Austin's mom, I woke up alone in my childhood bedroom. It was the morning of her funeral and although I was trying to be the strong one, I knew I wasn't prepared to handle the day.

I picked out my most church-appropriate black dress and black heels before meeting Austin in the back alleyway for a much-needed 'for-old-times-sake' trip to Pub Jesus.

I hadn't been to mass at this church since last Easter, nearly eighteen months ago, but everything remained the same in the sacred building, beautifully decorated with flowers lining full pews. Our old classmates, acquaintances, and familiar faces showed up to offer their condolences to Austin, his dad, and their extended family. Harden's mistress made an appearance but sat a few rows behind the family, surprisingly realizing this wasn't the place to publicly debut her halfway-relationship with a pseudo-grieving widower.

The priest gave a nice homily about life after death and a woman, who Austin said was his mom's best friend, delivered the eulogy. I had a tough time focusing on her words. I was trying to keep most of my attention on my best friend, especially after realizing I still hadn't seen him cry over her death.

But, one part of her eulogy caught my attention immediately.

"Candy was the sweetest, most thoughtful, and most caring soul I ever met," she said. "She put everyone else's well-being ahead of her own."

I looked at Austin, trying to decipher if he was as confused as me. I didn't know this woman, but I was beginning to believe the extent of her friendship with Austin's mom didn't scratch much below the surface.

Candace Packard cared about herself and only herself. And, although I never would say such things out loud, I knew Austin was thinking the same as we listened to the eulogy.

After the funeral, we went back to the Packard's home for the repass. Someone sent catered food and everyone spent time together, remembering Candace's life, and offering support to Austin and Harden. My parents never dealt with something like this but I was immensely impressed by the way they kept things organized, taking all responsibility from the Packard family.

About a half-hour into the repass, in the middle of a conversation with Griffin Kingsley about his upcoming child, I felt someone tap me on the shoulder.

"Maeve, can we talk for a minute?" Missy asked.

I didn't know what kind of drama was coming but I knew I didn't want to deal with it.

Trying to be the bigger person, I agreed, following her to the backyard.

"What's up?" I asked as we sat down, unsure what she possibly wanted to talk about.

"Has Austin said anything about our relationship to you?" she asked, with her usual attitude.

"When? Today?" I asked. "No, he's been a little busy grieving his mother."

"No, in general."

"I know you guys are hanging out but I haven't asked much else."

That was the truth. Austin knew I'd be there if he needed me but, for the most part, we didn't speak of his relationship with Missy.

"Well, we're not just hanging out," she said, attitude continuing. "We're dating and I have a problem with him running to you with his issues. He should be coming to his girlfriend for that."

This wasn't a conversation for right now.

"First, the 'issue' you speak of right now is the death of the person who gave birth to him, not a disagreement about where you're going for dinner. Second, you know Austin is practically part of my family so I don't know why you're surprised that he'd come to me first," I rambled. "Third, this is a conversation for the two of you to have but I promise you don't want to have it today."

Trying not to say something I'd regret, I walked away.

I spent the rest of the afternoon watching the clock, knowing I was headed to the airport from Austin's house.

I didn't know what waited for me in New York. I still hadn't heard from Declan and I hadn't responded to any of Greyson's texts over the past few days, too overwhelmed with everything happening to care about rooftop parties or funny conversations with co-workers. I didn't know if I was going back to a job or a boyfriend.

Saying goodbye to my parents in the driveway, I think my mom could sense my stress. I wasn't ready to leave Gulfpoint or my grieving best friend.

"It's going to be alright, Maeve. The world won't stop spinning if you take five minutes to yourself," my mom said. "You don't have to have all the answers or have everything figured out right away."

I knew what she said was right. I was running around nonstop lately and time to myself was relatively nonexistent.

"Austin's going to be alright. You know that, right?" she added. "We'll take care of him."

I nodded.

I wasn't sure how everything was going to work out but I really wanted to have some faith that it would, if anything, for Austin.

Chapter Twenty-Three

The morning I got back to New York from my last minute but far from fun trip to Gulfpoint, Declan called me into his office for an 'urgent' meeting. I hoped it was to discuss what I missed at the End of Summer Bash but when I saw Maribel sitting in his office, I knew I wasn't being called in for a good reason.

"Do you want to explain why you missed Monday's event and work yesterday?" he asked, not even saying hello.

Didn't he read my emails?

"Like I said in my two emails, I had to deal with a family emergency that ended up being a death so I had to stay in Florida for the services."

"Do you have a copy of the obituary with your name in the family section?" he asked, completely serious.

Was that a normal thing to carry around?

Plus, either way, he wouldn't see my name in the obituary. Austin was like family, not actually legal or blood-related family. But, as far as I was aware, asking for proof of death was reserved for the college kid who had the same grandparent die multiple times in a single semester, not a one-time situation for an adult.

"No, but I can pull up some media coverage if you want," I said, pulling out my phone and searching 'Candace Packard' on the internet.

A dozen articles showed up almost immediately.

"It wasn't an immediate family member who died? You went to Florida on a holiday weekend for the funeral of someone who was married to a celebrity?" he asked, astonished. "If it was your mom or dad, I'd maybe be a little more lenient, but I can't just let everyone miss work, or events, every time someone they know dies."

"Her son is my best friend so yes, I went," I said, even though I didn't feel like I had to explain myself or justify my reasoning.

"That seems unnecessary," he said.

I wanted to walk out of his office, but I was still trying to live by the whole 'be the bigger person' thing so I stayed seated and thought about my words before speaking.

"I apologize for letting you know at the last minute, but I emailed you for the first time as soon as I found out that I had to go back," I insisted.

"But why did you have to go back?" he asked.

I didn't know how to attempt an answer to that question.

Didn't he have friends? Didn't he know how to be supportive for the people he cared about in times of need?

I knew Declan Danvers was an odd guy but this was taking it to another level.

"My best friend is practically family. There was no way I'd miss being there," I said. "I apologize for missing the event, but I couldn't ask the doctors to keep her on life support longer just so I could be at a Sampson West party, one thousand miles away."

"See, that attitude won't fly around here," he said. "I can't make exceptions for some and not others, especially if that's how you feel about our events."

"This particular event was completely handled," I argued. "All that was left for me to do was be a physical body at the venue."

"I'm not even positive you were at that funeral," he said. "For all I know, you could have made that up so you could spend the last holiday weekend of the summer at the beach."

"Seriously?" I asked, dumbfounded. "You think I'd stoop that low? Just so I could go to the beach? Or just to miss a work event? After all I've done for this company?"

"Either way, pack up your desk," he said, dismissing me. "It's your last day working in publishing. I'll make sure of that."

Storming out of his office, I didn't mind that I got fired. I would have quit right on the spot if he hadn't figuratively handed me a pink slip. After an accusation like that, I didn't want to work for a guy like Declan Danvers.

Walking out of 1207 Park Avenue for the last time, a huge wave of relief washed over me, as if I let out a breath I didn't know I was holding.

I didn't have to answer to Declan Danvers or fulfill his absurd requests ever again.

I wasn't sure what I was going to do about paying my rent or bills but that could be an issue for Maeve of tomorrow to deal with.

I called my mom, dad, Wyatt, Greyson, and Austin when I got back to my apartment, looking for some insight on what to do about my new predicament, but every call went unanswered.

251

Not knowing what to do, I cleaned my apartment, including spots that hadn't been touched since moving in, well over a year ago. I dusted, mopped the floors, wiped down the stovetop and microwave, and soaked the shower floor with some vinegar concoction my mom swore by.

Once I got everything clean enough to eat off of, I got lost in my mind for the millionth time in the past few days. I wanted to go back to Saturday afternoon when my only concern was keeping up with the Georgia/Florida football game score. I wanted to be at the bar in Sand Harbor and take Candace's keys. I wanted to be with my parents or Austin and Wyatt. I wanted anything other than this new reality.

Knowing I was approaching a downward spiral, personally and professionally, and needed to talk to someone, I dialed Cecilia's office, hoping she'd have an opening at some point this week.

In a rare moment of luck on my side, Cecilia's receptionist mentioned they had a last-minute cancellation. There was an hour appointment open later this afternoon. She asked if I wanted to take it and I couldn't say yes fast enough.

With a few hours before I had to be at Cecilia's, I walked around the neighborhood, trying to get my head on somewhat straight. A couple of blocks from my apartment, I saw a poster for a blood drive and wanted to donate. There was a supply shortage at the blood bank right after Austin's mom's accident and, in the back of my mind, I couldn't help but wonder if she would still be here if there was blood available. It had been on my mind a lot the past few days, even when I tried to suppress the thoughts.

The blood draw process was quick, simple, and painless. The nurse was kind and thanked me for doing a nice thing, even after I insisted it wasn't a big deal.

When I walked into Cecilia's office, possibly due to of my lack of blood, I knew a breakdown was one thousand percent likely to happen during today's session.

"How have things been since the last time we spoke?" Cecilia asked.

I hadn't been to therapy since getting back to New York from Nantucket because Cecilia and I couldn't get our schedules aligned.

"A lot has changed since then," I laughed.

"Where do you want to start?" she asked.

"Well, I got fired today."

"What happened?"

"I went home last weekend because Austin's mom died. I missed a work event because of her funeral and, apparently, that's not allowed at Sampson West."

"Let's talk about that first," she insisted. "What happened with his mom?"

"She decided to drive after a night of drinking, crashed her car, spent a few hours in the ICU. They tried everything but she was taken off life support when they determined she didn't have any brain activity."

"How are you handling it?"

"I'm not sad which probably isn't good. I'm angry that she made such a stupid decision and I'm angry that Austin has to deal with the consequences of that decision."

"How is he handling it?" Cecilia asked.

"I don't think he knows how he's supposed to feel or act. She gave birth to him, but he's never seen her as a mother figure."

"What do you mean by that?"

"I think he sees my parents as role models in his life, instead of his actual parents."

"How do you feel about that?" she asked.

"Growing up, it was pretty cool living with my best friend and I'm glad he has my parents to look up to but there have been times when it hasn't been ideal."

"Like when?"

"There were definitely moments, especially while my dad was deployed or during days where my mom yelled a lot, that I wished my best friend didn't know literally everything about my home or family life," I explained. "I haven't felt like that in a few years, but it added some obstacles to our teenage years, for sure. Now, I just feel bad that he doesn't have a strong or healthy relationship with either of his parents."

"Do you think this loss will improve his relationship with his dad?"

"Honestly? Probably not," I said. "His dad is a former NBA player who brought his mistress to his estranged wife's funeral. He's always been concerned with fast cars and fast women so I can't see him and Austin building a substantial relationship now. Maybe if it was ten years ago but Austin's twenty-three. He's already learned most things a dad should teach his son."

"Did your dad teach him those things?"

"A lot of them," I said. "And Austin taught them to Wyatt when my dad was deployed."

"Sometimes people find ways to return the favor," she said. "That's why I became a therapist."

"Yeah?"

"After going to therapy myself, I realized I wanted to do whatever I could to help others in tough situations," she said. "And, as an outsider, it seems like that's what your family and Austin do for each other."

She wasn't wrong. Austin and I were always there in the tough times and I'd give up my job one million more times to be there if he needed me.

Shockingly, I made it through the entire session without shedding a single tear.

Walking out of the office, my phone dinged with an email notification. Opening the app, I saw a message from my dad with the subject **Just Some Thoughts**.

I walked to my spot to read the note.

Sitting on a bench, enjoying some quiet in the middle of the busy city, I opened the message.

> **Dear Mae,**
>
> **I'm sorry this is an email and not a handwritten letter, but these are some thoughts I wanted to get to you as soon as possible and that wasn't an option with snail mail.**
>
> **It was nice having you home this weekend, even if it wasn't for a nice reason. Maybe, we can go out on the boat or barbeque poolside next time you're in town (or honestly just do anything that doesn't include spending time at a funeral home.)**
>
> **Although the circumstances are terrible, I want you to know how proud I am of you for stepping up and being there for Austin.**

That's what your mother and I have tried to teach the three of you over the years.

Watching the two of you together this past weekend left me thinking a lot about your life and how you have grown into a wonderful young woman.

When we found out your mother was pregnant for the first time, we decided we didn't want to find out if we were having a boy or girl. For the entirety of her pregnancy, I was convinced you were going to be a boy, mostly because I knew how to handle boys. Plus, just the thought of being responsible for a little girl was terrifying.

But, when you were born, I couldn't believe how quickly I was wrapped around your tiny finger. I swear it happened as soon as you took your first breath and let out your first cry. I knew I wasn't going to let anything hurt you.

From the moment I laid eyes on you, I thanked God for you and for the fact that you looked just like your mother. I have thanked Him endlessly as you've grown up but over the past few days, I have thanked Him for your strength, your perseverance, your kind heart, your caring tendencies, and your friendship with Austin. Please don't lose any of that.

I love you more than you know.

Love,

Dad.

I re-read the email twice before wiping the tears from my eyes. I knew we were going to be alright. We were made to survive adversity.

Chapter Twenty-Four

I spent the rest of September searching for jobs and coming up empty. I wasn't getting denied or told what I should be doing differently, I just wasn't hearing anything back from anyone or anywhere. It was radio silent.

My savings account would get me through a couple of months and my parents offered to help out, but I couldn't let that be a long-term solution.

After filing for unemployment, I applied for everything that slightly matched a point or two on my resume. I sent messages to dozens of people on networking sites. I reached out to past professors, hoping they might know someone working for a company in New York City looking to make a new hire. I texted Sebastian to see if Judson had any openings. I asked my parents to reach out to people they knew from work. I even debated emailing Declan to reconsider my termination. I was desperate.

I checked in with my mom multiple times a day for the past few weeks and while we tried to figure out my unemployment situation, she let me know that Austin was having a really hard time handling his mother's passing, even if he made it seem otherwise.

Looking for a way to help, I invited Wyatt and Austin to spend Columbus Day weekend in New York City, figuring it would do both of them some good to get out of Gulfpoint and Georgia.

Although I was excited to spend the weekend with them, I was freaking out about them meeting Greyson. They talked over FaceTime a few times and played video games together online, but they still hadn't met in person. And even though I knew they'd get along, that didn't do anything to settle my nerves. But the uncertainty and nerves disappeared as soon as the boys got to town. The three of them got along like the best of friends almost immediately, teaming up against me every chance they got.

With multicolored leaves falling from the city's sparsely scattered trees and the briskness invading the air every morning and night, autumn in New York was breathtaking. I didn't know if it was the crunch of overpriced boots sending fallen leaves even closer to the ground, or the way everyone seemed to place an added importance to picking out the 'perfect fall outfit' every morning, but I would have lived the New York fall months on repeat if possible. I couldn't have been happier that Wyatt and Austin were in town to experience it.

"You really do like it here, don't you?" Austin asked as we walked through Central Park.

"I do," I smiled.

When I first moved to New York City, I lost count of how many times I got dangerously close to calling it quits. I was fine during the day, but waves of homesickness crashed over me most nights. No matter how much I wanted to love my life in New York, I missed the routine and simplicity of home. I hated that my apartment never smelled like my mother's baking, I missed driving around town with Austin, and I even missed Wyatt's annoying habits.

But now, I loved that New York was a hub of temporary moments. I loved that most people were from somewhere else, just passing by, each with their own story and their own problems. They weren't concerned with what was going on in my life, the same way that I wasn't worried about their daily routines. I loved that skyscrapers, crowded crosswalks, screeching taxis, and slowly-walking tourists had become part of my daily life. I loved that New York City was the land of brunches, public transportation, and seemingly unlimited food delivery – things I had gotten used to and things that didn't exist back in Gulfpoint.

There were still days where I missed the routines and simplicities of life back home, but I couldn't imagine my life any other way.

Part of me wanted to ask Austin to make the Gulfpoint to New York City move, but I knew it wasn't the right time for that. He had things he needed to sort out in Gulfpoint. He wasn't in the right mind space to start a new life in a city so far from home.

I still considered asking, but as soon as I opened my mouth, his phone dinged.

"It's my dad," he said, confused.

"Are you going to answer?" I asked, laughing.

He rolled his eyes before saying hello to his father.

"Yeah. No. I'm in New York with Maeve and Wyatt. You are? Yeah, we'll think about it. Okay. Text me the details."

"What's going on?" I asked after he hung up.

"My dad's hosting an event in New York City tonight."

"Really? For what?"

"I have no idea," he laughed. "But he invited us."

"Are we going?"

"Should we?" he asked.

"Why not?" I laughed. "As long as we can get Wyatt in."

I planned on spending the night at my apartment because Wyatt wasn't twenty-one yet and although he had his fake ID, I didn't want to be responsible for getting it confiscated after not scanning at a Manhattan bar.

"It's my dad's event," he laughed. "Wyatt can get in."

I knew that was the answer before even asking the question. Austin and I attended Harden's events for years before we turned twenty-one, mostly for free drinks, avoiding the red carpets and as much of the industry talk as possible.

But I was surprised that Austin agreed to attend. Their relationship always missed the cliché father-son components but things between the Packard men were more strained than usual since Candace's funeral. Harden was spending a lot of time in public with his mistress-turned-girlfriend and although he and Candace were separated at the time of her death, the people of Gulfpoint found plenty of reason to gossip about his new relationship. I knew Austin resented him for inflicting small-town whispers.

With a few hours until the party, I was sitting on my couch watching Wyatt, Austin, and Greyson play the latest war video game, in person instead of online. I couldn't help but think of a day when I was twelve and Wyatt was eight. We were in our basement, in the middle of an intense round of some racing video game, when we were startled by a slamming door. Pausing the game, we rushed upstairs to find the source of commotion. We searched the TV room, our mom's office, and the kitchen before finding our parents in the formal living room. The living room was always off-limits to Wyatt and me because our mom was afraid that one of us would ruin her white couches with juice or crayons. But on this particular day, as the music from our video game continued on loop, the room's four gray walls were witness to unavoidable news – our father was being deployed overseas with the United States Army. It was the first deployment where we really understood what was going on and goosebumps ran through my body as I remembered the details of the day I was forced to grow up faster than most twelve-year-old kids.

I did my best to avoid most things related to Harden's career but growing up, my parents' only rule was that Wyatt and I could attend Harden's events as long as we didn't have to walk any red carpets. Our lives were already complicated and they didn't want us subject to criticism by mainstream media. To avoid camera flashes and pushy interviews, Austin, Wyatt, and I would hang out with Harden and Candace's assistants, but today, because we didn't meet up with Harden ahead of time and because we were adults who didn't require supervision, our only way to enter the venue was via the red carpet.

Austin hadn't been photographed at events or games since we were seven, after our classmates started seeing him as Harden Packard's son instead of the kid sitting beside them in class. When my parents realized the effect on Austin's friendships and self-esteem, they sat down with Harden and Candace and suggested a break from the spotlight. Austin's parents didn't notice what was going on but they agreed with my parents and after some convincing, the basketball and media worlds hadn't knowingly seen Austin since.

Thankfully, his absence from the limelight left us relatively unnoticed on this red carpet, only having to pose for a couple of photos before making our way inside.

Like most events Harden hosted, this one was extravagant, too over-the-top for my preference but similar to the ones I used to help plan at Sampson West.

Greyson had a work event that he couldn't get out of and although he was disappointed that he'd be missing an event hosted by one of his childhood idols, I was relieved that he wasn't able to make it. Selfishly, I was at ease knowing I wouldn't have to deal with any fan-like tendencies from my boyfriend and that I could enjoy some solo time with my brother and best friend.

Once we got inside, Harden was nearly impossible to find, but that was expected and was likely one of the reasons Austin agreed to attend.

I heard whispers from other partygoers about the girl who walked the carpet with Harden, and I assumed he brought his mistress-turned-girlfriend, whose name I still didn't know or care to remember, along to the event. That was even more reason for us to try to avoid him.

Austin had a look in his eyes during drinks two and three and I knew something was up.

"What's wrong?" I asked.

"Do you know I still haven't cried about Candace?" he laughed.

I knew the game he was playing. When he got drunk, any respect for his parents disappeared and he referred to them by their first names.

I knew we were approaching a very dangerous territory.

"You know that's not good, right?" I asked.

"I'll be fine."

There they were, his famous last words.

"Remember when you said you thought therapy would be good for me?" I asked.

He nodded.

"It's your turn," I insisted. "You need to talk to someone unbiased about what's going on."

"I don't need therapy," he argued.

"I remember saying the same thing the first dozen times you recommended it to me," I laughed. "And look at me now."

"Still a mess but with someone to talk to about it once a month," he smirked.

"Self-care is the best care!" I exclaimed, knowing I'd get him to agree, probably not tonight but eventually.

As the party continued, I still wasn't sure what this particular event was benefitting, but I was pleasantly surprised to see Judson Sanders standing near the bar.

"Hey, Judson!" I said, walking up to him, realizing I wasn't even sure if he'd remember my name. "It's so good to see you."

He paused for a moment. I saw his mind register who I was and how we knew each other.

"Maeve!" he exclaimed. "What are you doing here?"

"Harden is my best friend's dad," I laughed.

"What a small world! I just found out he's dating my ex," Judson said. "And now, I wish I would have known that before I planned this party."

"Harden?" I asked, assuming Judson didn't date Missy McHale but also knowing not to count anything out when it came to that girl.

He nodded.

"Yikes," I laughed before feeling someone tap me on the shoulder. "Oh, Judson, this is my best friend, Austin Packard. Austin, this is Judson Sanders."

"Nice to meet you, dude," Austin said, clearly with no idea who Judson was, evident by his use of 'dude.'

Austin only used 'dude' while talking to guys he assumed were interested in me, insisting it was a form of intimidation, an explanation I never quite understood.

"Sebastian Barrett works for Judson. His company handles the biggest events in the entertainment industry," I explained. "They actually planned this one for your dad."

"You did a great job, thanks," Austin said, sticking his hand out, deciding Judson wasn't a threat.

"I'm sorry for your loss," Judson said to Austin.

"Thanks, I appreciate that," he replied.

"I don't think I've seen you since that photo on the front page of the sports section after Atlanta won the championship," Judson laughed.

"I was in that picture too," I laughed.

"No way?"

"Take a look at it later, I'm the little blonde girl next to this kid," I said, pointing at Austin.

"She uses me for the fame, bro," Austin laughed.

I smacked his arm before Wyatt called him away.

"How are things going at Sampson West?" Judson asked when we were alone.

"Uh, they're not," I hesitated to answer.

"No?"

"I missed the End of Summer Bash because I went back to Florida for his mom's funeral," I said, pointing toward Austin. "Declan called me into his office the morning I got back to the city and that was, in his words, my last day working in publishing."

"I always knew Declan Danvers was a douchebag but that's stooping low, even for him," he laughed. "So, what are you doing now for work?"

"Making a whopping $375 a week from New York State on unemployment," I said out loud for the first time, embarrassed.

"That's not a livable paycheck," he said, clearly shocked.

"Trust me," I laughed. "I know."

We talked a bit about my work experience and the samples I gave to Sebastian earlier in the year. He explained that his current public relations assistant was starting maternity leave in a week and he needed someone to handle press releases, blog posts, and exclusives.

He insisted that Sebastian vouched for me, before reiterating how much he trusted my childhood neighbor's judgment and input.

Judson explained the position would give me access to some of the most sought-after assignments in the entertainment world. Although the hourly rate wasn't exponentially high, I'd be getting paid to attend parties, listen to new music before it was released, see movies before they hit theaters, and interview some of the world's biggest stars. He presented me an offer on the spot that seemed too good to pass up, so I accepted it immediately.

My parents always said the most important thing in life was who you know, not what you know. After receiving the offer, thanks in large part to Sebastian's recommendation, I realized they were probably right about that, too.

Waking up the next morning, I couldn't help but let my emotions get the best of me. It was Austin and Wyatt's last day in New York City and I knew, no matter how much I wanted to avoid it, my best friend and brother would be thirty-thousand feet in the air in less than twelve hours. I wanted nothing more than to buy a ticket to join their New-York-to-Gulfpoint flight, even searching the web for last-minute deals, all of which proved unsuccessful.

Austin, Wyatt, and I had spent their last day in the city searching for an ice cream shop comparable to SaraBelle's, continuously coming up short. There were plenty of ice cream places in New York, visiting the top five on the Internet's 'top shops' lists but none of them rivaled our spot back home.

With only a few hours left together, Austin went onto SaraBelle's website and as soon as the page loaded, we all looked at each other with wide eyes and started to laugh. It took all of five seconds for us to realize there was another SaraBelle's Ice Cream Shoppe in New Jersey.

Another quick search informed us it was only a thirty-five-minute train ride from New York City.

Austin and Wyatt needed to be at the airport by 4:00 p.m. so we decided to leave for SaraBelle's at 11:00 a.m., giving ourselves enough time for the train ride to New Jersey, ice cream, and the train ride back.

We arrived at New York Penn Station a little before eleven and grabbed some coffee and round-trip tickets, fully prepared to take on this adventure. As we boarded the gray double-decker train that would soon be gliding through New Jersey towns, I couldn't help but ignore that this was going to be our last adventure together for a while.

The actual train ride was uneventful, giving Wyatt, Austin, and I plenty of time to talk as we watched trees sail past the train's window. We got so lost in conversation, like usual, that we almost missed our stop. Thankfully, Wyatt paid more attention to the route and stops than Austin and me.

Gathering their luggage and getting off the train, we were met by a burst of fresh air, a rarity in the city, instantly reminding me of home.

Pulling out his phone's GPS, Austin said the shop was "not far" from the train station, insisting we could walk there. We learned very quickly that countryside "not far" was very different than city "not far."

After what felt like forever, we walked through the shop's front door right around one o'clock, the "perfect time for ice cream," according to my best friend who had just led us on the longest walk ever. The shop took my breath away. It was identical to the one back home.

Unfortunately, like our trips to SaraBelle's back home, time passed faster than ever while the guys and I were in the shop and before I knew it, we were back on the train, headed toward the city.

As soon as we heard "Next stop: Newark Liberty International Airport" over the loudspeaker, we knew it was time to start saying our goodbyes but also knew it was best to keep things as short as possible. The train arrived at the airport and my eyes started to water. Wyatt gave me a quick hug, followed by Austin.

"I'll see you soon, Fitz," he said.

With that, they left the train and headed for the airport's terminal. It took all of five seconds to miss their smiles, their laughs, and their constant nonsense.

Chapter Twenty-Five

Although my first day in the office was relatively calm as I learned the ins and outs of the organization, there was no 'easing into things' while working for a guy as busy and in-demand as Judson Sanders. By day two, I was right in the midst of things, taking notes in meetings, scheduling social media posts, drafting press releases, and organizing details of upcoming events.

Conveniently, I started working for Judson during Sebastian's 'spend a couple of weeks working in New York' part of the month so we ate lunch together most days. He introduced me to everyone around the office and invited me to their almost daily post-work happy hours. It didn't take long for me to feel like I fit in, something I didn't get to experience during my time at Sampson West.

I knew Judson promised I'd get to experience massive events but that didn't even scratch the surface of things I did during my first month working for the media mogul. I also attended store openings and premiere parties, sat at dinner parties with athletes and actors, and got invited to galas and games.

At first, I was worried this new work schedule would interfere with my relationship but that wasn't the case. The end of the year was Greyson's busy time so he worked extended hours, compiling year-end reports and forecasting for the following year. And, on the rare nights and weekends that he wasn't at work, I got to bring him as my 'plus one' to events.

By mid-November, I was part of company group chats, had inside jokes with my cubicle-mates, knew which nights were reserved for team trivia and which were for team bonding via karaoke, and, most importantly, I didn't feel like the new girl.

Judson had a strict 'no events on Thanksgiving' rule so the entire office got the holiday off but Thanksgiving weekend was fair game. As the newest employee on the team, I needed to be back in the city by Saturday afternoon to attend an event on Saturday night. With such a short turnaround time, it didn't make sense, logistically or financially, to go back to Gulfpoint for the weekend.

Understandably, my parents weren't thrilled that I was missing another family holiday, but I told them I'd make sure I was home for the entire week between Christmas and New Year's, a promise I made before checking with Judson.

A few days later, with Thanksgiving quickly approaching, I knew I needed to ask about potentially having an entire week off, only a couple of months after starting.

"Hey, Sebastian?" I asked, knocking on his cubicle wall, hoping I wasn't interrupting anything. "Do you have a minute to talk?"

"Of course. Is everything okay?" he asked.

"I think so," I laughed. "I just have a question about how the holidays work around here."

"Thanksgiving or the December holidays?"

"Mainly the last week of December," I said. "I was hoping to use some PTO to go back home to Florida, but I didn't know if those were blackout dates because we have events to host?"

"You won't have to use PTO, but you should absolutely book your flight," he insisted. "Judson closes the office that week."

"Really?" I asked, confused and impressed.

"He believes the end of the year should be spent enjoying the rewards of the past twelve months," he explained. "So, he urges his staff to spend that time with their families and friends, relaxing, in preparation for the following year."

"Don't clients usually request events for that week?" I asked, genuinely curious as to his reasoning behind a full-office shutdown during prime party season.

"It's a known thing now in the party world that we close down," he said. "Judson started doing it years ago when he realized most people and most companies prefer to host holiday parties between December 1 and 20."

On the Monday of Thanksgiving week, I still didn't know where I'd be spending the holiday. Ralph always said I could have dinner with him and Miss Ruth whenever I wanted, but I wasn't sure Thanksgiving dinner was included on that offer. Deciding that probably wasn't my best bet, I considered eating Chinese food and binge-watching movies in my apartment, an idea that didn't go over well with Greyson.

271

"You're not going to celebrate Thanksgiving alone or with your apartment building's security guard and his wife," he laughed. "Come upstate with me."

"I have to be back in the city by Saturday afternoon though," I reminded him. "Don't you want to spend the entire weekend with your family?"

"Thursday morning until Saturday morning is plenty of time at my grandparents' house," he laughed. "Trust me."

I hadn't met Greyson's grandparents yet. They had been at their winter home in Florida, not too far from Gulfpoint, for Easter and according to Greyson, they weren't the 'spend the Fourth of July partying in Nantucket' type.

Somewhat reluctantly, I agreed.

On our drive to upstate New York, Greyson explained his grandmother was a bit senile and his grandfather had Alzheimer's, both with a tendency to forget their grandson. He laughed as he reminded me to speak louder than usual and apologized that we'd have to sleep in separate bedrooms, two things I was fine with.

Most of Greyson's aunts and uncles at Thanksgiving dinner were the same who had been at his house for Easter, so I only had to be introduced to his grandparents. Their home was beautifully decorated for the holiday, a task I assumed Natalie handled. She and Terry were as pleasant as ever, welcoming me into their family holiday without hesitation and without making me feel like an outsider.

But it was weird not being home. I was so used to my childhood home being filled with our immediate and extended families on Thanksgiving. My mom and aunts would be in the kitchen all day, stressing about when was the right time to put the turkey and sides into the oven. The guys would be screaming at the television with each interception, dropped pass, and touchdown. And after dinner, Wyatt and I would argue about who 'cheated' while breaking the wishbone.

At one point in the afternoon, after being introduced to Greyson's grandfather for the third time, he asked if I was "the fat girl" that Greyson dated during high school. I chuckled and insisted that wasn't me, but I wasn't sure he believed that.

At Easter dinner, Greyson's aunts said I was the first girl he brought to a family gathering so I felt like I needed to ask my boyfriend about this "fat girl" I had been mistaken for.

"I told you my grandpa doesn't remember things correctly," he laughed.

"I know. But did she exist?" I asked, finding the entire situation hilarious.

"Yes and no," he said. "She definitely wasn't my girlfriend."

"Who was she?" I laughed.

"Every cheerleader was assigned a football player to make banners for and stuff like that," he said.

"Yeah, every school has that," I laughed.

"No, I'm serious," he said.

"I know, me too. That's wasn't just a Crescent Peak thing, I promise."

"Well, either way, my grandpa saw her holding my banner at every game and he only knew high school relationships as the quarterback dates the head cheerleader," he said. "So, he always assumed we were dating."

"You were quarterback?" I asked, amazed that I didn't know that by now and more amazed because Greyson didn't seem like a quarterback.

"No, I was the kicker," he laughed. "And she definitely wasn't the head cheerleader and we never dated."

I liked hearing stories of Greyson's high school years. It made me wonder if he and I would have been friends back then. My gut feeling was 'yes.' His family continued to reminisce throughout the evening and although I was pretty bummed that I wasn't at home, they gave me a nice place to spend a holiday.

"Maeve, are you into cars?" Terry asked on Friday afternoon.

"A little, or enough," I laughed. "My dad has been working on an old Ford for years so I know a little about that and enough to call AAA if I ever break down."

I knew that was a safe enough answer, deciding to leave out that I had sex with his son in a backseat or that Austin and I 'stole' his dad's Ferrari for a joyride when we were fourteen.

"An old Ford?" he asked, eyes widening. "Want to see my collection? Maybe take a few pictures to show your dad?"

"Sure," I agreed, assuming he just wanted to show me some photos of a car or two.

"Follow me," he said. "They're out back."

"Dad, where are you taking my girlfriend?" Greyson asked as we stood up.

"To see the cars," he replied, pointing toward the backyard.

"Oh god, I'm coming too," Greyson laughed.

I didn't know what I was getting myself into but I didn't have much in common with Greyson's dad so, if this was going to earn me a few brownie points, I was game.

The 'car or two' I was expecting was actually nearly a dozen old Ford cars and trucks, some looking like they were from before electricity was invented.

"Maeve, what was your first car?" Terry asked as we stepped into the garage.

"A Toyota Corolla," I said.

In the weeks leading up to my sixteenth birthday, I mentioned to my mom how badly I wanted a car, even though I knew it was a completely unrealistic request. The day came and went and much to nobody's surprise, I remained car-less. But a week later, as we were getting ready for school, Wyatt forced me to the driveway and my jaw dropped as soon as the garage door opened. Parked in the middle of the driveway was a brand-new Corolla, topped with a red bow. And although I loved my new car, I burst into tears as soon as I realized who was behind the wheel, in utter disbelief when his combat boots hit the pavement.

Both Greyson and his father got emotional as I retold the story of my first car and my first surprise homecoming.

"See this car?" Terry asked, pointing to the Mustang. "That was my first car."

"That type or that exact car?" I asked.

"That's the one," he laughed. "I took Natalie for our first date in this car."

"That's the sweetest thing ever!" I exclaimed.

"All of these cars have a story," he insisted.

"Dad, don't bore her with them," Greyson moaned.

"No, I want to hear them," I insisted.

He went down the row of cars, explaining the years they were made, the model names, and a bit of their history. He had a 1931 Ford Model A, a 1939 Ford Anglia, a 1948 Ford F-Series, a 1955 Ford Thunderbird, a 1965 Ford Mustang, a Ford Model T, and a Ford Bronco.

Terry said his grandfather worked on the Model A production line in Detroit, the Anglia belonged to his father, and the Thunderbird had always been his dream car.

"Do any of these cars look familiar?" he asked.

"My dad's old Ford is a 1954 F-Series, so I know a lot about that one," I laughed. "And I obviously know Mustangs and the Bronco from O.J.'s infamous police chase."

"That's why I bought the Bronco," he laughed.

We spent the rest of Friday lounging around, exploring the property, and laughing by the firepit. My homesickness had started to fade as hours passed. By Friday night, I was glad I chose upstate New York over Chinese food alone in my apartment.

When we woke up on Saturday morning, I had to be reintroduced to Greyson's grandparents, twice each before breakfast was served. We didn't have long left at their house but Greyson made sure there was time for breakfast, insisting it was his aunt's specialty. After my first bite, I agreed.

Greyson's grandfather mistook me for "the fat girl" again over French Toast and omelets.

I laughed. Greyson had shown me a photo of his former cheerleader and although I knew I had eaten a lot over the last few days, we looked nothing alike.

I rushed back to New York City for an event that I hadn't been involved in the planning. I was only standing in day of so one of the senior executives could be off for the entirety of Thanksgiving weekend. So, when I saw "Chloe's 21st" being hosted at one of the city's hottest nightclubs on the Saturday night of a holiday weekend, I never assumed Chloe was a three-pound, three-year-old dog.

I rushed back to New York for a dog's third birthday party. According to Judson, the woman who hired us to plan and supervise the gathering was the heir to an oil company overseas who was worth "multiple billions of dollars." Because her Shi Tzu was turning three, or twenty-one in dog years, the woman wanted the event to be equivalent to a human's twenty-first birthday party.

I couldn't believe this was what my life had become.

Chapter Twenty-Six

J udson wasn't lying about early-to-mid December being full of holiday parties.

After the post-Thanksgiving puppy party, every day and night were spent bouncing between events. There were brunches and happy hours, luncheons and dinners, Secret Santa's and orchestra performances, and that was only during the first week of the month.

I brushed shoulders with superstars, asked for quotes from high-powered executives, sat beside diplomatic leaders, and networked with millionaires.

I lost track of the days, exhausted after every event. I cringed every time I saw a morning, afternoon, and evening event written on a single day. Not to mention, in addition to the parties, there were still movies to watch, music to review, and television premieres to prepare for.

Wyatt was on winter break, Greyson had some time off from work, and because my entire family hadn't been to visit me together yet, they came to New York the weekend before Christmas.

My dad was deployed when I moved to New York City and still hadn't seen my apartment or neighborhood in person. My mom helped me move in but hadn't been back since. Wyatt and Austin, on the contrary, knew Ralph by name and knew the best places to get snacks, bagels, and pizza near my apartment.

But, past visits aside, this would be the first time any of them got to experience winter and, more specifically, Christmastime in the big city.

I wanted to act like a tourist while they were in town. I wanted to show them the Rockefeller Christmas Tree, the Fifth Avenue window displays, and the people ice skating in parks throughout the city. I wanted them to experience the magic that invaded New York City's streets from Thanksgiving until New Year's Day.

When Judson asked where I was planning to take my family, I mentioned wanting to see the Radio City Christmas Spectacular with the Rockettes and The Nutcracker performed by the New York City Ballet.

I thought we were just making conversation to pass the time, leaving me shocked when he offered me six VIP tickets to both shows.

"Judson, I can't take these!" I insisted.

"Sure, you can," he laughed. "They send me like hundreds of complimentary tickets each year and they always go unused."

"Are you sure?" I asked. "Can I pay you for them?"

I didn't want him to think I was taking advantage of the company. I was genuinely just trying to make small talk.

"Absolutely not!" he insisted. "If you want to write a review for the blog, I'm sure they'd appreciate that, otherwise, just enjoy the shows!"

"Thank you so much," I said. "I owe you!"

Due to a storm coming out of the North, my family's flight was delayed and instead of arriving in New York shortly after lunch like planned, they didn't land until right around dinnertime.

Greyson and I treated everyone to dinner at Sal's Steakhouse, partially because I knew everyone would like something on the menu but also because I knew the two of us could afford to split the bill.

I knew my parents would like Greyson, and although they had already talked on the phone a few times, I was still nervous for them to meet in person. I didn't want my mom to get too personal or my dad to start telling embarrassing jokes. In the same way I never had to get introduced to parents before the Raske family, my parents never had to be introduced to my friends or their families.

"Greyson, what does your family do for the holidays?" my mom asked.

"It depends how much it snows," he laughed. "Some years, we've had fifty people at my house because the weather's been clear and other years, there have been blizzards, so it's only been my parents and me."

"Could you imagine that?" Austin asked, turning to the rest of the group. "Imagine your plans changing because of bad weather? Thank god that's not a thing at home!"

I couldn't tell if he was being serious or just wasn't thinking.

"Uh, Austin," I said. "What about hurricanes?"

"Oh yeah," he laughed. "I guess those suck a lot."

Chuckling at Austin's latest revelation, I knew we needed to change the subject.

"Would you want to come to Gulfpoint for a few days after Christmas?" I asked Greyson.

Austin kicked me under the table, as if to double-check that I realized what I just asked. I tried to play it off like this wasn't a big deal but we both knew I never brought a boyfriend back to Gulfpoint before. It was one thing to have a relationship with Greyson in New York City or to have him meet my family but bringing him back to my hometown was a huge jump in a relationship, especially a hometown where everyone had an opinion.

"I'd love to!" Greyson replied.

I kicked Austin back, under the table, adding a point to the Maeve column of whatever we were keeping track of this week.

My parents were staying at a hotel, not too far from my apartment, but Wyatt and Austin asked to stay on my couch and floor, well aware that I wouldn't be able to say 'no' to them.

Greyson had to be at the office early the next morning to finish up some year-end reports so I told him it'd probably be best if he stayed at his own apartment that night, knowing there wouldn't be much sleep with the three of us reunited. He agreed, took Ringo home, and insisted he'd meet up with us before the Christmas Spectacular at Radio City.

Austin, Wyatt, and I pulled an all-nighter, a decision I regretted when we met my parents for breakfast and started our day venturing around the city, starting in Central Park.

My mom wanted to take a carriage ride through Central Park and although I felt bad for the horses, I didn't want to ruin my mom's New York City dream. So, we piled into a carriage and rode through the park.

As the ride began and we passed a sea of people, my curiosity skyrocketed. There were teenagers causing trouble, people jogging, panhandlers looking for money or food, children running around, couples on dates, and families out for walks. I wondered about their stories.

How many of the people we passed had lost someone they loved? How many got denied from their dream schools or lost their jobs because of the current state of the economy? How many lived a life I simply couldn't imagine?

I was a college graduate in the process of chasing my dreams but what about the woman walking past us with a stroller and dark circles under her eyes? Was she stressed from a grueling job or did the baby in the stroller keep her awake all night?

Further down the path was a man playing with a young girl, no older than five. Did he realize the girl in pigtails looked at him as if he created the stars in the sky? Did he notice the way her eyes sparkled as she called out "Daddy, catch me!" while jumping off a bench? Did he understand that he would forever be the most important man in her life?

This was my first horse-drawn ride through Central Park and although I probably wouldn't make it a frequent activity, I enjoyed and appreciated the different perspective of the city's park.

After tipping the carriage driver, and getting to give a carrot to the horse, we made our way to Times Square.

We didn't stay in Times Square long, especially after I convinced them that they didn't want to spend any money in any of these stores. Wyatt didn't understand why until I explained that something that cost ten dollars at home would cost thirty dollars in the middle of Times Square.

"If you weren't coming home, would you have come to Times Square for New Year's Eve?" Wyatt asked.

"Absolutely not!" I laughed.

I hadn't lived in New York long but I knew Times Square on New Year's Eve was pretty high on the list of places to avoid. Being crammed with millions of people, with no access to food or bathrooms, seemed like the furthest way from how I wanted to celebrate a holiday, especially a winter holiday in the Northeast. I assumed most of the people who came to town for the occasion had a good time but I preferred to watch the show on television while pregaming for whatever festivities were in store that year.

As I led them through the New York City streets, dodging mucky puddles of dirty snow from the storm earlier in the week, my dad asked a million questions about the neighborhood, a majority of which I couldn't answer. I didn't know where the nearest police station was, why this building was shaped in a particular way, what the sidewalk paint meant, or why scaffolding hung over almost every building façade and sidewalk.

Continuing toward Fifth Avenue, I wanted to show them the department store window displays. They were one of my favorite parts of the city and I knew they, or at least my mom, would appreciate them. Every window displayed a different theme, from a winter wonderland to Santa's workshop. There were hydraulic elf figurines moving gift boxes and sparkling silver snowflakes hung by rhinestone strings. Some displays were minimalistic while others were bursting with color, each drawing a crowd. People stood in front of each window, taking photos of the smallest details, ready to tell their friends back home what they saw in New York City.

With about an hour to spare before we had to be at Radio City for the Rockettes' performance, I showed my family the Winter Village at Bryant Park. The boys sipped beer samples at The Lodge while my mom and I wandered through the vendor booths. There were vendors from near and far, selling everything from stocking stuffers and soaps to handmade wood signs and hand-sewn scarves.

After buying a few gifts, we met up with my dad, Austin, and Wyatt near the ice rink, watching everyone packed on the ice. There were families, people on dates, little kids skating circles around their parents, and people with no idea how to skate. There were dozens of people on the edges of the ice, deciding if they were going to be brave enough to skate, and countless people, like us, standing outside the rink watching.

I tried dance when I was younger but didn't last in lessons for longer than a year. But I was always impressed by the Rockettes and ballerinas, so I thought both shows were beyond incredible. It was even more special to experience the shows with my dad. He brought me to my first dance lesson and encouraged me to dance my heart out every day since, sitting through every subpar dance recital. Even though there weren't many impressive moves from mini Maeve, he was always the first to stand and applaud, sometimes before the music stopped, a habit that still existed eighteen years later.

Afterwards, we went to the world-famous Rockefeller Center Christmas Tree. The concrete area near the tree looked a lot bigger on television broadcasts and in movies. There were hundreds of people crammed in the tiny space, everyone trying to get the best view of the oversized tree. Little kids, bundled in jackets and high off holiday spirit, ran around as couples posed for photos that would receive a few 'likes' on social media. Adults were doing mental headcounts, making sure nobody in their party got separated from the group.

"Would you guys want to visit a soup kitchen tomorrow before your flight?" I asked.

Growing up, our parents constantly reminded Wyatt, Austin, and me to give back to our community at every opportunity because, no matter what struggles we were battling on any particular day, we were more fortunate than most people in our country and in the world.

Back home, we tried to spend at least a day or two every year at food pantries as a family. But, in Gulfpoint, there weren't people lining up for food assistance like they were in New York City. In all of our years volunteering in Gulfpoint, we packaged hundreds of bags of food, mostly for families with sick children, but we never saw the people we were helping. I knew we could see the impact directly at a New York City soup kitchen.

"We had to move our flight to early in the morning, sweetie," my mom said. "I have an important case starting on Monday that I have to finish prepping for. We just can't risk another delayed full day of travel, I'm sorry!"

"It's okay," I told her, somewhat disappointed but also aware that we'd be reunited within a few days.

I flew back to Gulfpoint on the morning of Christmas Eve and it was nice being back in town for something other than a funeral and for longer than seventy-two hours.

My first night back in town was spent at the same place as my last trip, our Catholic church. Wyatt, Austin, and I became 'Easter and Christmas churchgoers' over the past few years but my mom told Austin he didn't have to tag along today, assuming it'd be hard for him to be at the place of his mother's funeral. I knew he still hadn't properly grieved Candace's death, but I also saw the smirk on his face when he realized he had a very valid excuse for getting out of attending Christmas Eve mass.

After gifts were opened the following morning, Austin went back to his house to wish his father a Merry Christmas and Wyatt and I settled on the couch with a stack of old photos.

"Remember this one?" he asked.

It was a photo from a few years back of Wyatt and me at a ski resort in upstate New York. Growing up in Florida, we only saw snow in movies and neither of us knew how to snowboard but we begged our parents to take us wherever we'd be able to see the most snow in person. Our mom vetoed North Dakota so we ended up at a resort in Canandaigua, an upstate New York town I still didn't know how to pronounce. This particular photo was taken only a few hours before our dad shared that he would most likely be deployed for a majority of the upcoming year. It brought a flood of emotions, from joy and love to anxiety and devastation.

We'd been through a lot, separately and as a family, since then. Now, reunited in our childhood home, I was appreciative of everything, good and bad.

Continuing the reminiscing, Wyatt pulled out some old home movies and popped them into the VCR that I didn't know still worked.

An hour later, our front door opened, and Austin reappeared in the doorway.

"How was he?" I asked.

"I don't know. He wasn't there."

"What? Where is he?" Wyatt asked. "It's Christmas."

"Who knows," he said, defeat evident in his eyes. "But it's great that he didn't think to let his only son know he wouldn't be in town for a holiday."

"I'm sorry," I said, genuinely feeling bad for my best friend.

"It's okay," he said, plopping on the couch between Wyatt and me. "I have you guys!"

Austin's dad missed Christmas most years while he was in the league, usually spending the holiday in a game or traveling. But he was retired now, and his only son had lost his mother only a few months ago. He should have been in town for his kid.

Before Greyson got to town, knowing he wouldn't be here long, I created a list of places we needed to go. It was a list that got longer with each passing moment and I knew we'd never get to everywhere I wanted. Restaurants and mom-and-pop-shops took up a majority of the spots on the list, mostly because I knew authentic Southern food and genuine Southern hospitality didn't exist in New York City.

Austin, Wyatt, and I drove to Gulf Coast International on the morning of December 27 to pick up Greyson for his two day stay in Gulfpoint.

"Where's Ringo?" Wyatt asked as soon as Greyson opened the car door.

"With my parents," he laughed. "He wasn't ready for a flight."
Wyatt huffed.

"You just saw him like a week ago," I reminded my little brother. "Plus, I'm the one who told Greyson to leave him in Massachusetts so if you're mad, be mad at me."

"You suck, Maeve," he laughed, completely serious.

I kicked the back of his seat, laughing at how childish he acted every so often.

"Greyson, are you staying for New Year's?" Wyatt asked, changing the subject away from Ringo.

"I can't," Greyson said. "My friends and I do a huge New Year's Eve thing back home."

In the days leading up to his arrival, I hoped that Greyson would change his mind about flying back to Crescent Peak for New Year's Eve. I spent multiple holidays with his family and hoped he would have wanted to do the same with mine.

"That's lame!" my little brother said. "You're like 0 for 2 right now."

"Wyatt!" I laughed, secretly pleased my brother said what I had been thinking. "It's literally no different than what we do here."

"Oh," he said after a brief pause. "That's true."

"How do you like Gulfpoint, so far?" I asked on our first drive through town.

"This place reminds me a lot of Crescent Peak," Greyson said.

"With a beach and a lot more tans," I laughed.

Chapter Twenty-Seven

"What has been your biggest takeaway of the year?" my dad asked.

This was something we did every New Year's Eve, whether face-to-face or on FaceTime.

My parents would ask what we learned or what we were grateful for and we were supposed to choose something meaningful, although it didn't always work out that way. I tried to play by the rules on this particular tradition, but Wyatt and Austin usually came up with some snide remarks. There were three or four years in a row where one, or both, of them would say "good grades mean more video games" was their biggest takeaway. My mom always rolled her eyes at that response but, especially if it was a year my dad was deployed, she never made them think of another answer.

This year, Wyatt and Austin both credited the importance of family as their greatest lesson learned and I was impressed by their seemingly sudden maturity.

"What about you, Maeve?" my mom asked.

I considered taking the easy way out, using the same answer as the boys, like they had done to my answers for so many years in the past. But, although I never doubted or questioned the importance of family over the past twelve months, that wasn't my biggest takeaway or my greatest lesson learned, especially as I thought about everything that happened this year. I thought about the people I loved, the bonds I built, the tears of joy, and the tears of sorrow.

"My greatest accomplishment was just making it through the year," I laughed, although I wasn't joking.

"Maeve, none of us doubted you," my dad said.

He was right. I was the one who doubted myself the most. It wasn't the high school mean girls, the petty college guys, my longtime friends, or the strangers I passed on the streets. It was me.

"Did you make a resolution list this year?" Wyatt asked a few minutes later. "Or did those stop when you moved away?"

"Of course, I made one!" I laughed. "Don't Mom and Dad stop giving birthday gifts when we stop making lists?"

But I completely forgot about the resolution list over the past few months.

I knew I had a screenshot of it somewhere in my phone.

Scrolling through my camera roll, trying to find the photo, I wanted to show my brother and best friend how much had been crossed off. After a few dozen swipes, I found what I was looking for.

<u>Maeve's Resolution List</u>
Spend more time with genuine people
Reconnect with an old friend
Fall in love
Do something that scares you

Donate blood

Send handwritten letters

Volunteer

Travel without posting on social media

Meet new people

Ask work for a raise/more responsibility

Invest some paychecks

Find a new hobby

Stay in touch with yourself

Clear out the clutter at home

Find a new job you love

Talk about feelings

Learn to cook

Be a New York City tourist for a day

See more live music

Go somewhere you've never been

Do something kind for others

Go an entire day without checking emails

Enjoy the little things

Reading over the list, I was shocked. There was nothing left to cross off.

I spent more time and stayed in touch with the people who mattered back in Gulfpoint. I reconnected with Sebastian and formed a friendship that I believed would last. In the beginning of the year, I was afraid to stand up for myself, but I did that one hundred times in the past few months. I started sending and receiving handwritten letters again. I asked for more money at work and got a raise, and eventually fired. I gained a somewhat serious interest in photography. I volunteered and met new people at the shelter, along with Greyson's friends. I finally cleared out the clutter in my childhood bedroom, learned to cook, went somewhere I'd never been, saw live music, and started going to therapy. I donated blood, found a new job, invested some money, travelled without posting, left emails unanswered, fell in love, and learned to enjoy the little things.

A year and a half ago, people insisted my life was at its peak, but I refused to believe things wouldn't get better than college. I refused to believe life was all downhill after professors dragging on, soggy dining hall food, and seemingly unnecessary homework assignments. As I sat here, surrounded by my favorite people, I knew I was right.

Things were great. My dad was finally home from war, for good. My mom was always only a phone call or plane ride away. My bond with Wyatt and Austin only strengthened during difficulties. I was in a relationship that made me happy. I worked for a company I loved and, other than a few storms, I was getting good at dodging raindrops.

Acknowledgements

Writing this book has been everything but easy. It has taken years, interrupted by schoolwork, surgeries, baseball seasons, a chronic debilitating disease, loss, and life in general. I became impatient during this process and came close to giving up a few times, but thanks in big part to the COVID-19 quarantine, *Dodging Raindrops* is here!

I need to thank everyone who believed in this story from the very beginning, even on the days when I didn't. I especially need to thank everyone who encouraged me through new plots, new titles, complete re-writes, cover design ideas, writer's block, and everything in between.

I could fill the pages of another book with names of the people and experiences that contributed to this story, some knowingly and some unknowingly, but there are a few people and places who deserve special mention. Without them, *Dodging Raindrops* simply wouldn't exist.

Mom and Dad, there will never be enough words to explain how much I love you, how much I appreciate everything you have done for me, and how much I owe to both of you. Thank you for being my biggest supporters in everything. I would be completely lost without you. I love you both tremendously.

Nicole, there isn't a better big sister in the entire world. Thank you for showing me the ropes, for pushing the envelope, for leading by example, and for being my built-in best friend. There is no question that being your little sister has always been (and will always be) the coolest thing about me.

Gran, Grammy, and Poppy, thank you for instilling that family always comes first, for supporting every decision made, and for being the first to call on good and bad days.

Annie, Uncle Bob, Aunt Nan, Mame, Uncle Andy, Aunt Lisa, Uncle Doug, Uncle John, Aunt Libby, JJ, and Jess, thank you for being the best role models a girl could ask for. My days are easier knowing I can call you whether I have a silly question or need serious life advice.

Kerry, Bobby, Chris, Kyle, Michael, Katie, Kevin, Danny, Lauren, Kevin, Kelly, Kyle, Jenna, Laura, Shannon, Madeline, Mike, and Sarami, I'm so grateful that my favorite memories include all of you. We have shown up for each other during the best and worst times of our lives and I'm forever grateful to have all of you on my side.

Danny, I'll never forget the conversation we had on my twenty-first birthday about the idea of writing a book. I think you were the most excited about its potential. Losing you taught me a pain I never wanted to experience and a pain I'm still trying to process but I promise your light and legacy will live in me forever. Head up, eyes forward.

Katie, Thank you so much for all of your work on the cover design of *Dodging Raindrops*. You took a poorly drawn sketch I threw together and exceeded every possible expectation. I'll be forever amazed by your inner strength and your artistic abilities!

Emma Rose, Caroline Kay, and Jack Daniel, you are the most perfect additions to our family and I'm so excited to watch you grow into whoever you want to be.

Ava and Joey, watching the two of you experience the world through bright eyes has been the greatest gift. I hope you always find excitement in things like sticker books, animal noises, and afternoon dance parties.

Bridget Smith, Devon Wuagneux, Ellen Wuagneux, Erin Redding, Jenn Weiner, Jess Cassetta, Lynn Murphy, Meg McQuaide, Nikki Panuska, Pam Rodriguez, and Sheila McCombs, thank you for giving *Dodging Raindrops* a first look, for your feedback, for being so supportive, and for sticking around on this seemingly never-ending process.

Megs and Kellie, thank you for giving that shy girl an opportunity so many years ago, for teaching me how to find my voice, for reminding me to always run with an idea if it seems like a good one, and for your irreplaceable friendship. I can't wait to celebrate *Dodging Raindrops* appropriately – over bottomless mimosas at O'Donoghue's!

Jake, thank you for the countless pep talks, for yelling at me every time I tried to delete this story, for keeping me on track and in nice cars, and for being my Day One, always and forever. I can't wait to see where the next chapter brings us, I know it's going to be a good one.

Rutgers, thank you for turning one-time strangers into my closest friends. Thank you for the good days and the terrible ones. Thank you for giving me a place to find myself. Fourhees Fam and Hardenberg Girls, thank you for being such a crucial part of my story. Thank you for the parties, the study sessions, the tears, the laughs, and the drama.

And, to everyone on my side from Goshen, Wyckoff, the Boulders, WeKnowTheDJ, and Ear of Gold, thank you for living my dream alongside me, for sitting through countless baseball games, for reminding me that hard work always pays off, and for proving "small town, big dreams" is more than just a phrase.

Made in the USA
Middletown, DE
01 September 2020